FOOLING SHEEP

FOOLING SHEEP

SIMONE LAMONT

NEW DEGREE PRESS

FOOLING SHEEP

ISBN

978-1-63676-650-8

For Bapa

The greatest lover of books I've ever known.

Thank you for supporting me before I even wrote a single word.

CONTENTS

INTRODUCTION

"I think, therefore I am."

—RENÉ DESCARTES

Often known as the "cogito," this philosophical dictum serves as proof of existence through one's ability to doubt. It implies that although your senses might deceive you, and all your beliefs may be false, you must exist in order to be deceived in the first place.[1]

The purpose of this novel is not to define personhood or human existence. I am neither a philosopher, nor a computer scientist, nor even a fully grown adult if I'm being honest. But what I will try to do with Olivia's story is make you think and make you doubt. The inspiration for this book lies in my own interpretation of a modern-day Turing Test.

Alan Turing, the man often credited with creating the first computer, was a mathematician in the 1940s and '50s. He speculated about artificial intelligence long before it became

---

1 Lex Newman, 2019, "Descartes' Epistemology (Stanford Encyclopedia Of Philosophy)," *Plato.Stanford.Edu*.

a reality. In his 1950 paper "Computing Machinery and Intelligence," he wrote about a thought experiment known as the Turing Test, or Turing's "imitation game." The goal of this test is to essentially prove if a machine has strong artificial intelligence. In other words, the computer's intellectual capacity is that of a human brain.[2]

The idea of the test is simple: a person has a conversation with a human and a computer under the conditions of the test, so they do not know which is which. Based solely upon the responses to the questioning, they attempt to distinguish which one is the human and which is the machine. If the computer fools the person into believing they're talking to a human, it passes the test.[3]

Of course, there are many critiques to the validity of this thought experiment, such as the "Chinese Room" from philosopher John Searle. But additionally, some developments apply the Turing Test to human learning (top-down and bottom-up processes), ESP and superintelligence, and even gender and sexuality studies. The purpose of this novel is merely to apply these ideas to the context of my own life and create another thought experiment in the process. *Fooling Sheep* could be, in and of itself, a Turing Test for the reader.

Or it could just be a story about high school. That's fun too.

---

2 Andrew Hodges, 1997, "The Turing Test, 1950," The Alan Turing Scrapbook, 1997.

3 A. M. Turing, "Computing Machinery and Intelligence," *Mind* 59, no. 236 (1950): 433–460.

"Most people are other people.
Their thoughts are someone else's opinions,
their lives a mimicry,
their passions a quotation."

—OSCAR WILDE

CHAPTER 1

I watched myself die over and over again. That was what triggered my memory.

"I just remembered my dream." I turn to Wes.

"Uh-huh." His eyes are still glued to the TV screen, and they flit from one image to the next.

"You're not listening to me." The dream had come back to me in slow bursts of visuals all night. This last death where my character burst into flames finally put it all together like a puzzle. It drove me crazy, this lingering emotion that I couldn't quite place. "Do you want to hear about it?"

"Honestly, no." He jabs at the buttons of the controller furiously, and I hit him with one of the many pillows that make up our video game nest. He's been my best friend since childhood, so he's the only person I feel comfortable shamelessly attacking. Maybe my little brother is the other exception. "Hey!" He flinches when I hit him. "I'm the only one left. Do you want me to finish this level for us or not?"

Our favorite video game, Immortal Soldiers, is our Sunday pastime. My father loathes the violent shooting game. I know this level of the game well enough to know Wes is going to get killed soon, so I huff and decide I'll wait patiently. This is the part where we round a corner, and out of the rubble and ash of the crumbling cityscape a monstrous killer robot rises up and blows us to bits with its mechanical machine-gun arms. I know this part of the game like it's one of my own memories. *Why can't I remember the rest of the dream?* I just had it.

My mother's voice travels through the doorway from the dining room. "Olivia, Wes, can you turn your game down? We're trying to have a conversation in here."

"Almost done, Mom! Wes is shit at this game anyway."

"What was that?"

"Nothing!"

Wes giggles. But right as he does, the killer robot appears on the screen and he's gunned down in a graphic explosion. He curses and throws his controller to the floor. "Every damn time. I swear, we play this every weekend and we never get past this part."

"Maybe it's because you play like crap."

"You *invented* playing like crap."

"You used that one last week, genius." I love teasing Wes. My mom used to yell at me when we were younger because apparently Wes was a sensitive boy, and she was worried I would hurt his self-esteem. I'm just surprised she thought my sarcasm was good enough to permanently damage someone.

"Don't pretend like your humor has advanced since fifth grade." He picks up his controller again to keep playing.

"Says the one who's still wearing that comic book shirt. Didn't your mom buy you a whole new wardrobe for senior year? When are you going to stop dressing like a middle schooler?"

"When I get a girlfriend and have to."

"So, never. I'm going to be wheeling you out of the senior center in your superhero pajamas then."

"Hey, weren't you going to tell me about your dream?"

"Oh, that's right!" I frown, wondering how my thoughts had drifted so far away. "I forgot it now."

"Via, you've been trying to remember this all night. Maybe if you hadn't spent so much time ripping on my incredible sense of style—"

"Wait! I think I remember. I was looking for something, and then I died."

Wes's amusement fades. He sets down the controller lightly. "That's um… dark."

"Yeah well, I don't even remember how, so…" I trail off and he still doesn't look up at me. "Hey."

"Hey what."

"I'm gonna miss you."

"Come on," he nudges me. "You're just a town over now. It's like a thirty-minute drive to see your favorite nerd."

"Still. Senior year is going to be so weird without you, especially in this house. It looks like it hasn't been renovated since the seventies." I notice a shadow cross his eyes. "And what about you? Are you sure you're going to be okay without me?"

He looks down at his wrists and pulls his sleeves down over the scars.

"I didn't mean that," I say quickly. "I just meant…"

Behind us suddenly, the sound of bare feet thumps down the hall. Josh is in his usual hoodie and basketball shorts. His dark hair bounces up and down on his cute round head. He looks so much more Japanese than I do, just like our father. Right behind him is Danielle, who sports the same blonde, highlight-streaked hair as Wes. It's a miracle our younger siblings get along. Otherwise they would spend all their time bothering me and Wes instead of keeping each other busy.

I hop up from my spot in front of the TV and grab Josh by the hood. He squeals in protest, but I pinch his cheeks anyway.

"Get off me!" his voice cracks in that pre-pubescent teen way. "I told you not to do that!"

"What, this?" I pinch his cute little chubby cheeks again. He's kind of fat for his grade, but I love that about him. I hope he never grows out of it, because then he's going to be way better looking than me.

He smacks my hand away. "Go play with your boyfriend."

"Go play with your girlfriend."

"She's not my girlfriend."

"That's okay, just be friends for now. Friendship is the best foundation before marriage."

I always enjoy how this makes Josh and Danielle squirm. It's the way young Wes and I would squirm when our parents would tease us about the same thing.

"Guess what? I'm telling Dad you didn't do your summer homework." Josh makes a face and then scampers down the hall into the dining room.

"Hey!" Panic rises up as I chase him through the doorway. *God, seventh graders have no respect for pinky promises.* As I scramble after my brother, I trip over half-empty boxes and piles of books that wait to be unpacked. I curse to myself and recover just in time to see Josh dart into the dining room.

My brother bursts in, and the commotion jolts the attention of all the adults. My parents crowd around one end of the dining table with wine glasses in hand. They stop their conversation with Wes's parents and wait for an explanation. I stare blankly at my mom and dad, Tom and Emilia Prescott; my father insisted on adopting her last name when we moved to America. He also insisted that we never run in the house.

"Via didn't do her summer homework. She lied," Josh blurts out. "She made me pinky promise not to tell you."

"I am never telling you anything again," I hiss.

My father gives me a stony glare. His stern complexion is one I have learned to resent this past year. The same withering look tells me I can't have sleepovers with friends, I can't take the car out at night, or I can't stay up playing video games with Wes. If I got as much of his genes as Josh did, I wonder if I would have that same capacity to glare.

My mom says, "You can't start out your senior year already behind on work, Olivia. I told you I would give you some slack last semester, but this is a new school."

Josh gives me a devilish grin and escapes the dining room.

I cross my arms. "I'm not going to that school. All the other kids are going to be total computer nerds. We already had this conversation."

"You know it's not up for discussion anymore. This school is the whole reason we moved towns."

"We moved for Dad's new job. Don't pretend like this is about me."

"This is a great school, Via. It's going to get you into some very good colleges. But that's only if you actually *try* to do your work." My dad purses his lips.

"Dad, I—"

"We just don't want what happened last year to affect your senior year."

I feel my chest tighten. "Why do you always have to bring that up? That has nothing to do with anything, but you always go back to it."

"Don't be so harsh to your father," Mom warns.

"I was in the hospital for a week, and he's acting like I have brain damage or something," I snap. I know they hate when I get into this around Wes's parents, but they're the ones who always blame everything on "the Incident." My grades, my lack of a social life, even my sarcasm can apparently be traced back to that night in January.

"Can we talk about this later? It's not a very cheerful dinner table topic." Her gaze levels on mine.

"You're right," I say. "Lawrence and Beth don't want to hear you parent me anymore."

"Oh, that's what that was? Parenting?" Wes's father, Lawrence, teases. Thankfully the tension is relieved. For now.

"Lawrence!" Beth scolds her husband and almost knocks over her own glass in the process. She's drunk, although on a scale from one to last year's New Year's Eve, not that bad. "Olivia is right, though. We don't want to hear about that. We want to hear about your new school, tell us more! Is it true about the—" she hiccups, "the you-know-what?"

When she says this, I glance over at the other end of the table where a pamphlet for Park Falls Technical High School sits open. I pick it up, and a picture of a student robotics lab stares up at me.

"Just read the pamphlet they gave my mom." I throw it down in front of them and storm out.

CHAPTER 2

In the end I didn't really have a choice in the matter. Wes and his conspiracy theories are right. Free will is an illusion—at least, when you're seventeen.

I stand at the side of the hallway as a current of students push past. The smell of fresh paint and the sounds of banging lockers fill the newly built school. A large poster on the wall stares back at me, and I shake my head. It's a large silhouette of a nondescript person, and a cheesy question mark is plastered in the middle. Something about those cartoonish letters that read "Who is the Agent?" makes my skin crawl. These damn things are all over, as if it wasn't already on all of our minds.

The large double doors to the gym swing open. I filter in toward the back of the crowd. Four years of high school later, facing the vast rattling bleachers, I still get knots in my stomach when I think about where I'm going to sit. My eyes dart from nameless face to nameless face, and I don't even know what I'm looking for. I finally climb up to an empty seat at the end of one of the rows. My backpack lets out a loud thud as I set it at my feet, which causes a girl in the row in front of me to whip around. She has dark hair and even darker eyebrows. Those brows attack me with a look of either curiosity or judgement; I can't tell which one. She finally looks away as a round man in a suit steps up to a microphone in the center of the court. The buzz of chatter lulls.

"Welcome to Park Falls Technical High School, everyone! I will be your principal this year, Principal Conners, and I am *very* excited to embark on this journey with you." The short man beams up at all his students. The buttons on his shirt look as if they're going to burst from his rounded belly, and his cheeks glow red above a bushy beard. *He smiles too much.* I look around to see if other students are thinking the same thing. "Just like all of you, this is my first year at Park Falls High. Everyone is new here, and everyone will be learning their way around. This school is a really exciting place to be, so I hope you all know how lucky you are to study here. We have a unique STEM-based curriculum, access to advanced technologies, and, what I'm sure all of you are most excited about…" Principal Conners pulls out a remote and with a click of a button, the sleek projector screen behind him lights up with the same image from the posters around school. "The Agent!"

Whispers ripple across the bleachers. I notice some groups of kids roll their eyes while some visibly bubble over with excitement. I just think about what my father would say right now, how impressed he would be. The very thought leaves a sour taste in my mouth.

"Yes, that's right, thanks to YouTech Laboratory we have been given the opportunity to participate in the very first humanoid artificial intelligence simulation. You get to be a part of history!" Principal Conners's enthusiasm bellows. He changes the slide to a stock photo of kids working on robotics. "Think of this as an extracurricular project, something to stimulate your minds outside of class. Don't let it affect your everyday studies, but treat it like a game that will stretch your creativity and open you up to deeper thinking. There could be a robot sitting among you right now!"

This is the biggest bullshit I've ever heard. Arms crossed in my seat, I look down at the girl in front of me. She doesn't even pay attention and just scrolls through her phone. I resist the urge to pull out mine and text Wes.

"I know you all have many questions, which can be answered at a later time. My door is always open. So, without further ado, I would like to introduce the representative from YouTech Laboratory who will be working with our school. Stephen Richards!"

There's a weak applause, and another man crosses the gymnasium floor. Almost a complete contrast to the jolly principal, Mr. Richards is a tall man with a suit that looks like it was tailored just for him. The lines of his jacket are as sharp as his hooked nose, the color of the fabric as dark as the shadows in his deep-set eyes. He almost looks like a hawk, staring down his prey from behind the microphone with a beady gaze.

"Thank you for the introduction, Principal Conners. I will be working with this school throughout its first year, making sure everything is going smoothly and checking in on all of my… work. I'll mostly be running operations out of the lab's headquarters, but occasionally you may see me lurking in the hallways. Don't be alarmed. You are all unknowing cogs on a greater machine. This simulation is merely a test of our own technology and should not affect your day-to-day lives."

"This guy is creepy as hell," one of the boys next to me says to his neighbor.

"Seriously. I bet *he's* an Agent, look at the way he talks," the kid replies with a chuckle.

When the assembly is over, I follow the stream of students out of the gym like cows being corralled to slaughter. As I turn the corner into the cafeteria, I'm greeted by the hum of conversation and the scrape of hundreds of chairs. The room stretches far in front of me. The low ceiling creates an almost cavern-like chamber. Tables hug every square inch of the space, and I weave through the clumps of students until I find myself at the section in the back. Seniors are sprawled across tables in clusters. They ooze arrogance and confidence that I don't understand and could never mimic.

All of them look painfully human. I desperately search the array of groups for recognizable faces to sit with, and I can't help but find myself in search for some kind of giveaway. Some kind of cache that one of them is the Agent. They all look too normal, too much the same. If anything, *I* look like the Agent, standing here awkwardly with nowhere to go. *Why do they all seem to have friends already? Aren't we all new here?*

It's hard to look confident when you don't have a place to sit. I try not to look lost as my hands find the straps of my backpack. I feel discomfort creep under my skin the longer I stand with nowhere to go. It's like a ticking clock. I wish Wes was here.

"Olivia?"

It's Sydney from my first-period biology class, the only one I had before the assembly. I feel a rush of relief as she waves me over. I pull up a chair and squeeze in next to her, but there's not enough space for me to really fit. The other girls acknowledge me; I only know half of their names.

When I sit down, I notice the familiar attack of dark eyebrows from across the table. It's as if they were drawn on to have that affect. It's the same girl who sat in front of me at the assembly. She just glares at me as the rest of the group asks questions.

"So, which high school did you come from again?" one of them asks without looking up from her phone.

"Lakeland," I say.

"Never heard of it. How are you liking it here?"

"It's okay."

"Do you think any boys are cute?" Sydney asks.

"I don't know."

"What was the name you said you liked to be called?" another girl chimes in.

"Via," I say.

"Anyway," Sydney moves on. "Did you hear what that one kid, Max, was saying at the assembly? I overheard him talking about what his mom does at the lab. He said she works on the Agent. Apparently, he knows all kinds of stuff about it."

I see the girl with the bold eyebrows make a scrunched face, as if she mocks Sydney.

"He says the Agent is more likely to wear plaid because a computer is drawn to that kind of pattern."

"That's wild, but that's not what I heard. I heard that it can't wear a watch," one of the other girls says.

"I heard it can't draw. Or listen to music."

The rumors continue to pile up one by one as each person at the table comments on different things they heard or different things their parents know. I stay silent, wondering how anyone could believe any of that. I check my phone for texts from Wes, but nothing.

"I have to go to the bathroom. I'll be back." I stand up to leave.

"Do you want us to go with you? We totally will," the girl with the eyebrows says.

"I'm fine, thanks."

I navigate through the cluster of students until I'm out in the hall and then check my phone again. No texts. My sneakers scuff on the tile of the hallways as I wander through the school. I head into the stairwell and up to the second floor. Windows peer into classroom labs with expensive amenities and barely touched equipment. Occasionally I come across other kids eating their lunch in classrooms or in groups out in the hall, and they stare at me as I pass them. I duck into the library instead. I walk through modern bookshelves and rows of high-tech computers that nobody is using. The silent shelves give way to a section of study desks in the back, and a single boy has his head buried in a laptop. He glances up when I approach a desk near him. Through large-framed glasses he gives me a startled look. I catch a glimpse of the You-Tech Laboratory building on his screen before he slams the computer shut. I murmur something along the lines of "Sorry" before I turn and flee.

Back in the cafeteria, I still picture the boy's startled brown eyes. I sit down at my original lunch table once more.

"So, which high school did you come from again?"

"Lakeland."

"Never heard of it. How are you liking it here?"

"It's okay."

"Do you think any boys are cute?"

"I don't know."

"What was the name that you said you liked to be called?"

"Via."

For the rest of the day this conversation repeats on loop, again and again until the words I respond with sound strange in my own mouth.

* * *

Friday during one of our free periods is the first time in a while I feel like I'm in middle school again. The girls openly talk about a party in front of me without inviting me. The one with the dark hair, who I now know is Klara, passive-aggressively compliments my outfit. With her prying eyebrows that cut into my soul, it somehow comes off as an insult. I feel like the old me for the first time in a while—that middle school version of Via who was a nerd, a version of me I've run very far and fast from.

But then I go to class and remember the one good thing I still share with that Olivia—math.

I've always liked math. But more importantly, I've always been good at it. If anything has carried me through school with a decent chance of getting into college, it's this. For a lot of people, it's just a fun thing to complain about. But I find it reassuring. There are facts and formulas and limits. Everything is logical and makes sense. You know when you have the right answer, and you know when you're doing it wrong. Clear rules can be defined and followed without any blurring of lines. In the end, it all works out like a nice neat puzzle. Most importantly, though, it is never subject to opinion.

In the social climate of Park Falls Technical High School, everything is subject to opinion.

At lunch I don't wait for Sydney to wave me over. I just pull up a chair to their table. As usual Klara bores into me with that unwavering gaze. I expect the usual stream of questions, the same ones I've answered all week; no matter how many times we have this interaction, I know we're always back to square one.

But then I realize something is different. Today, everyone stares at me. The whole table.

"Cute shirt, Olivia," Sydney says.

"Thanks..." I look down at my flannel, and that's when I realize. Plaid.

"I think it's really clever, making fun of the rumors and everything." Klara raises one of her eyebrows, and the whole table laughs half-heartedly.

"She's right, that's so cool," another girl smiles. "I love how you just don't care what other people think."

I look over at Klara, whose eyebrows attack me, and then at the rest of the smiling girls. I try to focus on my breathing. *One, two, three, four...* I glance around the buzzing cafeteria where everyone is wearing shirts and jackets and sweaters—none of them plaid. And everyone is wearing a watch too. Everyone except for me.

"I forgot I left my tablet in biology today." I push out of my chair. All sets of eyes look up at me. As I leave the table, I feel the back of my neck prickle with other people's inquisitive stares. I slam into someone's shoulder out in the hall and he stumbles with a shocked laugh. His long coat and unkempt hair are just a blur to me as I apologize and keep moving. I throw open the bathroom door across the hall to find girls already inside. I go over to a sink and wash my hands, pretending to scrub them meticulously until they leave. Only when I'm alone do I pull out my phone and type a message.

Hey Wes, what's up?

I lean against the sink counter and wait for a response and look into the mirror at my reflection. *Stupid.* I take off the flannel and wrap it around my waist. Suddenly my phone buzzes. I look at the text from Wes.

Sorry, can't text right now. I'm at lunch with the guys.

I tap the screen with my nails. *Of course he's busy at lunch. That's normal.* Just then I hear voices outside the bathroom, and I slide into one of the stalls before they come in. The door rattles as I close it.

"I'm not saying I believe any of the rumors. I know the whole plaid thing is dumb," I hear one of the girls say. I recognize the voice as Sydney's.

"Oh, I know, totally," the other voice responds over the running sink. "It's just, you know, she's kind of quiet anyway. She's cute, but her vibe is a little weird."

"Right? And none of us went to school with her before, so it could totally be her."

The two girls leave the bathroom, and I'm left alone in the cramped stall. My reflection in the shiny new door wavers, and under my breath I count, "One, two, three, four..." My phone buzzes and I expect a text from Wes. But it's not. It's from an unknown number. It says: *five, six, seven, eight.*

Heart pounding, I push open the door and peek out of my stall. Nobody else is in the bathroom.

CHAPTER 3

I amble through the hallway of my house, wading through boxes and trying to find something in the all-consuming dark. My hands search the walls, eyes straining to see, but the hall never ends. I can't find what I'm looking for. In the distance I see a flicker of light and feel a twinge of heat on my skin. Maybe a fire? I step closer, tears bursting into my eyes from the intensity. That's when I see it. A shadow sits in the center of the house, a black hole in the space between licking flames. I think it's a person. The cloaked figure turns slowly, but just as I'm about to see its face, I wake up.

Startled from the dream, I sweat as if I can still feel the fire on my skin. I swing my feet onto the cold floor and go downstairs in the dark. There are no boxes or flames, just art that hangs on the walls. My parents are asleep, and Josh is asleep. I should've known it was just a dream. Anything that illogical and nonsensical isn't something I like to dwell on. But still, that feeling. I pull out my phone and it illuminates the lurking shadows. The text from the unknown number stares back at me in my half-asleep state. *Five, six, seven, eight.*

* * *

Sunday is the day I get to see Wes again and finally get to tell him about my horrible first week at this insane school. I thought he would be eager to hear about the program, rambling on about all kinds of science fiction jokes and conspiracies, but he's oddly unexcited.

"So, it was normal?"

Feeling the sting of his disinterest, I tug at my sleeves. "Well, *normal* isn't the word I would use… there's been a couple wild theories out there. Like for example, this one kid thinks the entire program isn't a state-sanctioned experiment at all, but an invasion. Robots disguising themselves as humans and then taking over society from the inside out. Pretty crazy, right?"

Wes shrugs. "I don't know. You don't think any of it could be true?"

A laugh catches in my throat. "Do you?"

"Sure, why not? Don't you think it's a little weird that of all the places they could have chosen, they put their headquarters in Park Falls? A town in the middle of nowhere?"

"Maybe they were looking for a place where nothing happens." In mathematics, you want to eliminate all the variables so there's less that could change and go wrong. Less confusion. *I should tell him about my dream. I should tell him about the texts from the unknown number.*

"We should go out and see the headquarters," Wes says suddenly.

"Like, where my dad works?"

"Yeah, aren't you curious? Maybe we could do a little snooping about the Agent, uncover some dirty secrets from YouTech Labs. I don't know."

"Did I hear something about YouTech Labs?" My dad darkens the living room like a cloud. Immediately I pause the game, and he frowns. "Wes, you know we have a house rule about taking your shoes off."

"Sorry, Tom, I didn't—"

"We were actually just leaving." I drag Wes to his feet. *What a kiss-ass.* "We're taking the car."

"Where are you going?" he asks, lips pursed.

"Via, I don't like when your dad looks at me like that," Wes hisses as I pull him toward the doorway. "You're making him mad and he's giving me that look. I don't want that look. That look isn't a good sign for me."

"Okay, bye, Dad!" I close the door behind us. "You wanted to go on a little investigation. Right? Then let's go."

My family's faded red Subaru sits in the driveway like a stain. Wes slams the door of the passenger side, which rocks the small car on its wheels. "You know you better watch out, or one day Tom will actually murder me. Then you'll really have no friends."

I start the car and pull out of the driveway, all the while picturing the stern face I know awaits me at home. It worries my parents when I take the car out for no reason. They think every time, it'll be a repeat of what happened in January.

Our ride hums and pulses under my grip on the steering wheel. Thick vibrant forest whips by, and soon we're out of the suburbs and into the darker woods. The road winds further away from the booming suburbs, past the thriving downtown, and up into the wilderness where newly populated cabins and vacation homes are littered along the lakeside. YouTech building their headquarters here was the best thing to ever happen to Park Falls, and my family is just one of hundreds to flock to these rolling woodlands.

Wes gives me directions from his phone. My palms start to sweat a little bit, and I notice an anxious flutter in my chest. *I don't care about seeing the lab. I don't even care about figuring out who the Agent is. This is for Wes.* As we're getting closer to the destination, the lanes narrow, and the pines close in on the road. I see Wes fidget. *I should tell him about school. I should tell him about the girls and the rumors and the unknown texts.* I drum my fingers on the side door but keep my eyes focused ahead. *One, two, three, four...*

"You're doing it again."

I tap the leather harder. "Doing what?"

"I can tell because you make that face when you're stressed. You're counting."

"I'm not stressed." I shift in my seat. "How's therapy going?"

"Screw you." Wes's lips twist into a smile. "How's your dad's new job?"

I glance down at the GPS directions. "I don't know. He doesn't talk to me unless he's lecturing me about homework. But you should see him after he comes home every day. I think he's more unhappy at the lab than I am at this new school."

Wes shifts in his seat, and the car grows silent. Then he points. "I think it's just up here."

I slow the car as my tires crunch on the gravel of the poorly maintained road. There it is. It's even uglier than my classmates said it would be. A tremendous slab of smooth concrete and sharp glass, the building juts out from the dense pines like a sword from a wound. It's massive, a colossal eyesore tucked away deep into the northern woods. *To think that every single Park Falls student has a parent who works here, and yet nobody knows what goes on inside...*

"You know, I read something the other day about You-Tech's research on advanced machine learning and AI models.

They have some of the best software engineers in the world. I read that the programmers who build the new Agent for this program can't even tell the difference."

I roll my eyes at Wes, and then I'm drawn back across the road toward the YouTech building. *I know we're watching them, but why do I feel like they're watching us?*

"I read about this test where an Agent was made to look exactly like the brother of the software engineer who programmed it. Then they put the brother and the robot in the same room, and the guy couldn't even tell which was which. Isn't that… terrifying?"

My head shakes. "I still don't buy it."

"Don't buy what?"

"It's bullshit. Just like this school, just like the Agent. Couldn't the brother, the one in this experiment, just ask the robot about a really personal memory?"

Wes brushes his hair out of his face. "Memory is a weird thing. It's kind of subjective."

The car grows silent. Suddenly I wish we were back in our nest of pillows in my living room, playing Immortal Soldiers and hitting Wes for giggling.

"What are we even looking for?" I scour the edges of the building, the vast parking lot. *We don't have a specific question or a goal yet. That's like solving a math problem without knowing the formula—it's pointless.*

"I don't know. You tell me." He turns in his seat. "You're the one who's in their simulation. What do your friends say?"

"I don't have any."

"It's only been a week. It can't be that bad." Wes sighs. "Get a boyfriend. Then you can sit with him and his friends."

"I'm being serious! It's like everyone already knows each other, and somehow I missed it. You know what I'm talking about. Like there must be something weird about you that you just don't know. What do they see that you don't? You torture yourself trying to find out why certain people don't want to get to know you, and there's just no logical explanation."

"Maybe it's high school and people are just dumb."

"Fine." I crack a smile. "But it was easier when I only needed you."

"You always wanted other friends, Via. The only reason you didn't have any is because you gave up."

"I gave up?" *Why did he say it like that?*

"Yeah," he shrugs. "You always had me, so you stopped trying to get close to other people."

Blood rushes to my cheeks. "I didn't give up. You know what happened." Mind reeling, I tighten my grip on the steering wheel. "After *the Incident,* my dad wouldn't even let me go to the grocery store, much less go to a party or a football game. I couldn't get close to people even if I wanted to, not after that night."

"Really, we're doing this again? Look, you're not the only one whose social life took a blow." Wes leans back and puts distance between us. "I started going to therapy twice a week, and my parents don't let me out of their sight most days. And when they do, they think I'm going to—"

"This isn't about that. It's about this new town and how it sucks."

"No, it doesn't, it just—"

"You don't know, Wes! You don't go here!"

He looks down. "You're right. I don't." I feel a pang of guilt in my chest as I see him bite his tongue and move away from me in the car. "I didn't mean to bring up the Incident. I'm sorry."

We don't ever talk about that night last January, the one he was there for. But when we do, it's like we're no longer on the same wavelength. Something about this eerie laboratory and being this far up in the woods makes us both on edge.

"Let's get out of here." I turn the keys and start the car. As I do, something catches my eye on our side of the road. Through the tree trunks and down from the road, a boy with jet-black hair and glasses stands by the lake.

"What is it?" Wes notices I've stopped.

"I think… I think that's a kid who goes to my school. I have English class with him," I say. The boy just stands there and stares out at the water. My mind goes back to the library when I saw him and he slammed his computer shut.

Wes shakes his head. "I hate this place. What would possess someone to come up here alone?"

* * *

After going up to the lab on Sunday with Wes, after so many new suspicions have appeared, I have this restless feeling in my gut that I can't shake. Math is all about patterns and rules, objectively reaching the same conclusion. And my life is becoming more and more like… English.

In English, there are no clear lines or facts. Everything is dependent on your interpretation, and there are really no right answers. Virtually any theme can be taken from any book, and anything you write could become a piece of literature. At least, that's what I've experienced. Half the time the entire class is just bullshitting themselves through essays and oral presentations. The other half of the time the students are the teacher's favorites, and they could say complete crap and still get A's. It's ridiculous. Almost as insane as thinking there could be a robot next to me this very moment. Which I do think about. A lot.

It's probably Jimmy Andrade.

It's Monday afternoon, and everyone seems to be sociable after the weekend. But not Jimmy. I watch him as he sits in his chair like he's hiding from something. His neck retreats into his collar like a turtle in its shell. His face is very symmetrical with a chin that's as square as the black rims of his glasses. He has jet-black hair that's neatly lifted up in the front, not a hair out of place. He's always fidgeting with a pencil or tapping his knee. If a single strand of hair falls down to his forehead, it's immediately swept back into place.

As I observe him sitting in front of me, I can't help but wonder what a boy like that was doing standing by the lake across from YouTech headquarters.

"Sorry we're running a little late today," our teacher, Ms. Xavier, scrambles around the room setting down folders. Her scattered energy matches the eclectic variety of patterns in her outfit, and she's placed stray hair clip in a seemingly random fashion on her short bob. *God, English teachers. How did she even get hired at a technical STEM high school?* "I'm just going to hand back your essays on Macbeth before you leave," she says.

I can see my dad's face now if I get a bad grade on my first big essay. I look over at Jimmy and watch him survey his paper.

"Do you think if the Agent was in this class, it would do well on this paper?" I lean forward.

Jimmy looks startled when I talk to him.

"I just want to know in case a robot is ruining our curve."

He shifts uncomfortably and then fiddles with his pencil. "An Agent might be able to analyze Shakespeare. Artificial intelligence creates art and composes music all the time. What constitutes art is subjective, so whether the computer is truly understanding what it's creating with intent or just going through the motions and mimicking, it probably doesn't matter. Students just imitate previous analyses of Shakespeare without understanding anyway, so why would an Agent be any different?"

"Right." I turn back to the test. *So much for sarcastic banter.* This is the kid in class who will ask the teacher about the homework when you were hoping she forgot. Sarcasm is my love language, but I'm at a loss here. I have no other social skills to carry me.

"What did you get on your essay?"

He holds up his paper shyly, as if embarrassed. "A minus."

"Poor you. Where will you go when your family disowns you?"

He smiles to himself this time as he registers the joke. It's very subtle, like he laughs at something only he understands. "What about you?"

"I got a D. My grade for the class is now officially a C minus."

He hides a wince. "That's not too horrible."

"It caused you physical pain when I said the letter D. I saw it on your face. You know it's bad." I zip up my bag.

"Alright, well, see you tomorrow." Jimmy adjusts his glasses and then heads out the door. I watch him leave and push away that itch to ask him questions about the lakeside. I sling my backpack over my shoulder and head in the opposite direction of the hallway. I don't make it far before I stop and turn back.

"Jimmy!" I race to catch up with him down the hall. He looks over his shoulder in surprise, as if nobody has ever called his name at school. "Listen, this might be weird, but could you tutor me?"

"Um... tutoring?"

"I just know my dad is going to kill me if I don't get my grades up. I don't play any sports or anything, and no offense, but I don't think you do either, so we can do it whenever."

"You're serious?" his face contorts with confusion.

"Of course I'm serious. I want to get into college," I laugh nervously.

"But why me?"

"So you… don't want to?"

Jimmy shoves his hands in his pockets. "If you want, I guess I could."

"Worth a shot. Right? How about Thursdays?"

Jimmy adjusts his glasses. "Yeah, yeah I can do next Thursday." When I start to walk away, he says, "Um, where exactly?"

"My house," I say. "We'll text about it later."

"You don't have my number."

"I'll be able to reach you. Don't worry. Nothing a little light stalking won't solve."

"Oh," is all he says. Then I lose him in the congested crowds of the hall.

Why did I do that? Do I really need a tutor? This only happens in the movies when someone is using it as an excuse to get with someone else. I don't have a crush on Jimmy, but when I picture the kid's face after I asked him, it makes me happy. The way his forehead wrinkled right above his glasses, and how he shoved his hands in his pockets. Part of me enjoys making him uncomfortable. In a weird way it makes me feel more at ease to have the upper hand. Maybe this makes me feel better because I might have finally made one meaningful connection at this school.

Or maybe, as much as I think this whole Agent investigation is ridiculous, deep down I know something is strange about Jimmy Andrade.

CHAPTER 4

"Please, it's not that big of a deal," I beg Jimmy as we emerge from the library together.

"I know. I just don't like being in the cafeteria." He adjusts his glasses. "The library is a lot quieter, which is surprising actually because most of the amenities at this school are state of the art and very underused—"

"Jimmy," I stop him by one of the large windows that frame the trees outside. "It's one lunch."

"You're just tired of sitting with the girls. If it bothers you so much, find another table. The social hierarchy of this school is still developing."

"But see, that's the thing. It feels like it's already set in stone." I hop up onto the window ledge and press my backpack against the glass. "I have no idea why, because everyone's supposed to be new kids here. We're all strangers to each other!"

"Not everyone." He stares at the floor.

Before I can respond, four boys erupt from the classroom door on our left and one of them clips Jimmy's backpack in his haste. Jimmy's glasses almost fly into me while I'm perched on the ledge. The group stops abruptly, and I recognize the smaller kid as Alex from my economics class.

"Sorry, man, didn't mean to hit you," one of the boys murmurs. He's impressively built for a high schooler with his t-shirt stretched tight over lean muscles and olive skin. His dark hair falls in waves around his forehead. I just barely catch a glimpse of hostility in the moment he locks eyes with Jimmy. Alex looks at the ground, and the three boys behind him shift uncomfortably.

"It's fine." Jimmy's square jaw clenches. They stand there and simmer for a moment longer. Then he says, "I'll be in the library, Via. See you later."

He brushes past the group and hurries down the hall. I press my lips together as I watch him go. Then I'm left alone on the window's ledge with just the boys. Alex nudges his friend, "Come on, Elliot, let's go."

With one last backward glance, Elliot turns and heads for the stairwell. Alex gives me an awkward smile as the rest of them follow. *What was that all about? Did Jimmy and that boy Elliot know each other?*

The hallway empties out slowly for lunch in the lazy flow of a Wednesday afternoon, but I stay rooted in my spot. I glance out the window toward the trees as my gaze searches deeper into the woods behind the campus. I tap my foot on the wall and then pull out my phone. No texts from Wes or anyone else. I sigh and put my phone away. *There's no excuse for me not to go to lunch.*

The similar buzz of conversation and clanking of chairs animates the cafeteria. I wander in alone. Klara and all the girls circle the table with their heads down, glued to their phones. I suddenly feel exhausted. I am not in the mood for that. I don't want to sit there and pretend to be on my phone just to avoid looking like the odd man out, wondering what kind of rumor I've missed the mark on this time.

And that's when I see the group of boys I just ran into.

"Hey, Alex," I approach their table without thinking twice.

Alex looks up at me in confusion, and the three other boys are startled out of their conversation. One of them is Elliot, and the other two I don't know—a redhead and a boy engulfed in a game on his phone.

"Did you want to go over the economics homework or something? I know it's pretty weird, studying a utopian market in space. But Ben did it already because he's in the earlier section." Alex points to the ginger kid.

"No," I tug at my sleeves. "I was just, uh… do you mind if I sit with you guys?"

Do you mind if I sit with you guys? That was a pathetic thing to say. I sound like I'm desperate. I should've been more casual.

"What's your name again?" Ben asks.

"It's Olivia," Elliot responds without hesitation, and I'm surprised he knows me.

"Yeah, Olivia." I pull up a chair.

The boy who games on his phone hits Ben. "Why would you ask that? Plus, it's not even Olivia. It's Via. She said it like three times in robotics home room."

Ben sneers. "She literally *just* said Olivia. I'm pretty sure she knows her own name, Cole."

"It's called a nickname, dipshit."

While they continue to banter, Elliot leans over to me and says, "Sorry about that thing earlier with Jimmy. I didn't want to come off as rude."

"No, it's fine," I shrug. "But watch out, I might start a rumor that you're the Agent."

He laughs with his whole face. His eyes squint and dimples flex around his smile in a very different look from the one he gave Jimmy earlier.

"Oh wait, I almost forgot." Cole suddenly types furiously on his phone. Ben kicks him under the table, which makes him groan.

"Dude, not now," Elliot hisses, but Cole passes the device over to me anyway. I grab it hesitantly.

I stare at the screen, and it takes a moment for me to register what's in front of me. It's one of those tests that comes up when you log onto a site or order something online. It's the one that asks you to type out the letters you see.

"Is this... one of those 'I am not a robot' things?"

"Jesus Christ." Alex buries his head in his palm.

"A CAPTCHA test, exactly," Cole says and laces his fingers together. I realize he's still waiting for me to do it. I clear my throat and type in the letters quickly, giving it back to him when I'm done.

"See, I told you it wouldn't work." Ben holds out his hand, and Cole reluctantly fishes a five-dollar bill out of his pocket.

"I am so sorry about them." Alex gives me a sheepish look, and Elliot throws chips across the table.

My face still burns red, but I smile faintly and pull a sandwich out of my backpack. CAPTCHA tests or not, at least I don't have to deal with the rumors or the whispering anymore. It's not what I pictured, but it's something.

* * *

"Alright, your move." I smack the tacky plastic chess piece onto the cut-out board. *If this school can afford high-tech projectors and devices, why can't it buy nicer chess boards?*

Klara doesn't look up from her phone. She doesn't even pretend to be paying attention to the game, much less hide the fact that she scrolls through her social media in the middle of the exercise. *Why did I have to be partnered with her, of all people?* The morning light filters in through the classroom window and fills the negative space between partners.

I clear my throat, and her sharp eyebrows perk. "Did you say something?"

"No, it's just... uh, it's your turn."

"Oh, you're actually playing?" She sits up. "I thought everyone was just pretending because Principal Conners is watching."

It's true, the round man popped in through the doorway of our math class just to watch everyone play chess. It was his idea, I'm pretty sure, to make the whole school do a chess tournament as a "fun" cognitive lesson. Little did he know, everyone just wastes time and loses on purpose so they don't seem like the Agent.

Well, not that one kid in the corner. He's been winning every single game shamelessly. It's the same kid in a long coat that I bumped into the first week; I watch him shake his head of unkempt hair and slam another piece down in front of his opponent. *See, now* that's *a kid who doesn't give a shit about rumors.*

With a flick of dark hair that snaps me out of my thoughts, Klara places her elbows right on top of the board and rests her head on her hands.

"So, Olivia."

"Via," I correct her.

She flicks her hand. "Sure. Listen, a couple of the girls and I have been wondering... are you dating Alex?"

"What?"

"So, you *are* dating him."

"I'm glad you interpreted my confusion that way."

"Is that a yes?" Her sharp eyebrows perk. *God, those eyebrows could cut someone.*

"Sadly, no. I am still very much single. Thank you for reminding me." I hope she recognizes my sarcasm.

"Wait, you're not dating any of them?" the girl continues. "Any of them?"

"Ben, Elliot, Cole... none of them?"

"No..." I glance around the room. Everyone watches everyone and listens to everything. I hope they don't hear this conversation.

"Then why are you sitting with them? Do you have a crush on one of them?"

I feel personally attacked by her eyebrows. "I'm just sitting at their table. I don't like any of them like that. I just thought I'd... branch out."

"Huh, odd. Are you sure you don't even like Elliot?"

"Nope."

"Have you seen his body though?"

"Nope."

"You know, he kind of hangs out with nerds, but he's actually a huge basketball stud. Maybe that's not your type. That's assuming your type even *is* guys. I don't really know you that well. And of course, I have nothing against lesbians."

"Of course," I nod. *One, two, three, four...*

She takes my silence as a sign to talk. "Are you sure though? Because I heard a rumor that the Agent can't be gay, so that would kind of be a relief, you know."

"I really don't think I am." I press my lips together. *Five, six, seven, eight...*

"Well, you know if you ever do want to date Alex, just know that I think you two would be cute. I mean, I know he's short, but nothing you can't ignore." She looks down and removes her elbows from the wrecked board. "Oh, I think you were winning."

"Thanks?" I don't know what else to respond. *Did it take moving tables at lunch to get her attention?*

"You're totally welcome." Her mouth stretches into a shallow smile, the kind you practice in the mirror for photos. Luckily, the bell saves me from having to continue this interaction.

Kids pack up, and Principal Conners throws out enthusiastic remarks to everyone as they leave. "What did you think of this exercise? Isn't it great to expand your minds through complex games?"

I throw my backpack over my shoulder, and my feet barely move fast enough to leave the room. But Principal Conners catches me at the doorway and bounces like he's had too much caffeine. "Good morning, Olivia. I saw you were really getting into your game. Does this give you any *exciting* ideas about the Agent or how coders can mimic the human brain?"

"Well," I say. "I guess you'd have to be a pretty horrible coder to make a computer that can't play chess."

For a second he looks confounded, but then his beard twists back up into a smile, "You're absolutely right! Fascinating stuff, keep up the good work. You're burning it up!"

"Right. Burning it up," I say. My mind regurgitates terrifying memories from a dream.

Before Principal Conners can probe me about his little chess activity any further, I book it down the hall to my locker. I pass cheesy poster after cheesy poster and round the corner so fast I don't even see the person I knock into.

"Alex!" I exclaim as the boy drops his lunch, startled.

"You're fine," he laughs and crouches down to pick up the remains.

"I was planning to steal your lunch money, but this works too," I say. He gives me a confused look. "Sorry, bad joke." I shake my head and help him pick up his things.

"No, it's okay, I haven't had a bully knock my lunch out of my hands since middle school." When I don't react, he says, "Sarcasm. That was me trying to be sarcastic too."

I exhale and hand him his sandwich wrapped in saran wrap. *That was kind of funny.* "I appreciate you stooping to my level…" before I can continue the joke, though, something catches my eye. Alex's hand starts shaking, and the sandwich drops to the floor. He hastily pulls his hand back and I see the whites of his eyes. I look away.

"So, uh, I'll see you at lunch later?" Alex says quickly.

"Yeah, of course." I watch him walk away. Before he disappears into the swarm of students in the hallway, I see him reach up and clutch his right hand with white knuckles.

CHAPTER 5

"I found another really interesting article about AI today." My dad stalks into the kitchen where I struggle through homework. The soft glow of the light deepens the shadows on his face. "I sent it to you. I think you'd like it."

"I won't read it." I don't glance up from my computer. "Just tell me what it's about."

He opens the fridge and grabs a diet soda. "You really don't read any of the articles I send you? You used to love that kind of stuff."

I glare at him as his soda bottle fizzes. The sound pricks at my nerves. "Emphasis on *used* to. And now thanks to your work, my entire life has become about this stupid Agent and this ridiculous—" suddenly I see a new notification on my computer screen from the unknown number. My heart races.

"Are you learning anything interesting in your classes?" Dad tilts down the screen of my computer before I can see what the text says. My mind reels.

"Dad, I'm not in the mood for this tonight. It's a Wednesday. I need to get my assignment done."

"But you seemed pretty interested in your homework just now. You must be learning something."

"I played chess today in math. I did an AI personality test in English. We don't do anything normal. This school is a joke." I lift my screen again and look for the notification.

"An even better reason to read the articles I share with you."

"I haven't been bored enough to read something you shared with me since…" My eyes settle on the text from the unknown number, and it says: *January 29th.* "The hospital," I breathe.

"That's right, you read a lot in that hospital." He purses his lips together and takes a gulp of soda. I gaze up from the computer and realize I've made him uncomfortable by mentioning the Incident. I close the notification quickly and swallow hard. *One, two, three, four…* I try to focus on my homework, try to ignore that date, and type.

"Look, I know I can't share things with you about my work like I used to. I keep sending these articles so we have something to talk about. It is frustrating, but—"

"Do you even like your new job?"

When I ask him this, he takes off his reading glasses and cleans them on his shirt. He doesn't respond.

"All you do is proof other people's work at the lab. Right? And I know Mom misses teaching at the university. Don't pretend like you're happy to leave it all behind. I know you aren't."

"You can't go backward in life, Via. You always have to move forward." His face hardens into that stern look, and the shadows on his face set in stone. "Your mom and I sacrificed a lot to move here and put you in that school. We're doing this for—"

"For my own good, yeah, I know." I shut my computer. My bare feet slap on the kitchen floor as I storm out. My dad continues to sip his soda in silence.

* * *

"You really don't have to do this."

The parking lot rests in the shade of the trees around the school, new pavement with hardly even a crack in sight. Jimmy trails me as I weave between glinting cars, and behind us the shiny building of the high school blends into the trees as if it was part of the forest.

I sigh, "It would be ridiculous for you to take the bus to my house when I'm driving home anyway. Just let me give you a ride."

He pretends to think about it a little bit and buries his neck in his collar. "Okay. But just for this first session."

"You know, I'm surprised you don't have a car. Everyone here has a car. You can't live in Park Falls without one. How are you going to get home from parties when you're drunk?" He gives me a nervous look. "Kidding, I was kidding. I don't drink and drive. I barely drink."

"Okay," is all he says. We make it to my car and open up the Subaru's faded red doors. He starts to climb into the backseat.

"What are you doing?" I ask. He hesitates, shakes his head, and then closes the door and gets into the passenger seat. I laugh. "You're my tutor, not the president of the United States."

We barely make it five minutes out of the school parking lot before I see a flash of gold hoop earrings on the shoulder of the road. Klara walks slowly next to the afternoon rush of cars, her head buried in her phone. She seems small against the wall of trees.

I slow down, and Jimmy shifts uncomfortably. "What are you doing?"

"Is that Klara?"

He squirms in his seat. "You're going to give her a ride?"

"What, are you scared of her?" I tease.

He adjusts his glasses. "But weren't you just saying how—"

"I know what I said, shush." I roll down the window when we pull up to her. "Klara?"

Klara looks up from her phone and squints into the sun. Then she points between Jimmy and me. "What is this? Are you two dating now?"

Jimmy withers next to me. I ignore her. "Why are you walking?"

"My dad gave all my older brothers cars, but I guess he doesn't trust me with one. I take the bus now." She recoils in disgust. "Ew, right?"

I look at the road behind me for oncoming cars. "Do you need a ride?"

Jimmy gawks at me incredulously.

"That's super sweet of you, V." She melts into that superficial smile. I bite my tongue and resist the urge to tell her that's not my name. "But it's really okay. I haven't been to my cycle class in ages. I need the exercise. Plus, you don't want to go to my house. It's *way* up the road."

The sharp edge in her eyebrows makes me stop. *Why does she not want me to see her house?* I glance at the phone in her hand, which is like an extension of her arm. *Who is she always texting?*

"Are you sure? It'll be a lot faster than the bus," I push on.

All of her innocent glow fades away and leaves nothing but a cunning twinkle in her eyes. "I really don't like getting in cars with other people. You never know what can happen. There have been some pretty crazy accidents up the road. Especially in the winter, with all the snow on the ground."

My pulse quickens. *January 29th.* "Alright, see you around." I drive off and glance back at her shrinking figure in my side mirror.

"That's weird. Why was she talking about winter…" Jimmy murmurs. I feel my phone in my pocket and drum my fingers on the steering wheel.

A bit down the road, I pull off to the side and park the car in a dirt clearing among the trees. I can just barely see the bus stop from here.

"Wait, what are you doing?" Jimmy gulps.

"Nothing." I squint out the windshield.

After a few minutes, Klara's figure comes back into sight. I duck a little in my seat. Jimmy glances around anxiously, and I grab his collar and pull him down too.

"We're spying on her?" His voice cracks with fear.

"This will just take a minute." I peek back up and watch her dark ponytail disappear into the bus. As it roars and pulls away from the stop, I start the car again and creep out onto the road. We follow at a sizable distance and slowly wind away from the school and downtown. Now we're deeper into the woods. We pass glittering lakes and swathes of forest that just began to change to fall colors as the bus continues to climb.

"We're following her. Why are we following her? This is stalking. This is so wrong on so many different levels." Jimmy's leg bounces nervously.

Finally, the neighborhood changes. The bus pulls up to a stop right outside of a series of elaborate fences and towering pines. I watch Klara step out of the doors and skip along with her phone still in her hand. She halts in front of one of the wrought-iron gates, and I see a strange emblem with a set of initials stamped in the center of the bars.

"People in Park Falls have family crests? That seems strange. Isn't pretty much everyone new here?" I think aloud.

"Maybe she's just really rich. Can we go now?"

"Relax, you'll still get paid for this. Think of it as an extension of our tutoring session." I put the car in reverse and back away from Klara's looming property. Jimmy shrinks back into his collar and studies me with those large brown eyes.

* * *

When we get back to my house in the suburbs, Jimmy seems to relax a little. But as I lead him up the drive and into the entryway, he just shadows me awkwardly with his hands shoved into his pockets.

"So, this is the living room. Over there is the dining room, and behind that is the kitchen. Down that hall is the stairs. That's about it. My parents are still working, and Josh is at hockey, so we have the place to ourselves."

"It's nice." Jimmy looks around at my parents' display of sophistication and fine arts.

"Yeah, it's all new. It's a miracle it looks like this, finished and decorated with stuff. We just started moving at the end of the summer."

"Cool."

"When did your family move?"

"We didn't. My house is still in the district zone, only like fifteen minutes away. We got lucky." He takes his hands out of his pockets and taps them on the sides of his pants. "Um, where do you want to work?"

"We can just go into the dining room." I lead the way after I grab my backpack from the chair against the wall. I slide to the end of the table and pull out my stuff. Then I notice that Jimmy just hovers. "You can sit, you know."

"Right." He shakes his head slightly and then drops down quickly in the chair next to mine. His awkwardness makes me smile a little, like the way he didn't know how to handle me following Klara's bus.

I take out my laptop to show him my assignment. When my screen lights up, I suddenly remember the notification from the unknown number. "Quick question before we get started. What's your number?"

"Oh, here," he pulls out his phone. Immediately I see that it's not the same as the anonymous messages.

"Okay, thanks. Let me pull up my essay." I type on my laptop and then clear my throat. "By the way, I went up to YouTech Labs the other day. Just to check out the new headquarters. It's pretty cool, very Area-51 vibes. Do you ever... go up there?"

He adjusts his glasses. "No, why would I? Only our parents have clearance."

"Well, I don't know, there are some cool lake houses up there, nice views..."

"Do you do this all the time?"

"Do what?"

"Never mind," he says. "I think we should focus on the essay. It probably needs a lot of work since you got a D on it." Reluctantly I drop the questions and slide my computer over. He leans forward to read.

I wait impatiently for him to finish as I pick at my nails. I suddenly feel very vulnerable. My eyes scan the entirety of the room as I pretend to ignore the slight tension. Messing around in school, it was fine. Following Klara's bus, it was fine. But at this moment, when he reads my essay in my house on my computer, I realize how little I know about this boy. I basically know him just as well as I know the anonymous number texting me.

"Hey, if you want some water or anything, you can help yourself." I gesture to the kitchen.

"Oh, sure. That would be great." Jimmy pauses a moment and then stands up. He points at the doorway.

"Yup, right over there. Glasses are in the cabinet above the sink," I call to him. The second he leaves, I slip his laptop over to my side of the table. I'm not usually one to snoop through a teenage boy's computer (I learned the hard way when I found Josh's search history), but I can't help myself. I glance up toward the kitchen where Jimmy still finds his way through the cabinets like a lost puppy. The lock screen of the computer stares back at me, and I curse silently. I am no hacker. There are billions of possible password combinations for any given nerd… I try space movie references and then comic book names, but nothing. Then I stop, remembering Wes saying something about his favorite superhero the other day.

The Balancer.

The computer unlocks, and I laugh to myself. The Balancer is every teenage geek's favorite superhero nowadays because he can stop time and do all this crazy stuff with his mind. Personally, I don't get it. But my laugh turns into a frown when I see the window that's open on his screen. It's a picture of the YouTech Laboratory building; the same one on his computer that first day of school in the library.

"Why are you looking at my laptop?"

My eyes shoot up to the doorway. "You're doing it too."

"Doing what?" He fidgets and fixes a strand of his hair that's fallen out of place. I scroll down the page as he rushes around the table in protest. He's too late because I go through it all. It's a directory of investors in the Agent program. The picture at the top is a graying man with a familiar emblem next to his name.

"That's the crest we saw at Klara's house. That's her dad. He's their key investor?" I look at the name Charles Brooks and then back up at Jimmy. "And you thought I was crazy for following her... when you were doing the exact same thing."

He lowers his voice as if someone will overhear. "This is not the same thing as stalking."

"Oh my god, it so is. You're trying to find out who the Agent is."

"No, I'm not. I'm just researching." He snags his computer back from me.

"You're stalking your classmates. You're just as much of a stalker as—"

"Wait," Jimmy's panicked expression suddenly breaks. "How do you know The Balancer?"

We stare at each other for a moment and the entire house goes silent. But before I can help it, a chuckle escapes my mouth. Then another, and then I dissolve into laughter. Jimmy's lips tug at a smile—just a tiny smile, as if he's trying to hold back—but then a full-hearted laugh bursts out of his chest too. Soon enough we both shake in laughter, maybe because we completely underestimated one another. He becomes less of a stranger with every smile.

A notification buzzes on my phone. It jarringly interrupts our amusement.

"You got a text," Jimmy nods. His laughter ebbs away when he sees my face.

"I know. It's fine. I don't need to read it now." I turn the screen over and compose myself. It's too late, though, because I already saw what the anonymous text says:

Don't look for Alex.

CHAPTER 6

Jimmy strains to push open the heavy front door of the school and hold it for me. The faint sunlight feels good on my face after being inside all day. It warms my skin as we make our way to my car, but even still, no amount of blue skies on a Friday can shake away the feeling of dread in my gut.

"You didn't see him all day either?" I glance back at the entrance and watch for Alex's face. All I see is a stream of escaping students and the boy in a long coat from the chess tournament smoking a cigarette. *Why don't I know that kid's name yet?* My passenger-side door squeaks as Jimmy opens it.

"No. I told you, I don't really associate with those guys," he says.

"Which, by the way, is something you haven't explained to me," I point out.

I throw my bag inside the Subaru and scan the crowds in the parking lot one more time. Nothing. I shake away the feeling one last time and turn my attention to Jimmy. I hand him the cord to plug in his phone for music.

"You're the DJ," I insist, but he hands it back to me without hesitation. "Hey, no, I'm serious this time. I won't judge, I just want to know what kind of music you listen to. I've given you rides for three days in a row now, please."

"I like *your* music, though. Mine is… weird." He buries his chin in the collar of his flannel.

"Don't worry, guys, I'll take the aux," a voice says as one of the doors shuts. My seat tremors, and Klara has just thrown all of her bags across the car. She props her legs up on the middle console.

"You've got to be kidding me," I murmur under my breath.

"You didn't wait for me, Olivia."

"Via. It's Via."

"Yeah that's what I said. More importantly, I have some questions." Klara leans forward, and her head pokes between ours. "First, what are we feeling for music today? Something a little more vibey?"

"Klara, why are you in my car?" *She doesn't talk to me in school and pretends she doesn't know me. Then I offer her a ride once and suddenly I'm her chauffeur?*

"No, you're right. It's a pump-up day. Secondly, why does he get shotgun?" she points at Jimmy.

"Nobody's calling shotgun because there is no shotgun. This isn't a carpool. It's just me and Jimmy going to my house."

"Alright, alright, I just need a ride to the bus stop." She sprawls back on the seat.

There's silence, and then Jimmy says, "Shotgun."

"Hey!" Klara sits forward again, but I start the car and swerve out of the parking lot before she can protest anymore. Her face scrunches in mockery as she sits back and pulls out her phone. I watch her type through my rearview mirror.

"So, Klara… your dad bought all your older brothers cars, but not you?"

She doesn't look up. "I know, tragic. I think I'm his least favorite."

"You must be pretty well-off then. I mean, your family," I say. Jimmy twitches in his seat. He knows what I'm doing. "What do your parents do at the lab?"

"Are you gonna turn the music up or what? I can barely hear it." Klara's eyebrows perk like daggers through the rear-view mirror as I meet her stare.

Jimmy fidgets. "Focus on the road, please—"

"Alex wasn't at school today," I say. "Did you know that?"

"No, I didn't."

"He's not even responding to Elliot's texts. Weird, right? I didn't peg him as the kind of kid to ditch."

"I don't know much about Alex." Klara thumps the seat in front of her. "But Jimmy does. They went to the same high school. Maybe you should ask him."

"The bus stop is right here." Jimmy points out the window quickly. I sneak a glance at him as I pull over to let Klara out. His head is turned away. *Why didn't he say anything about that before?*

"Hope you find Alex." Klara flashes a practiced smile before she closes the door.

"We will."

* * *

"Wait, so what are their names again?" Wes says from our video game nest.

"Elliot, Ben, Cole, and Alex."

"And the kid who's tutoring you. He's not one of them?"

"No, his name is Jimmy."

"Whoa," Wes laughs. "When I told you to get a boyfriend, I didn't mean get five. That's a little extreme. Don't you think?"

Before I can hit him with one of the pillows, all four of our parents clutter the hallway. My mom smiles in at us. "Alright, we'll be back from the movie in a couple of hours."

Wes stands up. "I can drive home. Danielle isn't coming back from her sleepover. Right?"

"Why don't you stay here tonight, Wes?" Lawrence coughs.

Wes stops. "What do you mean? Can't I just sleep in my own bed?"

"I think it's better if you spend the night here with Olivia," his dad insists.

"Do you not want to?" I fidget. "We can play video games and stuff, but if you don't want—"

"Whatever, it's fine," Wes waves dismissively. But he seems unsettled as he watches our parents put on their jackets. He brushes the hair out of his face repeatedly in annoyance.

"I don't want you guys like zombies in front of the TV when we get back." My dad points at Wes. "And, you, on the couch."

Wes gives his mom a pleading look, which makes my throat tighten. Beth says, "Don't look at me. I've said it before, and I'll say it again. I want grandchildren before I'm dead."

When the adults are gone and Josh is upstairs, I nudge Wes. "Hey, what if we go for a drive?"

His eyes, glazed over in a distant trance, snap up to mine. "A drive? Like… another investigation?"

"No, no, I was just thinking we could get out of the house. I'm a little rattled by this whole Alex thing because nobody has heard from him since last night—"

"That's perfect. We can go looking for him!"

I glance over at my friend. "What?"

"You were just telling me earlier tonight how you think Klara is super suspicious. You think those anonymous texts are coming from her, right? Why don't we drive by her house and see if anything's there?"

"You sound crazy. I'm not going to break into some girl's house."

"Not just some girl. She's the daughter of YouTech Lab's main investor!" His whole mood has changed as he jumps up and paces around the pillows in a manic flurry. "There could be all kinds of top-secret stuff in that house. Plus, the fact that Jimmy was looking into her family means something. And now that we know he went to school with Alex before this year... I really think he knows something about the program we don't."

I pluck at one of the pillows. "Why are you so persistent about this?"

"Come on, let's do it. It's a Friday night and we're seriously going to sit here doing nothing?"

In my dreams I'm always looking for something. I always walk into that burning house. And it always leads to my death.

"Fine. Let's do this quickly though." I grab my jacket on the way out. Quietly as not to wake Josh, we sneak along the driveway and climb into our charming deathtrap of a car. As I drive through the night, I strain to remember the way to Klara's house. My eyes search every turn and road sign in the dark, my muscles tightened in anxiety. *This is a horrible idea.*

After what seems like ages, I catch a glimpse of the Brooks's family emblem and pull the car over across the street. The Subaru turns off and plunges us into pitch black.

"Okay, what's the plan?" Wes leans in.

"There's no plan. We aren't secret agents. Klara always has her phone with her, so maybe I'll go sneak in and look at her computer. From there I can see if she's been sending the texts, but then I'm gone. You're my lookout, okay?" I exhale shakily and step out of the door. I didn't even realize I had been holding my breath.

I hustle across the street and approach the looming iron gates. In the night, they glint sharp and tall. *I'm just doing this to prove there's nothing crazy going on, no conspiracies. Wes doesn't need anything else to worry about in his life.* My hands and feet find sturdy holds on the cold metal. I pull myself up to the top of the shaking bars and heave myself over. Adrenaline rushes through my body when I hit the ground on the other side.

My phone buzzes with a text. It's from Wes: *Who is this badass and what have you done with Via?*

I roll my eyes and continue into the property. The driveway lined with cars leads back to a modern one-story house with a low sweeping roof. Only a few lights are on, but after I circle the gardens a few times, I can see directly into one of the illuminated windows. Must be Klara's; it's definitely a girl's bedroom. As I carefully pick my way closer through the shadows, I see there's nobody inside.

With a light jiggle I realize the door is locked. I don't know why I thought it would be open. Maybe I'd hoped Klara would be there to let me in and I could pretend I was stopping by to see her.

I pull out my phone and search "how to pick a lock." As I scan through articles, I receive a text from Wes: *Hurry up. We don't have all night.*

I frown and type back: *You try picking a lock, smartass.*

I take the hairpin off my head, thankful I had one with me, and try to figure out the directions. *It's just like a math problem. Just follow the steps. It's very logical.* After a few missed tries of investigating the pins of the lock, I hear a sound from inside. I duck into the garden bushes. After a moment I reach up and try again, and as I'm crouched there it finally clicks open, to my disbelief.

The lights in Klara's room are still on, so she must be here somewhere. I hurry over to her desk and open her drawers. The laptop is nowhere to be found. *Maybe it's elsewhere in the house?* I hear a man's voice from down the hall followed by footsteps. Panic rises in my throat like bile. I close the dresser drawers hurriedly, slip out, and creep down the hall. The walls are lined with photos of all of Klara's brothers and framed articles about the Agent program and Brooks Investments. I don't see anything with Klara in it.

A light flickers on above me, so I dart through a large stone door at the end of the hallway. I'm swallowed into this new room and open my phone in the pitch black. I type furiously: *Wes, abort mission. There's nothing here.*

Text bubbles pop up: *All the lights are starting to turn on. What are you doing in there?*

My heart pounds. I can hear the deep rumbling of Charles Brooks's voice coming down the hall. *He must know someone is here.* I frantically look for a light switch.

Another text from Wes: *Get out of there!* When the lights turn on, my eyes search for an exit. There's a back door on the opposite side of the room. As I throw myself toward my escape, something stops me. This isn't a bedroom. Instead of furniture, every corner is occupied by a complicated setup of machines with the YouTech logo branded on every panel. It looks like a huge computer. *That must be a lot of data. Why would it not be in the laboratory?*

Before I can investigate any further, the sound of footsteps echoes right outside. I jump over to the beckoning doorway and my hand slips on the handle as I twist it. It opens and I fling myself out into the night. I hear shouting but I'm already shrouded by the darkness. I stagger too far to the left as my internal organs pound. *Why is it so hard to breathe? Why does my heart feel like it's going to explode?* I sprint across the grass toward the gates.

"Dude, what the hell?" Wes, my supposed getaway driver, is in a frenzy when I barge into the passenger side.

"Drive!" The car rattles under my weight.

Wes shifts the gear and we shoot off like a flicker of a ghost, but he can't even pay attention to the road. "Did you find anything? Did they see you? Holy shit, this is the most intense thing we've ever done. This is like Immortal Soldiers!"

"Shut up, Wes." I try to catch my breath. "I didn't even find her laptop."

"So the mission was a failure then?"

The beams of our headlights blaze into the void. I want to say yes, because it *was* a failure, but I think I accidentally stumbled upon something much stranger. Wes turns his head toward me every few seconds, like a nervous clock that ticks in the silence.

We finally pull into the driveway, and I breathe a sigh of relief that my parents' car isn't there. I crawl out of my shaky vehicle, but Wes doesn't get out yet; he's still shaken from the night's events.

However, as I approach the front door, I squint to see a person is sitting on the steps. *It can't be the police; how did they already find out about the break-in?* I realize it's a kid. For a brief moment I imagine it's Alex. But then I see a glint of earrings and sharp eyebrows.

It's Klara.

"You've got to be kidding me." My head whirls.

"Thank God. I've been waiting for you to come back for so long." She stands up to greet me. I swallow down the fear in my throat.

"It's ten o'clock at night, Klara." I push past her and unlock the house. The key shakes in my hand.

"I know. I'm starving. Do you have any food?" She walks right by me through the door the moment I open it. I glance over my shoulder at Wes, who is still in the car. *Is he okay?* Inside, I hear Klara find her way through my house.

"How did you know where I live?" I follow her into my kitchen. "How did you get here? Also, why are you here?" I clench and unclench my fist. *There's no way she knows I was at her house. She must have been here the whole time.*

"My dad is being such an ass." She rummages through my fridge. "He tried to put me on lockdown in my house. He does this every time I mess with some of his work equipment, like he's worried I'll break something. I wish. Man, I hate that stupid program."

I think about the large computer in her house. *So it's equipment for the Agent program?* She pulls out a yogurt. "Where are your spoons?"

The front door rattles shut, and Wes finally comes inside. He calls from the hallway, "Via, who's here? And if you're getting food, can you get me some too?" Klara's eyes widen underneath piqued eyebrows. She freezes and mouths, "Who is that?"

"Be there in a second!" I call. Klara sneaks over to the doorway and peeks in at Wes.

"Did you know there's a cute boy in your house?" Klara turns back to me.

I close the kitchen door before she can spy on him anymore. "Yes, of course I know there's a boy in my house. And the boy's name is Wes."

"Is he your boyfriend? Do you have a boyfriend I don't know about?"

"Wes? God no, he's basically my brother."

"There's a difference between *basically* your brother, and *actually* your brother." Klara goes back to her yogurt. I pull out a spoon from the drawer to hand to her. My palms are sweaty. I just want her to leave. She takes the utensil and stabs into the yogurt. "So, Olivia—"

"Via."

"So, Via, what is he doing here?"

"He's spending the night because our parents are out."

Via practically chokes on her spoonful of yogurt. "I'm sorry, he's sleeping here?"

"Every weekend he comes over here with his family. We just have dinner and play video games and his mom drinks all our wine. Sometimes his parents make him spend the night."

"And there was never a point where you thought he was attractive?"

"We've known each other since we were five."

"Look me in the eyes and tell me you've never thought about hooking up with him."

"No!"

Klara raises her eyebrows and sucks on the spoon.

Suddenly, the kitchen door swings open. "Hey, what's taking so long? I said to get..." Wes trails off when he sees who it is. "Oh, she's still here." He pulls his sleeves down over his wrists.

Klara takes the spoon out of her mouth. "I'm Klara."

"Hi there... Via, can I talk to you for a minute?" Wes pulls me out of the kitchen. Klara's dark eyebrows follow us out. When we're in the living room, he whispers, "Is this the same Klara that we just—"

"Shut up. She doesn't know." I glance back at the door.

"You constantly rant about her. I thought you hated each other. Why would she be at your house?"

"I don't know, something about her dad—"

"Hey, guys, I hate to break up this little shit-talking session," Klara opens the door and interjects. "But what's the sleeping arrangements for tonight? Do you want the couch, or should I take it, or…"

"Wait, no no no," I stammer.

"I think I'm going to take the couch, actually. It's been a long week and I don't want to crash on the floor, so I think I'll be more comfortable out here. You two can just go up to Via's room and figure out something there. Don't worry about me. I'll be fine."

Wes turns to me with a face twisted in panic.

"Alright great, glad we got that all figured out," she says. "Unless, of course, you two aren't comfortable sharing a room together. Which shouldn't be a problem, considering you're *basically* her brother. Right?"

Before she even gets an answer, she bounces over to the couch and starts rearranging the pillows.

"She's messing up our video game nest," Wes hisses as we head up the stairs to my room. "I don't trust her. What if she's doing the same thing we were doing at her house? You need to stay away from her."

"Look, I know this whole Agent thing has you on a conspiracy mission. But maybe she just has something going on at home. Maybe her home life is messed up and she doesn't want her friends to know, so she came here."

"You don't want to spend the night with someone who's toxic for you." Wes grabs me by the arm. "Trust me on this."

We create a makeshift bed for him, and I turn off the lights. It seems like lifetimes as I try not to restlessly shift underneath my covers. In the dark silence I can almost hear the gears turn in his head. But eventually he drifts into sleep because his breathing falls into a pattern that finally relaxes. Through the shadows my eyes find his sleeping figure. As I watch his chest rise and fall gently, I think about the morning his parents found him in his bathroom bleeding out on the floor. That was only a month after I was in the hospital. I think about how they never look at him the same way again. How he's changed in their eyes.

He's changed in my eyes too; I'll never stop seeing those scars.

And then, through the dark, a buzz from a notification. I jolt as my hand fumbles anxiously on the bedside table. To my surprise the text isn't from the unknown number. *Oh god.* I rip my sheets off my body. Quietly I step over Wes and grab a coat on my way out.

I know where Alex is.

CHAPTER 7

Why would Alex text me his current location? This late at night, the parking lot of the hospital is dark and eerie, and shadows from the woods reach out toward my car like skeletal claws. My heartbeat picks up as I make my way to the doors. Memories of the last time I was here creep toward the front of my mind, and I push them back down.

"Hi, I'm here to pick up a friend. His name is Alex?"

The orderly at the front desk glances up from his screen. Tired eyes scan me up and down. "Last name?"

"What?"

"His last name," the man repeats.

Shit, I don't know Alex's last name. How do I not know his last name?

"Do you know when he was admitted?" he sighs.

"Um, no."

The man gives me an exasperated look. My face gets hot. *Why can I hear my heart pounding in my ears?* I remember this lobby, the texture of the chairs, the vending machine in the corner. *One, two, three, four…* "Brockman. His last name is Brockman."

I exhale shakily as he types into the computer. "Okay, Alex Brockman… right, here he is. He was admitted to the

ER last night. But we just discharged him fifteen minutes ago. He already left."

"Wait..." A million questions race through my head. "Is he okay? Did he leave alone? Were his parents here or anything?"

"I'm sorry, but I can't help you. All I know is that the patient signed the discharge papers and left here fifteen minutes ago."

"Right, thank you." My mind whirls. *He can't have gotten that far on foot. Maybe he took a bus?* It's at least a thirty-minute walk to anywhere in Park Falls from here. He should not be out in the woods alone. I hurry, relieved to escape the familiar smell of hand sanitizer. The parking lot basks in the silver sheen of the moon.

My car shakes when I slam the door. I turn the keys with urgency, and it rumbles to life. I pull out of the deserted parking lot, thinking about my parents returning from their movie to an empty driveway. I imagine that look on Dad's face, the one I haven't seen since the Incident.

A figure appears in the road like the grim reaper. It interrupts my thoughts suddenly as my breath catches in my throat and I barely manage to swerve out of the way. I pull over onto the shoulder of the other lane. The car lurches to a stop and my headlights bathe the empty road in piercing light. A boy walks down the yellow dashes on the asphalt.

"Alex!" I stumble out onto the road while my car still hums. He doesn't seem to hear me. "Alex, it's me." I catch up to him and reach out for his shoulder.

He whips around at my touch and his eyes find mine. He looks like a ghost in the pale glow.

"What are you doing in the middle of the road?" My chest heaves. "Do you know how dumb that is? Someone could have hit you! I almost hit you!"

"I'm fine," he says blankly.

"No, I'm serious, you can't just be on the road like this at night. Someone could get killed. You're freaking me out, Alex. Are you sure you're okay?"

"I said I'm fine, I just..." he trails off and seems to lose his thought.

"Why did you text me then? Do you need a ride?"

He doesn't respond. The blinding lights and moonlit trees reflected off the pavement are a familiar nightmare that sends shivers down my spine. I push a flood of memories away.

"Can I call someone for you then? Your parents? Or what about Elliot?"

"I need to find my brother." He turns as if in a trance.

"Your brother?" I shake my head and strain to keep up with him. "Alex, you were just in the hospital. Let me take you home, or at least call Elliot."

"Don't call Elliot. Or anyone." The whites of his eyes shine in fear. And that's when his hands shake. His head snaps down and he stumbles away from me faster. "Shit. *Shit.*"

Panic rises up in my chest. *He shouldn't have texted me. I barely know him. I don't know what to do. We're not even really friends. Why didn't he call Elliot? Why me?*

"Hey!" I grab his arm and stop him. Alex jolts, and his eyes flash down at my arm and then up at me. It's the same way Wes looked at me the night of the Incident in January. I shrug away the feeling. "We'll find your brother. Okay? I won't ask any questions. Nobody else will know about this."

His lip quivers. He grips his hands tightly.

"Let me take you to Elliot's house. If you don't want to go home, let me take you there." *Elliot will know what to do with his friend.*

Alex just nods and mumbles something about his brother, who I have never even heard of until now. *How did the hospital staff let him leave like this?*

* * *

"Thank you so much for picking him up." Elliot shuts the beautiful mahogany door to his house.

"I'm sorry I had to wake you up. I just didn't know what to do." My voice is hushed, as if I'm worried Alex might hear me from inside. We stand outside his large stone house on the front porch, back in the suburbs. Despite the fever dream that is this night, I can't help but feel a twinge of annoyance. Nobody should look this good after being woken abruptly in the middle of the night. Elliot's olive skin practically glows in the porch light. His side part gives way to a wave of hair that falls in front of his face as if he'd planned it that way. Maybe I'm just tired, but I can't hold eye contact.

"No, you did the right thing." He grabs his hair with both hands. "I am such a shitty friend. I should've been there. I should've known something was up."

"Hey, nobody could have seen this coming. Not even you. I mean, I don't think his parents knew he was in the hospital."

Elliot's lips pout into a frown. "What was he doing in the middle of the road though? Only crazy people do that."

"Yeah, crazy people." I picture Alex just now, the way his hands shook, his eyes swelled with terror. Another memory comes to mind, one of me standing in the middle of a dark road while snow drifts through the biting air in flurries.

"You know we went to the same high school, right?" Elliot steps closer. "Alex and me. We've been friends for a while. I know him better than anyone."

I cross my arms and shift from one foot to the other. "Yeah, I understand."

"So, do you know why he texted *you*?" Shadows cross his eyes. "I mean, no offense, it's just that I didn't think you guys were that close."

"I didn't either." I shrug.

I see a hint of something behind his gleaming facade. I just can't tell what it is. A troubled expression twists his chiseled features, and I realize I've never seen him like this at school. Elliot Kang is the perfect balance of basketball jock and playful dork in a school where it's impossible to be flawless. What does he ever have to worry about? Before Alex, nothing.

"Alright, well, I should go. I'll see you at school tomorrow." I press my fingers to my temple. "Except why even bother? I'm going to get like three hours of sleep at this point."

"Uh, wait, before you go," Elliot scratches his head. "It's not really about Alex, but I never got the chance to ask you because we're always around the other guys."

My heart races. *What would he want to ask me away from the others? Is it another Agent rumor?*

"This is a weird thing to bring up now, but…" Elliot plays with the strings of his hoodie. "You're friends with Klara. Right?"

Klara. The girl whose house I broke into, who is currently sleeping on my couch. "Friends is definitely one word for it."

"What, uh, what do you think about her?"

"Like… is she the Agent?"

When I say the word, he flinches. "No, no, forget about that. What I mean is, what would you think about me asking her out?"

It has been a long night of surprises, but this is really the strangest plot twist of all. I stifle a laugh. "Wait, you like Klara?"

His cheeks redden. "No, I don't know, she's the one who likes me. She's the one who's been texting me all week."

"Oh my god, you're serious. You want me to set you up with Klara?"

"Why are you laughing?"

"I'm sorry. It's just sleep deprivation." I attempt to hold a straight face. *Pull yourself together, Via. He's being vulnerable. He's opening up to you about normal high school things.*

Elliot hunches his shoulders, so he suddenly looks small. "Never mind. Forget it."

"Hey, listen," I nudge him. "I'll see what I can do."

His eyes smile, and it makes me feel better for a brief moment. But then I look back at the door. We're out here laughing about crushes, and Alex was just discharged from a hospital for God-knows what. The last time I was at a hospital was when I got the call about Wes, and it was the scariest day of my life—even scarier than my own medical stay. *What kind of a mess am I getting myself into?*

"I should go." I head toward my car. *God, my parents are going to kill me. I left Josh and Wes alone with a stranger.* I remember something and turn back to Elliot. "There was one more thing."

Elliot perks. "Yeah?"

"Alex said something earlier, on the road. He said he was looking for his brother."

"That's weird."

"I know. He just got out of the hospital, so I don't know if it had anything to do with his brother, or—"

"No, I mean that's really weird." Elliot pouts his lips.

"Why?" I ask as the shadows bounce off his features.

"Via, Alex doesn't have a brother."

* * *

I barely even know how I got home between the exhaustion and the confusion. But I don't see my parents' car when I pull into the driveway. Thankfully it must be a late night for them too.

My mind is so scattered that I forget to take off my coat when I get into the house. I go straight upstairs to the hall bathroom, and the door bangs as it closes. I turn the sink faucet on, but I forget what I was going to do.

It's like déjà vu. I relive the exact same night all over again. It was January and the snow fell in large flakes all around me. I could see Wes's figure on the road ahead as he stood on the center lines—before the scars, before the therapy. The darkness swallowed his figure. I called out to him. He turned around at the sound of my voice, the side of his face lit up by oncoming headlights.

"Via, are you okay?" The bathroom door opens. It's Wes.

"Um, yeah." I turn off the sink quickly.

His groggy eyes trace the sink and then my jacket. "Did you leave? You look kind of rattled."

I think about Alex's shaking hands. "No. I just, uh… I was cold."

The house is silent. His forehead creases with concern. "You know you can tell me anything. Right? Even crazy, dumb things."

"I know." *I wouldn't even know where to start. I can't tell him about the hospital, or it might trigger him.*

"Alright, just making sure," Wes says. "Now let's go to bed before Klara wakes up and then I'll never forgive you."

I give him a faint smile and follow him back into my room. On the way down the hall, I pause at one of the doorways. I glance inside. Josh's figure rises and falls in the dark as he sleeps. Something about seeing my brother calms me.

CHAPTER 8

Heavy sunlight pours in through the windows of the library. It's the kind of filtered glow that slithers in earlier as winter approaches. The whole array of tables in the back are blanketed with a lazy silence as I drag my way through the coding assignment. Jimmy listens to music with earbuds next to me, already finished with his work.

I'm not focused on the code at all. *How am I supposed to care about fundamentals of computation when I still haven't heard from Alex? Why hasn't Elliot told me any updates since this weekend?* My imagination fears the worst.

"Hey, let me listen," I whisper to Jimmy.

"No way, finish your assignment." He leans away from me and hides a thin smile. "This is why you need tutoring."

The light giggle in my chest warms my mood like the afternoon sun. Regardless of the fact that he won't let me see what music he listens to, it feels like Jimmy and I have really developed a sense of comfort and normalcy together. I need that stability after the rattling incident with Alex only a few nights ago.

Suddenly the quiet of the library is disrupted, and I can hear the voices of Ben and Cole drift through the bookshelves.

"All I'm saying is, you would never get to see boobs again if you were blind," Ben says as they wander over to our section.

"Please shut up." Elliot hits him.

"Oh god, what led to this?" I close my screen, grateful for an excuse to stop. That's when I notice Alex with them. Something about the boy is… off. He scratches his arm and doesn't look at any of us. His eyes flit around the room in a daze.

Meanwhile Jimmy, flanked suddenly by the four boys, flinches out of his music and retreats into his collar.

"Basketball star over here thinks he's too cool to talk with us about superheroes, just because a girl actually likes him," Cole teases. "We're arguing about whether The Balancer or UltraSonic would win in a fight. It's for my ESP project in English class."

"What project? I have English later today." *Am I imagining it, or does Alex have dark rings around his eyes?*

"It's another one of Principal Conners's exercises, but surprisingly this one is really sick." Ben flops onto the chair next to me. "We get to design our own experiment to test varieties of ESP. They're letting us use all this wild equipment from YouTech."

"ESP?" I tilt my head.

"Extrasensory Perception," Jimmy takes out an earbud. "It's a term for various mental abilities that go beyond the five basic senses. Telepathy, clairvoyance, precognition, sometimes even telekinesis."

"Yeah but that stuff doesn't really exist though," I say. "I mean, it's all just supernatural phenomena. It isn't science."

All the boys look at me with wide, hurt eyes. It's like I've crushed their dreams or told them Santa Claus doesn't exist. Meanwhile, Alex just spaces out at the window.

"Alex, what do you think?"

He snaps out of his distant trance and blinks at the group. "Um, sorry. What do I think about what?"

Elliot and I exchange glances. Jimmy fidgets next to me and disappears back into his music. *I wish I could just ask Jimmy about all this. He has to know more than I do, but I don't want to bring up something painful.*

"Alright, well, we're gonna be late to class," Cole clears his throat. "Just wanted to see what you smart people were up to instead of eating lunch with us."

Ben and Cole trip over each other as they leave, and Alex follows rigidly.

I leave Jimmy and my table suddenly and pull Elliot into one of the book aisles. "Hey, is Alex okay? He seems... stressed."

"He's fine. It's probably just homework. He's taking a lot of engineering classes." Elliot's eyes linger on my arm and then glance away at the books.

"But did he say anything to you Sunday night?"

He shrugs. "Not really. We don't talk about that kind of stuff. You know?"

I'm stabbed with a pang of disbelief: *How do high school boys never seem to talk about anything real? Maybe he's covering for his friend.*

"Hey, you're still coming to the Halloween party this weekend. Right?" he changes the subject. "I need you there. It's my first date with Klara."

"How many times have I told you, a party is not a first date." I roll my eyes.

"Please, Via," his lips pout. "I think she's starting to get bored of my texting."

"Klara gets bored of herself talking sometimes. I wouldn't take it as an insult." The bookshelves seem to close in and edge us closer.

"Okay, so I'll see you there?" He flashes his dimples and I glance down at my feet. "It's at Chad's place, right down the road from the YouTech headquarters."

This sparks my interest, and for a minute I contemplate going. Then I shake my head. "No, I'm not third wheeling with you and Klara."

"Fine, then bring Jimmy." He playfully bounces out into the aisle. "We'll make it a double date."

He's gone before I can make a snide comment or ask anything else about Alex. Still flustered from his last remark, I go back to the table where I left Jimmy. He takes his earbuds out, his jaw clenched.

"I didn't know you two started talking. What did he have to say?"

"Nothing much." I shake my head.

He adjusts his glasses. "I think I'm gonna head out."

"Oh, sure." I frown. "But weren't you saying you'd help me with my college essay after—"

"Yeah, I'll just see you in English." He shoves his hands in his pockets and strides out.

A heavy sigh escapes my chest. I want to say something to him, but the words are stuck in my throat. I reluctantly turn back into my laptop so I can get the assignment done but then realize that Jimmy left his phone and earbuds on the table. *I can probably catch up to him in the hall.* But when I lift up the device and watch the screen turn on, I see what he was listening to.

It's not his own music at all. It's one of my own shared playlists, on shuffle.

* * *

The door to the English classroom swings ajar. Principal Conners bursts through with a thunderous and buoyant energy. "Look at this, a beautiful think tank full of focused intellectuals!"

I groan and turn to say something to Jimmy, but his stare is locked straight ahead.

"I'm sure you've heard about this exercise from your peers already, and indeed you should be very excited for what you're about to explore. No less than… the wonders of the human mind!" Principal Conners exclaims.

Ms. Xavier pops up from behind her desk, her blouse a jarring mix of colors. She tries to match Principal Conners's enthusiasm and it makes my skin crawl. "Very exciting, yes. We were inspired to incorporate this project into the English curriculum because of the intriguing research that YouTech Labs has published on the subject."

"Totally, they have a whole astrology department at YouTech just for tarot card readings." I laugh to Jimmy.

"What was that, Olivia?" Principal Conners swivels his intense beam of attention on me.

"Oh nothing, I just…" Everyone stares. The room feels stuffy and suffocating all of a sudden. I clear my throat. "You want us to create our own test of an extrasensory perception, right? I just don't see how this connects to YouTech and," I glance around, "the Agent."

"No, no, this is great! We're really starting to dig deep and have a discussion here!" The stout man corners me like a moth to a light. "Olivia, I want you to consider this. As recently as 1949, extrasensory perception was regarded as scientifically proven! In fact, Alan Turing wrote on the subject himself!"

I tug at my sleeves. *Why did I say anything in the first place? This is humiliating.*

"Artificial intelligence has everything to do with ESP! Let us play the imitation game." He waves dramatically. "Take a human and a machine and put them in a room together. One is the sender, the other a telepathic receiver. From there it's just a matter of tuning in to each other's signals. That's what we're going to attempt, right here in this classroom!"

I try not to wither under his jubilant intensity. "I'm sorry, I just don't see how a thinking machine like a computer could ever account for things like telepathy and clairvoyance."

"She makes a great point, sir," Jimmy speaks up, coming to my rescue. My chest relaxes. "We just read an article the other day in my AI fundamentals course that a system can't think outside of its programming. How would it go beyond basic senses?"

"That's for you to explore, and us to find out." His whole beard twists into a smile.

"Now get into a line, everyone. We're going to try something here." Ms. Xavier gestures to the front, causing her bracelets to jingle. "We have this headset gifted to us from YouTech, just one example of equipment you may have access to for your individual projects. First, you will put on the headset and attempt to transmit a message. The message is simple: Agent. The screen in the front will project the word if it picks up a telepathic signal. You only have a minute before your turn is up."

"Brilliant! Who's first?" Principal Conners ushers us to the front. Nobody stands up. "Jimmy, my scholar, why don't you step up to the plate?"

Jimmy noticeably gulps and adjusts his glasses. The rest of the class whispers and giggles. He stands hesitantly and the teacher helps place the headset of wires and glowing discs over his carefully groomed hair. As his forehead creases in concentration, everyone falls silent. Even Principal Conners is wide-eyed like a child. *Come on, Jimmy,* I root for him. The projected screen shows a wiggling line at the bottom measuring brain activity, but no word comes up.

"Darn, looks like your book smarts have deceived us. Never fret! You will have many more opportunities to expand the powers of your mind!" Principal Conners searches hungrily for another victim. "Now, Laura, how about you?"

We go through two more rounds, but none of the kids can get anything more than a tremor of stress in the brain activity line. *Will we ever do actual English or math in this school? Or is it just weird activities and games for the rest of the year?*

"Olivia, I have a good feeling about you." Principal Conners wiggles his sausage finger at me.

"I'm okay. I'll just—"

"Nonsense! Let's unlock the secrets in that mind of yours." He practically pushes me up from my seat to the front.

I tug at my sleeves, and the hairs on the back of my neck rise as the headset is placed over my hair. The discs are cold against my temple. A warm glow tingles down my spine when it turns on, and I see the line on the screen begin to waver. *This is dumb, but I'm sure Wes would love it.*

"Focus, Olivia. Clear your mind. Concentrate on the image of the word like it's part of your memory."

When he says memory, the line on the screen fluctuates. Instead of my mind going blank, it spirals into memories of a night road in January. Snow falling around me. Wet asphalt reflecting the winter moon. The line on the screen in front of me spikes. *Come on, Via. Drop it.* Then the memory of Alex on the road. His silhouette in the headlights. I see the whites of his eyes. *Stop.* Then I'm back in my dream, flames lick closer and closer to me and the smell of burning flesh is so real I gag.

In that moment the ceiling lights flicker, and the room goes black.

A few kids shriek, chaotic murmurs and chatter erupt in the dark. My heart pounds, and I falter at the front of the room. My hands fumble on the headset as I rip it off my crown.

"Relax, everyone. Stay calm!" Principal Conners waves his arms. Almost as quickly as the power had shut off, it comes back on again. "Sorry about that. I forgot we were having a power drill today. It's a new building. You have to test these things."

Although we are in the light again, the talking doesn't silence. Every fearful eye is locked onto me. They wait for me to do something.

In the back of the room, Jimmy's brown eyes latch onto mine. He is the only one who doesn't look away.

* * *

I walk along the edge of a lake, and harsh sunlight blinds me as it glints off the frozen surface. My shoes shuffle out onto the ice, one foot in front of the other. I'm searching for something, but I don't know what. I step further away from shore and trace the cracks with my shoes. They're not my shoes. Then I hear a voice behind me—a young voice—as it calls my name. I spin around, but at first I only see ominous pines hugging the lakeside, whispering in the winter wind. Then I see it. A cloaked figure in the shadows watches me. For a moment its head twitches and blurs in a static, as if there's an error.

And then I fall.

The ice beneath my feet gives out suddenly. The freezing water strangles my cry for help, and I plunge into the depths. The blinding sunlight disappears above me and is replaced by murky waters and a dark void that stretches on forever. I thrash my limbs and strain to reach for the surface, but nothing can stop me as I sink below. I am swallowed by pitch black. Fear grips every muscle and my lungs tremor in agony. Finally I open my mouth to scream, but its silenced by the suffocating flood of water into my chest. Darkness closes in around me, and everything begins to go faint. I can't even make a sound as I'm dragged into oblivion.

I wake up with a choked gasp. Tears wet my cheeks. I feel my heart pound out of my ribcage as I desperately cling to my covers for stability.

"Will you shut up already?" Josh is at the door to my room. He rubs his eyes groggily as the hall light makes his round cheeks glow. "You're gonna wake the whole neighborhood up with your screaming."

"Sorry," I mumble something incoherent and find my footing. I push past him through the dark and slip into the hallway bathroom. My hands shake as they turn the faucet on, and I flinch when the water gushes out of the faucet. I change my mind and turn the sink back off.

"Jeez, what is up with you lately?" he grumbles.

"Nothing," I snap. My hands grip the sides of the sink. "It was just a dream."

CHAPTER 9

The air turns frigid almost overnight. The swaths of forest that cling to the lakeside seem to recoil in shock from the sudden chill. Even the walk from my car to the front door of the party seems like a frozen trek. The cold swallows me like I've just dropped into arctic waters.

I ferociously slam the car door shut so it almost falls off its hinges. *What is wrong with you, Via?* I see Klara shiver beside me, but that's probably because her "costume" is really just glorified underwear. It resembles some kind of slutty corset and fishnet tights. Pleased with herself, she says, "I am so honored that I get to be the one to take you to your first party."

The glowing cabin in front of us is a pulsing beacon of light amidst the slumber of the northern woods. No wonder Chad throws all the parties. As if his name wasn't fitting enough, his parents also moved into a picturesque lake house for work.

"Klara, this is not my first party and… you know what? I don't need this from you right now. Why am I even here?"

"To get laid."

"That's it. I'm leaving." My coat flaps behind me.

Klara grabs my arm. "I'm kidding. I'm kidding. You know I need you here."

"Yes, to be your designated driver."

"No, to be my friend." She raises her eyebrows in the dark. For once they don't attack me. Still, I'm not sure I believe that plastered-on smile so easily. "Plus," she continues, "this house is incredible. I mean, not as cool as mine, but our parents work together."

"Wait, really?" I try to sound casual. "What does Chad's family do?"

"Oh, I don't know. His mom is some project manager for the lab. She handles my dad's investments and all that. But honestly, I can't believe she lets Chad throw all these parties. Especially after they got such a nice house."

My mind whirls. *This is the house of someone who could be in possession of confidential records, information on the lab's projects.* "Fine, I'll go in. But I'm doing this for Elliot because the boy needs serious help."

"I think it's cute." Klara loops her arm in mine. "It's like in those classic romance books. He's throwing a whole party just for me, hoping I'll show up."

"This is Chad's Halloween party, Klara. And he throws a party every weekend regardless of your attendance." I laugh, "But I appreciate the literary reference."

When we open the door to the party, a wave of heat spills over us. The air seems to be a complete contrast to the sharp chill outside. It's like a cocoon, the atmosphere thick with sounds of drunken kids. The entrance is a mess of coats. I start to take off my shoes, but then I notice nobody else did. I guess it's just an Asian thing.

"Look who decided to come out." Elliot approaches us through the buzz of people. He wears a basketball jersey. *Wow, how creative.* "What are you guys dressed as?"

"I'm a girl who was dragged out of her warm house filled with Halloween candy and TV," I say. "And Klara is a stripper."

"Burlesque dancer," Klara hits me. "I've told you this a million times, Via."

"Sorry, my bad. A *high-end* stripper."

Elliot laughs, and his whole face squints. He shifts nervously and adds, "Klara, can I get you a drink?" And just like that, they both disappear. *Well, that was easy.*

When I dare to venture in alone, I realize that it's going to be a long night. As I feared, this party is one of those smaller ones of only about thirty seniors. The reality of the situation is that nobody can afford to supply infinite amounts of alcohol and trash their houses every weekend, so most of the time it manifests as these intimate get-togethers at a cabin in the woods. It sounds like the start to every horror movie ever.

"Cabin" is probably the wrong word for this house anyway. It's a sprawling estate with large maple beams that crisscross through a maze of cozy nooks. The main living room boasts high ceilings and tall windows that overlook the glistening lake below. For such an impressive party venue there are no crowds to get lost in, and ironically no notable Halloween costumes. *Now if only I could just slip away, maybe Chad's mom has an office...*

"Hey, are you new?" a boy cuts me off before I can escape.

"Max." I'm jolted out of my thoughts. "Are you serious? I have classes with you. You've known me for almost two months now."

"Oh, well I'm pretty drunk right now, sorry." He reaches out a hand. "We've never been formally introduced, but I'm Max."

"Yes, I know." I press my lips together, but shake his hand anyway. "Hey, do you know if Chad's parents have any rooms we're not allowed to go into?"

"I don't know." Max shrugs. "I'm too messed up to care."

I sigh and head through the doorway to find someone who might know. The dining room features beer pong and another table with alcohol that is swarmed with people. *When did these kids learn to mix drinks? Is that just something I should already know?* Next to all these intoxicated bodies, my movements somehow feel clunky and awkward. I am a sober void in the warm glow of every room. *Maybe this party was a bad idea. I'm not going to find out anything here. And why did Klara and Elliot even need me if they were just going to run off?*

Suddenly, a shoulder knocks into me from behind. The warm trickle of alcohol pours down my arm. I whip around and realize it's that guy. *That* guy. The one with the long coat nobody seems to know, now with a red solo cup held loosely in his hand. He ruffles his disheveled brown hair, and then stops when he notices me.

"We need to stop meeting like this." The boy steps back with a little bit of a sway as if pulled by an invisible string. *I know almost everyone at Park Falls at this point. How do I still not know his name?* His eyes glint with that same look from the first time we ran into each other, like he's trying to remember me. It feels insulting.

My skin pricks under watchful eyes as strong alcohol bleeds into my clothes. Now I'm alone, sticky with a bitter stench of something akin to cinnamon, and I feel like an idiot. "No, this is perfect. I really love smelling like alcoholism."

His mouth hangs open in a devilish smile. "You're being sarcastic."

"And you're being an asshole. Apologize already, and then you can get back to being an obnoxious drunk."

"Believe me, I was not trying to be anywhere near you," he says with piercing watery eyes and then pushes past me toward the stairs. A couple of kids in the corner snicker. *One, two, three, four...*

I clench my fist and escape the room. My thigh hits the corner of the table as my boots catch on the carpet. I make it over to a small bathroom in the hallway to take refuge. Every inhale feels strained and shallow as I close the door. My flushed reflection stares back at me. *Is this how I've looked all night? Oh god. I really need some sleep.* I splash water on my arm in an awkward motion. Every now and then my eyes flutter up to the mirror, and I notice the dark bags I tried so hard to hide with makeup.

Suddenly, someone is at the doorway.

"Need help?"

It's Elliot.

"I'm good. This jerk just spilled vodka all over my arm, but I think I got it." I look up. "Where's Klara?"

Elliot laughs so his whole face squints again. "She's going shot-for-shot with the forward on our basketball team."

"You mean the guy who's almost seven feet tall and two hundred-fifty pounds?"

"Yeah, him."

"Jesus, Klara." I lean on my arm that's propped up on the sink. "That girl is going to be the death of me."

"You're a good friend." Elliot closes the distance between us.

"Yeah, well, I'm starting to think you don't choose your friends." I shrug. *Why am I even spending time with Klara in the first place? Am I really doing all this just to find out who is sending me those stupid texts?*

"Here, let me." Elliot grabs a washcloth and runs it under water. Instead of handing it to me though, he washes off my shirt himself.

I lower my voice. "So you haven't... you haven't talked to Alex at all?"

He pauses only momentarily but then says, "No, I told you. He didn't even say anything to me that night."

"Don't you want to know what's going on with him?"

Elliot leans over to dab my arm meticulously with the wet cloth. Waves of black hair fall in front of his eyes. I watch him concentrate with pouted lips and furrowed brows. He changes the subject, "Who's the drunk who spilled on you?"

"I don't know. Some guy in a long coat. Maybe it's a costume, but I hope he knows that's a woman's coat." I look away as Elliot leans closer. His breath tickles my shoulder, and I clear my throat. "I barely see him around school, though, and nobody seems to know who he is."

Elliot shakes his head. "I know what kid you're talking about. His name is Dean. Don't worry about that guy, everyone ignores him anyway. He's been really annoying at every party this year."

"Why do they keep inviting him then?"

"They don't." He shrugs. This bathroom is too hot and stuffy. I quickly take the cloth before he can douse it in water again and before he can lean in again. "He lives a couple of miles down the road, so I guess he just comes over. He's always here and always drunk. The guy's a douche."

"I am in full agreement."

He looks up at me through strands of hair. "If you want, I can beat him up for you."

Before I can respond, Klara is at the doorway. "There you guys are! You won't believe how much I just drank. I'm giving it five minutes before I completely black out."

I shift my stance toward the wall and put my arm down by my side. "Live your life, girl."

Elliot runs his fingers through his hair. "I think it's time we get you home. I can drive, I haven't been drinking."

I'm grateful to him but can't help feeling like I want to grab Klara by the shoulders and shake her. She was looking forward to this party and making a move on Elliot for weeks now. But then she had to go and consume her body weight in alcohol.

The two of them leave, and I sit there for a minute. The room spins and I'm not even drunk. I grip the sides of the sink with both hands, listening to the muffled sounds of the kids outside. *Pull yourself together, Via. You can't go home alone. But you also can't stay in this bathroom all night.*

Right when I emerge in the hall, Max is in front of me again.

"Hey, are you new?"

"Max. We just talked like fifteen minutes ago. We've also had two classes together for a semester."

"Oh, well I'm pretty drunk right now, sorry." He reaches out a hand. "We've never been formally introduced, but I'm Max."

"Wow, this is déjà vu," I murmur, but suddenly my gut churns. It's that eerie sensation you can't quite place, the same way a feeling lingers after a dream. It's a hunch, a strange sensation that looms over you like something bad is going to happen. I try to shake it away.

Then, from behind Max, the blur of a familiar face catches my eye. It's Alex. His head whips around and scours the party desperately. He must have just walked in. My heart drops; he looks even worse than he did at school.

"Alex!" I fly across the room. "You're here. I didn't know you came to these things. It's just, I thought you were going to take it easy after… everything."

Alex doesn't even seem to hear me. "Where's Elliot? I need to talk to him."

"He just left to take Klara home. You better not interfere. I've been trying to get this to happen for weeks now and—"

"No, no, no," Alex curses to himself. His face is flushed and glistens with sweat.

I reach out and touch his shoulder. "Are you okay?"

He stares at my hand on his shoulder, then looks up at me. In his eyes I see a wild expression that I don't understand, and it shocks me. It takes me back to the night I found him after the hospital. I retract my hand awkwardly.

I think he notices. He shakes his head, and his expression softens. He gives me a brief smile. "Sorry, I'm fine. It's not a big deal. I just had something I wanted to tell Elliot."

"Okay…" I respond hesitantly.

He wipes sweat from his face with both hands. "Um," his gaze wanders around the party and he brushes off his hands on the sides of his jeans. "Do you know where the alcohol is?"

"Yeah, the dining room." I point.

"Okay. I'm gonna get a drink."

"Right. Sounds good." I watch him pace into the room with the beer pong. His head still sweeps across the scene around him like he's watching out for something.

Why do I have this bad feeling in my stomach… maybe it's just Halloween and I'm getting spooked. I was surprised when Alex even started coming back to school, but this doesn't seem like the right environment for him now. *This isn't your problem, Via. Just go home and watch a movie with Josh or something.* I navigate through gyrating clusters of bodies toward the entryway and almost trip over coats on my way out.

I race out into the cold only to be startled by a heated argument in the driveway between two people. To my surprise, it's Klara and Dean.

"Oh yeah?" Klara's enraged eyebrows leap from her face. "And you're going to tell me what I can and can't do?"

"It's you, and I know it. Don't be such a diva!" His long coat flares out.

"You're a coward. You know that?"

"I'm warning you. You better stay out of this or else—"

"Klara?" I step in. "Didn't you get a ride with Elliot?"

They both snap out of it immediately when they see me. Klara sways and regains her wide drunken smile. "Via! Yeah, no, he's just pulling the car around." She stumbles over to me. "Get me out of here. This kid is *such* a loser."

I glance over at Dean, who still seethes. His eyes narrow. "You. Do you actually never smile, or is that part of your costume?"

"Stay away from me. And Klara."

His mouth dangles into the grin of a Cheshire cat. "Consider it done."

What an ass. The memory of an outcast, angsty middle school Olivia stings like a wound. "Your name is Dean?"

"Yes, ma'am." He pulls out a flask from his coat and takes a swig. "And I'm not even going to ask what yours is."

"Good." I turn and throw my arm around Klara to guide her away from the party. The cabin already seems smaller as the lanky figure of Dean shrinks into the night. I plan to text Elliot and tell him I took Klara home. In the meantime, he can go in and take care of Alex. Everything will be fine. *One, two, three, four...*

This eerie feeling follows me like a shadow. Beyond all my senses, beyond all my reason, it broods under the surface. I just don't know what it is.

CHAPTER 10

On Monday it snows. The gray clouds built up thick over the weekend and now cast an oppressive shadow over the rolling woods. The lakes freeze over with a glossy film of ice. The first snowflakes are heavy and large, floating down gently from the white sky. It's a cold November morning in Park Falls, and everything is still.

When I walk into school, there's a murmured hush over every conversation. It seems quieter than usual. Everyone I pass in the hallway seems uneasy, on edge. There are no echoes of laughing or goofing off throughout the building. I shuffle into my first period class and take my seat cautiously. I don't want to say or do anything, because I'm not sure what's going on. As kids slowly fill the seats and straggle in after the bell, I notice that the attendance is small. The desk next to me is empty—Elliot's desk.

When Jimmy comes in, I stop him before he goes to his seat. I grab his arm and his brown eyes flicker down to me, startled. He looks like he's seen a ghost.

"Hey, where's Elliot? Mr. Perfect never misses a day, and I know because you constantly complain about it like he's stealing your crown."

My attempt to put humor into this situation fails. Jimmy glances around and then crouches down next to my desk. In a hushed voice, he whispers, "You didn't hear. Did you?"

"What?" I don't usually check social media before school starts. Now he has me worried.

"Look, I... just see for yourself." His face breaks a little, and an overwhelming sense of helplessness crashes over me. He adjusts his glasses and throws his phone down on my desk. Restlessly, he stands up and shoves his hands in his pockets.

On the screen in front of me is an article. It reads, "Local Teen Commits Suicide, Found Dead in Home."

My breathing stops. The picture next to it is Alex.

Our Alex.

* * *

They call an assembly at lunch. Everyone takes their seats on the bleachers with a solemn hush. The gym is eerily quiet, drastically different from the assembly on the first day of school. Principal Conners is in the middle of the basketball court where I watched one of Elliot's basketball games with a distant Alex last week. Distant, but still alive.

The round man has lost all his zest. His beard sags and he stands before us without movement, unusually still. "Today, we are having an important and serious discussion because of a tragedy in our lives. A young man in our school died over the weekend." He clutches his round chest. "When we lose someone in our community, we cannot always explain the loss. What we can do is take care of ourselves and show compassion to those around us," he says. "We will kindly ask all of you to be respectful and courteous, and not to spread rumors or overshare about the situation. The family has asked for privacy, and it is unkind and disrespectful to spread stories in the midst of grief. Find adults in the community and the school you can talk to instead," he says. "And most importantly, be there for those around you."

I grab Jimmy's arm next to me with white knuckles. He just stares straight ahead with his brown eyes low and jaw clenched like it's going to break.

"We have brought in counselors from all over the district to be here for anyone who wants the support, so please take advantage of their presence. Also, our representative Mr. Richards from YouTech Laboratory will be coming in, and he may take some of you aside to talk and ask questions. Please be cooperative because they're just trying to get a better sense of what happened in a secure and confidential way. Thank you all for being respectful and giving us your time."

When the assembly is over, I don't go to lunch. I don't want to sit at the table without Alex, or even without Elliot. I get in my sad faded car and I go home. Jimmy comes with me, but we don't speak the entire drive. Everything seems like a blur. A strange fog. We get to my house and we bury ourselves in my couch next to each other. This is not a tutoring session.

"Do you want to know what music I listen to?" he asks.

I nod. He takes one earbud, I take the other, and he puts on his playlist. It's classical music. I am surprised at first, skeptical, but soon my mind is taken like an ocean tide by the swell of emotions in each symphony. Anger and passion in soft crescendos fill my ears until I am numb. The only time we move is when Jimmy reaches over to his phone to change the song. I don't think I would've appreciated his music if it wasn't for this moment. Suddenly, I'm thankful he waited to show me until now.

After a while I catch Jimmy go into his phone for more than just changing the song. He cradles the screen, eyes fixated on a single photo. It's a young high school basketball team; it must've been years ago. The group of boys in their jerseys after a game pile close to each other in the photo. In the center, a young Jimmy has his arms thrown around Alex and Elliot. The three of them beam up at the camera with elated smiles I haven't seen on any of the boys since I've known them. They look happy.

* * *

The door slams behind me. I feel my entire house shudder. My brother Josh is at hockey right now and my parents are still at work, so the empty house mocks me in its silence. It's just me and the art on all the walls.

Today at school was a fever dream. Elliot didn't show up, which I expected the day after the news broke, but neither did Jimmy. I haven't felt this alone at school since my first couple of weeks. All of Park Falls seems quiet and lonesome as it mourns Alex's death in a suffocating silence. It's only been a day.

I throw down my backpack and stride into the kitchen to search the drawers for some kind of painkillers. I have the worst migraine, and my lack of sleep doesn't help the incessant throbbing. My fingers find their way around a small bottle and I swallow a couple of the pills without water. All I can think about is that anonymous text. *Don't look for Alex.* I grip the bottle and wait for the pounding and the dizziness in my head to stop. That stupid, unknown number seemed to know exactly what was going to happen. And it was sent to me, of all people. Even without it, though, I knew something was going to happen. I could feel it that night. Almost like it had already happened.

"Hey."

I jump and whirl around. Pills fly from my hand.

"Jesus, Klara, what the hell are you doing?"

"Wow, I really scared you." Klara raises her bold eyebrows. "You didn't wait for me after school. I had to walk. Normally I'd forgive you, but today I saw a kid actually throw up at the bus stop. I'm not even kidding."

I feel like I could throw up.

She frowns. "Are you okay?"

"Yeah, I'm fine." *One, two, three, four...*

"You're popping pills like Christian from fourth period. You're obviously not fine," she says. She snatches the pill bottle away from me, as if worried that I'm going to dump the whole thing down my throat.

"I just need to be alone right now," I say through gritted teeth. "What are you even doing here? Don't you ever go home?"

If my comment hurt her, she doesn't let it show. "We were gonna do our coding together. Remember? Because Jimmy couldn't make it today for tutoring, and you didn't want to do it alone. You said—"

"I know what I said." I hold my forehead. "I just... I really just need to figure out some stuff. Okay? I need a little time to think. I can't handle your Spanish rap and stories about Elliot right now."

"You sound like my mom."

I groan and storm out of the kitchen, heading up to my room. I hear her footsteps pound on the newly carpeted floor as she chases after me. *Five, six, seven, eight...*

"Via, I think it's better not to be alone right now," she calls after me.

"Go home, Klara." I stomp up the stairs. "Or go comfort Elliot. Isn't he like your boyfriend now?"

"We don't have to talk about Alex. I just think it's better if we hang out for a little and take our minds off of things. I know how you're feeling."

"Trust me, you don't."

Her footsteps continue to thump up the stairs after me. "Look, I get it, he was like your first friend at school. But if you don't talk to me—"

"Klara, I'm fine."

"I don't care. You're not listening to me. Let's just hang out for a little while. We don't even have to do homework."

"No."

"No, you don't want to hang out with me? Or no you don't want to do coding?"

"Yes!"

"So you *do* want to do coding?"

"Klara, I'm fine!" I stop at the top of the stairs to face her. "I barely even knew him. He was just this kid I sat at lunch with, okay? Elliot and Jimmy are the ones who knew him from before. I didn't know anything about him. Apparently he doesn't even have a brother, which, you know, I didn't ever bring up again because we weren't really that close. That would have been weird if I said something because it wasn't my business. And I know that. If I had said something about that night on the road, or the hospital, or the text, or his shaking hands, that would have been overstepping. Right? I mean I shouldn't even worry about it. It wasn't my problem."

Klara's dark eyebrows cut through my resolve.

"We've all messed up, Via. We've all done things we regret."

I tug at my sleeves.

"But I get it. I know it's not your problem. Nobody at this school is anyone's problem, really. We've only known each other for a couple of months."

"Right," I say. "It isn't my fault that something happened to him. I couldn't stop it."

"Sure, there was nothing you could do. Why should you even care?"

I swallow hard, the taste of the pills stuck in my throat. *Why is it suddenly so hard to swallow?*

Klara sighs painfully and scrunches her face in reluctance. "I can't believe I'm doing this, but…" she takes a few steps up the stairs. "Here's the thing about not caring. You think you know what you're doing. You think you know how you feel, that you're on top of it. And then suddenly, before you know it, everything's changed. It sneaks up on you and you don't even know how it happened."

Her words ring in my ears and I slide down with my shoulder against the wall. I crumple on the top stair. My fist clenches because I don't want this girl to see me cry.

She collapses down on the step next to me. "It sucks. Feeling things. It ruins everything. Doesn't it?"

My eyes sting, but I quickly reach up and rub them with my sleeves. Klara's eyebrows wilt and she slides her arm around me. I can see wheels turn behind those cunning eyes, levels of so much more than just Elliot and Spanish rap.

"Thank you," I murmur.

"For what?" She leans her head against mine. "I'm just that crazy girl who spends her free time breaking and entering in your home."

I choke out a laugh, for reasons she can't understand. In that moment I realize that Klara is the best type of person. I may not trust her father or the program he's involved with, but to be honest, I don't know if I can trust anyone. She may be pushy, intrusive, and inconsiderate, but that means I can count on one thing. She's always there—whether I want her to be or not. The thing about Klara is that she's there for you when you didn't even realize you needed someone. And thank God for people like that.

CHAPTER 11

"This is ridiculous." I sigh. "I don't understand why he's not allowed to come over."

My dad responds without glancing up from his reading. "He's not my son. It's not up to me to make the rules in this situation." This week it feels like he won't even acknowledge me. He always has his nose stuck in a different book. This one is something about Zen Buddhism.

"Wes is seventeen years old. I think he can go over to a friend's house without his parents' permission."

"It's only been a week since the suicide, and you know that's a sensitive subject for Beth and Lawrence. Apparently the therapist cautioned them about triggers."

"Dad, I think I would know what's good for my best friend." I cross the kitchen and lean against the granite island. This doesn't close the mental distance between us. "And it's not like I would bring it up around him anyway. I just want to see him. I feel like I'll go insane if I don't."

He flexes his knuckles as he sets down the book. "Have you ever considered that maybe he's having a hard time? I know *you* need him, but think about how others are being affected."

"But he hasn't been responding to my texts. I think it's probably Beth and Lawrence. They definitely took his phone away." I pull mine out. "Here, I'll text him again."

My dad takes off his reading glasses slowly. "Do you want us to call your old therapist?"

"No, are you kidding me? I severed all ties with Dr. Simmonds after he told me I was playing video games as a coping mechanism. That guy doesn't know anything." My fingers drum on the counter and then flit up to my mouth. I can't seem to sit still today. "But if I said it would be good for my mental health, would you let Wes come over?"

"Why don't you invite some of your other friends over? Like that girl Klara. She can always spend the night here. Or what about Jimmy? That boy is very hard-working, a good influence."

My hand itches like I want to punch something. "Sometimes I just need Wes. Okay? He's the only one who understands." I bite at my nails and check my phone again. *I need to tell him how Jimmy and Alex and Elliot went to the same high school. I need to tell him about Chad's mother, the strange Klara and Dean moment at the party, and what happened with the ESP exercise in school.*

"You seem tense. Why don't you go to sleep early tonight? Put that phone away for a little bit."

"Trust me. I don't like being on social media right now anyway." I flip through my music until I find Jimmy's classical playlist saved in my library. *Why won't he come to school? Why has he canceled every tutoring session? Why does it seem like everyone is ignoring me?*

He watches me with deep creases in his forehead and heavy eyes as if he stares at a childhood photograph. "Are you sure you're okay?"

"I'll be fine. It's only been a week," I reassure him. I almost convince myself.

"Alright," he says. "Say goodnight to your mother."

I exhale heavily, and he gives me that stern look I knew was coming. "Don't be like this, Via."

"She hasn't moved from that spot in days, Dad. It's freaking Josh out," I whisper.

"I know you can't understand this, but have some sympathy for her as a mother." The lines in his face twist into shadows. "A parent should never have to live longer than their child."

I falter under the pain in his expression. I nod and leave him under the kitchen lights. My feet pad softly into the living room where I can see my mom's back hunched over the coffee table with a glass of wine in her hand. Her chestnut hair is pulled back in that bun that always reminds me of her teaching days.

"Hey, Mom." I perch on the arm of the couch.

She stares deeply into the translucent glow of the wine. She's a flickering ember in comparison to her usual luminescence. She still has a scent like honey, though. I think that's what my old house smelled like, but I can't quite remember anymore.

"Goodnight, Mom." I breathe her in one last time before I slink down the hall.

* * *

On Monday, Elliot finally comes back to school. All weekend I've wanted to text him. He's the only other person who knew about Alex in the hospital. But I can't bring myself to talk to him about his dead best friend, no matter how much it unsettles me. My mind has been reeling in circles without Wes to vent to.

Elliot looks distant but he's still here. That's better than Jimmy. He comes in and out of classes but doesn't even take his earbuds out to acknowledge me. And he's always gone by lunch.

"Via, look what you've done. You've invited the enemy to our table." Ben pokes fun at Klara to lighten the solemn mood. Klara joined us in the cafeteria with a feeble attempt to make the table seem less empty. To no avail, because the whole school seems empty. Even though it's been a week, the tragedy hangs over the student body like a dark cloud.

"You can still throw chips at her from here." I shrug.

"Actually, she's here with me." Elliot takes the beanie off of his head and runs his fingers through his hair. "I know. I'm a traitor. I accept my punishment with dignity."

This is the first time Elliot has mentioned anything about being together with Klara, and the whole table exchanges sly glances. I'm happy for them, and to see Klara smile genuinely is a miracle in and of itself. But then that shy smile dies off. I follow her gaze to see someone approach our table. I frown because I didn't expect to ever see this kid again.

Dean's long coat swishes behind him as he pulls up a chair.

"What are you doing, Dean? I thought you were trying to stay away from everyone like the plague," Klara snaps. I'm brought back to the night of the party, just outside the cabin.

"Circumstances have changed." Dean crosses his arms on the back of the chair and eyes Klara. He hasn't even acknowledged me, which I should be relieved about. "I wanted to come and say I'm sorry for your loss. Alex was a good kid. It's a shame."

A vein on Elliot's neck protrudes forcefully.

Klara's eyebrows cut like a knife. "Oh please, you don't care about Alex. Why are you really here?"

"Can I speak to you privately?" His mouth dangles open. "It's somewhat… urgent."

"You heard Via at the party." She flicks her ponytail. "Stay away from me."

Dean's tongue plays on the inside of his cheek. "God, you really are the worst."

"Get lost, Dean," Elliot growls. His hair stands on end. "She obviously doesn't want to talk to you."

Everything about the boy is a devilish challenge, as if he wants to get beaten up. I find myself aggravated by the way his mouth hangs open after he finishes talking, the way his unkempt hair adds to the chaos of his disheveled appearance, and that stupid, pretentious long coat.

As if sensing my annoyance, for the first time since he sat down, his gaze swivels over to me. I look away from those unsettling eyes as a dark feeling rises up in my chest. It's the same sensation from Halloween.

That's when something catches my eye. Three men in dark-fitted suits hover in the doorway of the lunchroom. I watch Mr. Richards and his two henchmen scan the crowds of students with their sharp ties. They stand out like wolves in a flock of sheep.

"Those guys don't look like they're here to comfort people." Cole puts down his phone, which I never see him do.

"You've got to be kidding me," Elliot grumbles, momentarily distracted from Dean. "I didn't think Principal Connors was serious when he said they were bringing these guys in."

I look back over at the men and realize Mr. Richards has his gaze dead-set on our table. The weight of everything I carry in my mind crashes down on me.

"Interesting that they're here for the whole Alex tragedy. It really makes you wonder, how involved are they with the students at our school?" Dean stretches his tall legs. "What are your thoughts on this, Klara? I mean, your father is a key investor in the program. You must have a lot to say on the subject. You certainly had a lot to say to me at Chad's party."

Klara's voice drips with malice. "Screw you."

Elliot turns to her. "Wait, you guys talked at the Halloween party?"

"Oh, you didn't tell your boyfriend? Yeah, we had a whole chat." Dean shoots a glare at Klara and backs away from the table. "I'll go back to avoiding everyone like the plague now. Let me know if you change your mind, Klara."

Elliot stands up with his fists clenched, and his chair clatters on the floor behind him. Everyone at the table flinches. The whole cafeteria stops and takes notice of the commotion from the varsity basketball star. The shattered look on his face makes me want to scream. *What kind of a sick human would play with someone's emotions like this right after his best friend's death?* Bile rises up in my throat and I push it down.

Before Dean can respond, the men in suits stride toward our table. He tries to escape but is blocked by Mr. Richards's broad shoulders. A look is exchanged between them so vile that even I feel unnerved. Klara's eyes pique, and I know she sees this too.

"I'm sorry to interrupt, but I've been informed this is the lunch table where Alex Brockman used to sit." His beady eyes scour our faces. "You were his friends?"

"Friend is a strong word." Dean gives Mr. Richards a look up and down. "I'd go with acquaintance."

The man seems unfazed by Dean's impudence and studies him in a cool and calculated manner. "Principal Conners mentioned you were the students who had the most contact with Alex during school. Is that correct?"

"Yes," Elliot nods. "I went to the same school as him before. Jimmy did too. Jimmy Andrade."

I glance over at the empty chair next to me and notice the gaping holes left by Alex and Jimmy.

"We've already contacted Mr. Andrade about meeting separately. In the meantime, we will need to speak to all of you individually about the recent incidents involving your friend. It's nothing serious. We're just trying to get a sense of what happened."

I tug at my sleeves to hide my sweaty palms under the table.

Mr. Richards levels his hawk-like eyes on Dean. "Mr. Wallace, why don't we have our meeting now?"

I see something flicker across the boy's eyes. I could be mistaken, but it looks like… fear. He mumbles sheepishly, "Yes, sir."

"Excellent. Follow me."

Dean stares forcefully at the ground, and I wonder if he's going to resist. But then he adjusts the collar of his long coat and follows the men in suits. Strangely, I watch his face twist, and then he laughs to himself like the whole thing is funny. *There's something wrong with that kid.*

"Thank God. I hope they expel him." Elliot sits back down, and Klara links her arm into his with a scrunched frown. Regardless of Dean being gone, our table doesn't continue conversation. My stomach churns as I anticipate my own meeting with the wolves.

CHAPTER 12

I take a deep breath before I knock on the principal's door. My knuckles rattle on the unscathed glass. Inside, the blurry images of Mr. Richards and Principal Conners speak in hushed tones. Their silhouettes straighten. Principal Conners darkens the doorway with his round figure.

"Olivia! I see you're the last one to speak with our Mr. Richards." When I'm ushered inside, he tilts his head like a sad puppy. "Once again, I am very sorry about your loss. Thank you for consenting to have this conversation."

Did I ever consent to this? Did I ever consent to be any part of this messed-up school?

"And thank you for checking in with me, Principal Conners." Mr. Richards speaks right over my head. "I'll check for those records later. They should be in the trunk of my car."

"Great!" Principal Conners squeezes his belly to pass me and then gives me one last head tilt. "And may this be a path to healing and closure for you."

"Thank you." I glance around warily. *Is this some kind of free therapy? My mom would get a kick out of that.*

"Olivia Prescott, it's nice to officially meet you. As you know, I'm Stephen Richards." He reaches out a claw-like hand as the door seals us in. I hesitate to shake it. He retracts the attempt and instead settles into the room amidst the stacks of papers and the other school chaff of Principal Conners's euphoric clutter.

I don't know where to look as I take a seat. I'm nervous to meet Mr. Richards's stare, as if my eyes will reveal my suspicions. His predatory bird-like appearance makes me unable to sit still. His sharp intensity and hooked nose search for something behind my expression.

"Right." He lowers himself into the opposite chair and closes the cramped distance between us. He opens a slick briefcase and takes out a tablet. "How would you describe your relationship with the deceased?"

I eye the tablet and the chic pen he writes on it with. "We were in a couple of classes together, and we sat at the same lunch table every day. I've only known him since the beginning of the semester. I didn't go to school with him before."

"Yes, not many students came from the same districts for a reason." Mr. Richards nods. "Something about diversity and inclusion. I'm not really involved with the school board side of this operation. To be honest, it bores me."

"Oh. Right."

"While we're on the subject, can I ask you a few things about your opinions on this institution?"

"Sure." *He's pivoting away from talking about Alex.*

"During your time at Park Falls, have you learned anything particularly interesting about our program or the Agents? Outside of your classes of course."

"No, not really." *Why are my palms sweating? Just because suspicious things happen to me doesn't mean I have to be suspicious...*

"Alright, that's fine. Have any of Principal Conners's other exercises piqued your interest?"

I watch his pen scribble on the screen. "I guess I'm a little confused about the ESP and telepathy project. I'm not sure I understand how it has anything to do with the Agent."

"Our research is about so much more than just computers and robots, Olivia." He sets down his device. "If we're going to help each other out today, I need to make sure you understand that. Do you know what this program is about? And not what the school board has to say, or what that pamphlet tells you."

"It's just an artificial intelligence simulation. I don't know." My throat feels dry. "You're trying to see how human-like you can make the robots. It's like a game."

His mouth clamps shut; he can tell I have my doubts. *Is he offended? I'm just a kid. What does he expect?* "A game? Well, yes. I can see how Principal Conners's spectacle and all his chess tournaments would make you see it that way. As a professional who's dedicated his life to this cause, I can say this isn't how I would have done things. You see, our research is so much more than just a magic trick. What we're doing here, what we're trying to achieve, will advance all of humankind."

The last time I saw Wes two weekends ago, he made jokes about space battles and superpowers. Strangely this feels like a similar conversation.

"If you're trying to save the world, what are you doing in Park Falls?"

Something clicks in Mr. Richards's beady eyes. He chuckles. "I like how you think, Ms. Prescott. One day I would enjoy speaking with you at greater lengths about our research at the laboratory."

"I'm just here to talk about Alex."

His broad shoulders roll back. "I can see you're still rather skeptical of our work. I don't blame you. Most of our investors also had a hard time grasping the reality of an Agent walking among them." Then he suddenly stands as if to pace, which throws me off. Deeply engrossed in his passion, he continues. "You see, there are two types of artificial intelligence. I'll try to make this simple. One type is weak AI, which is the kind of intelligence in your phones or computers. But the kind we're reaching for, the kind of system nobody has achieved yet, is strong AI."

My eyes flicker down to his sharp suit, and I follow his darting eyes. "So it doesn't exist?"

"Not exactly. Strong AI is essentially a deeper intelligence, where the inorganic system of the AI actually functions like a human brain. It doesn't just think for itself. It also thinks exactly like our brains do. This kind of machine learning was thought to be impossible because you can make a computer imitate a human mind, but it's harder to instill actual understanding."

I glance over at the clock, and my knee taps restlessly. I'm waiting for the punchline, but he seems to only want to feed his ego and talk about his program.

"Have you ever heard of Alan Turing?"

"He was brought up in our exercise the other day." My stomach turns in knots at the memory. "Is that another thing your lab is trying to bring into existence? ESP?"

"Well, that much already exists. It comes in strange forms. The more we understand about the computational thinking system, the more we understand about human beings."

Did he also bring up Alan Turing and ESP with my friends in their meetings? Or just with me?

"So the Turing Test, that's why you built this school? To test the Agent?"

"We're doing what Alan Turing would have done if he was alive now. But instead of hypothesizing if a robot can be identified through a conversation, we're seeing if it can be identified through interactions in the real world among everyone else."

"But why high school? Why… us?"

"Why not? A high school is a perfect environment of self-discovery for this simulation. It was a risk for sure, to surround an Agent with unpredictable, hormonal teenagers. But it seems to be paying off."

"Did you finally realize high schoolers are more predictable than you think?"

He laughs in surprise. "Yes, that could be the case. A computer can't think outside of its programming the way a human does, but it can be guided by its surroundings. And this environment has proven to be the most successful trial yet. Up until now, nobody has been able to create a system that can pass the Turing Test. Even getting close is a success."

"Success? You call this successful?" My throat tightens. "A kid died."

"Yes, we are aware. But in any experiment, there are many… variables. That's why it's been so promising that right now we are farther into this test than we've ever been. Because despite these variables, we can finally—"

"I'm sorry," I interject, "but I'm not sure how all this relates to Alex. I thought I was in here to answer questions about my friend. I understand you're very passionate about your work, but I really have to get to class."

"You're right. I apologize." He straightens his tie and slinks back into his chair. "But we are a part of history, and I feel as though you may be someone who could understand that. You may not realize it, Olivia, but this project has been going on for far longer than you would think. Long before your parents began working with us."

Something about the way he says this prickles the hair on the back of my neck. "Then why did you really create this school?"

"Ah, now here is the real question." He taps his forehead. "And this is what brings us back to Alex."

I swallow a sinking feeling in my chest about where this is going. It's that lurking dread, the same one that started at the Halloween party—the last time I ever saw Alex alive.

"How well did you know your friend? You said you only sat with him at lunch, but did you know anything about his family life? His life outside of school? Anything personal about him that could help us better understand?"

What could be more personal than Alex in the middle of the road at night? Without his family, not wanting to go home, looking for a brother who doesn't exist? "No, I didn't know a lot."

"The reason I gave you so much background on our program is because we're deeply concerned with his suicide. That's why we're meeting with you and others who knew him. We need to find out why your friend killed himself. You see? It is imperative to our research, because we need to prevent this from having repercussions on our simulation."

"Repercussions?"

"Have you heard of copycat suicide?"

"Yes, I mean…" I shake my head. "It's people imitating suicides. Like on TV, or in their own life."

"Correct. Copycat suicide is when suicides come in clusters. It's like a contagion. And unfortunately, the age group most susceptible to this phenomenon is teenagers."

"Then you're worried other kids will commit suicide because of Alex?"

"It's possible."

"No, that's not it." My fingers tap on my knee. "You're worried about your Agent committing suicide."

He leans back in his chair. "To some extent. This is a strong concern for everyone at YouTech because we've already been experiencing glitches in our system."

"Glitches." I look down, remembering Alex's shaking hands. "Right."

"Just subtle things in the coding, small errors. The point is, if we don't figure out this problem, our entire experiment and even our whole program could be in jeopardy. We may never achieve the greatest leap in all of humanity's evolution." Mr. Richards leans forward. "Are you willing to help us eliminate our risk and figure out why Alex committed suicide?"

I swallow hard and fight down the queasiness in my gut. "I don't believe you. Why would you need our help if you have all these employees and all this equipment and technology?"

"I like you, Olivia. You're a very sharp girl with that head of yours." I see his long fingers curl around the tablet. "I have to say, not many people from Park Falls like to ask 'why' questions when it comes to things they don't understand."

"Yeah, well, I'm not really from Park Falls. Nobody is."

He laughs. "Fair enough. But still, something is curious about the way your mind works. I would love to study it. Did you know my background was in psychology? A PhD in behavioral neuroscience."

My heart pounds and I resist the urge to leave. *You have nothing to hide, Via. He's just some creepy lab scientist.*

"Studying minds and computers for all this time really does make you wonder. So many kinds of systems are out there that transmit information, so many AI models. The human brain cannot really be that simple. But then again, if it was, we would be too simple to understand it."

I study his expression with growing panic. *Does he know about my dreams? Does he know about the way I knew something bad was going to happen with Alex, like it already had?*

"If you're uncomfortable with all of these questions right now, I can give you some time to gather your thoughts. I know this is a lot to handle, processing the loss of your friend so soon. We can speak again on another occasion." He rises to his full height. "This is all for research, after all."

With that he buttons up his suit and strides out of the office. I stay behind for a moment and tap my knee on the carpet. *This is such a sick joke. I always knew this experiment was ridiculous, but this is a whole new level. I can't believe my dad works with these guys.* Then my eyes land on the slick briefcase on the ground in front of me. *He accidentally left it here.*

I glance around the office, at the desk and the tall file cabinet, and when the coast is clear I slide the case over and fiddle with the clasps. I hear a sound from outside in the parking lot and crane my neck to see what it is. I can see Mr. Richards right outside the window as he unlocks his shining black two-door convertible and opens the trunk. I watch him stop suddenly, pause for a moment, and then spin around back to the school.

He must have realized he forgot his briefcase.

Hastily I return it to its spot on the floor and slip out of Principal Conners's office. I pass through the front desks and my feet carry me out to the hall in a dizzying haste. The lockers blur by as I head for the outside doors. I hear the click of Mr. Richards's nice shoes on the tiles of the hall, and right as he passes me, we lock eyes.

He disappears back into the administrative office, and with a new determination, I push out into the parking lot. The double doors of the entrance clatter behind me, and shadows of clouds dance on the pavement. The chilled November air makes me shiver.

I am at the side of the sleek convertible, relieved to see he kept it ajar. But as I crack open the trunk and peer in at the boxes of files, I realize I have a bigger issue. They're all locked.

"Shit." I glance back at the window to Principal Conners's office, but don't see Mr. Richards's looming shoulders. *He'll be back any minute. I'll get in huge trouble for this.* I yank at the locks hopelessly. *One, two, three, four...* Then I feel for the hair pin on my head. "Okay, okay, this is fine. You've picked one lock. You've picked them all. Doors, file cabinets, it's all the same."

My hand fumbles with the pin and wiggles to investigate the lockbox. Every sound of a slamming door or student's voice back in the school makes me jump. With a click I release the breath I didn't even realize I held in. Hurriedly I unclasp the sides and sift through the information. All the folders read "Confidential." I hear my blood pound in my ears as my fingers flip across the pages. *Why would they keep this information on paper instead of digitally?*

I land on one that has this week's date on the top. I pull it out and scan the sheet, seeing unrecognizable numbers and data that don't mean anything to me. I shiver; maybe because of the cold or maybe because of the sickening feeling that swells in my chest. I don't even know what I'm looking for.

That's when I see something. At the bottom of the page is a brief description of a coding glitch that resulted in self-termination. It records the status of the system and keeps using the name Agent A-3. And then, at the very end, the unofficial name for A-3.

Alex Brockman.

I feel like I can't breathe. My eyes are stuck on that one page. They stare at the words but can't take them in. I continue to scan for some kind of confirmation that my friend wasn't a part of this, but it just continues to mention Agent A-3 and the glitch. It talks about it as if it's an unfortunate error or a small setback in the simulation. When I get to the last sentence, I realize this is only the beginning. The last line reads: "As of now all other active Agents remain operational. No further glitches detected."

I lose my breath entirely. *There's more than one Agent?*

And when I turn back to the school, I find that Mr. Richards's beady eyes stare out at me through a dark side window.

CHAPTER 13

I'm inside the game. I'm inside Immortal Soldiers as my own avatar, and I search for something. I don't know what it is, but I need to find it. I wander through the ruined streets as buildings crumble to ash and the pixelated sky stretches its gloom in all directions above me. A sense of hopelessness crushes in on me. *I'll never find it.*

And then the dream shifts. Suddenly the empty street is winding through the woods. I look down and I'm in a hospital gown, barefoot. My hands shake, slowly at first and then violently. Fear courses through me. Before I know what I'm doing, I peel at my skin. I start at the top of my pointer finger and pull away the flesh all the way below my palm to reveal metal underneath. I tear off the skin on my wrist, and then my forearm, up past my elbow. My whole arm is a metal skeleton; gears and hinges and steel pieces. I rip away the last layer and hold up the grotesque, robotic hand to the pixelated sky.

* * *

The harsh light of my desk lamp flickers. I'm snapped out of my head, back to the assignment that's due tomorrow. I tap my pencil on the blank page. *Who assigns handwritten homework these days?* My eyes wander around the room at the stark walls I've been meaning to decorate for months now and then back to the paper. I hear the *tap, tap, tap* of the pencil on wood, the sound of Josh's music from the room over. I flip over my phone and the screen glows. Nothing. Back to the page. The bulb flickers again, like a streetlight on a deserted road through the forest. I'm drawn into the feeling with each pulse of energy, and the loneliness swells like a tide.

The screen of my window squeals and my pencil drops to the floor. With a thud, Wes tumbles inside my room. "What the hell, Via. You didn't tell me that was going to be so hard to climb."

"You scared me." I pull my hand down from my racing heart.

"Sorry, I barely escaped without my parents noticing. Didn't have time to text you." He leans back against my bed frame and brushes long blonde strands out of his eyes. "What was so urgent? Couldn't you have waited until dinner when my whole family is here?"

"I couldn't wait that long. I needed you alone." I pace in front of him, and my toes curl on the carpet. "Okay, so here's the thing. I know this is going to sound crazy. Like full psychotic breakdown crazy. But I don't know who else to tell."

"Did you do some more investigating?" Wes claps his hands together. "I bet it's more dirt on Klara. Or wait, did you find out why Jimmy—"

"Alex was an Agent."

Wes freezes. His eyes go vacant. "What?"

"You heard me."

He slumps back against my bed.

"I didn't mean to find out. I just happened to see these records in a trunk because I was curious. Actually yeah, I did mean to find out, but I didn't know what it was going to be. Richards was meeting with everyone at our table, and I couldn't tell if he was lying to me because he was saying all this bullshit. It was really freaking me out. This whole thing is huge, Wes. It's not just about one Agent like everyone thinks." I stop and tug at my sleeves. "Say something. Aren't you the one with all the conspiracy theories?"

"I'm just a little… confused." His face is twisted, his neck rigid and tense. "I thought you didn't believe in all this stuff."

"It's not Santa Claus, Wes."

"I know, but… there's no way. I'm sure you got something wrong. Alex couldn't be the Agent. You said it yourself. The whole school is just one big joke."

"I wish I could tell you I was being sarcastic. For once, I'm dead serious."

"Are you sure this isn't some kind of coping mechanism to deal with Alex's death?"

"No!" I pull at my hair. *I think I have a perpetual headache now.* "I know what I saw. This isn't just something in my head. And you weren't there for everything else that was going on with Alex. You didn't see the way he was… different. Toward the end." My palms sweat just at the thought. *One, two, three, four…*

Wes processes in a world of his own. His hand flits up to his wrists and rubs along the scars. I don't like that he's not saying anything. I don't like that he won't look at me. *Maybe I should have told him about the night on the road with Alex and the hospital. But he already went MIA on me this week…*

"Who else knows?"

I shrug. "No one, I don't think. But I have this… feeling. I think it has something to do with Jimmy. He's always so weird around Elliot and Alex, and they were all at school before. They're hiding something from me."

"Do you think Jimmy and Elliot know?"

Before I can respond, there's a loud knock on the front door downstairs. *It can't be Beth and Lawrence already.* Josh listens to music in his room so he probably doesn't hear.

"Stay in my room." I bundle into my sweatshirt and slip out. For a minute, I picture Jimmy's soft worried eyes and hope it's him.

I open the door and my heart falls. "Oh, it's you."

Klara raises an eyebrow. "Expecting someone else?"

"No, it's just… why are you here?"

"You look like hell." She pushes past me with a judgmental up-down.

"Now is not the best time, Klara," I urge, but she's already halfway down the hall. She throws off coats and stylish bags along the way. "Seriously, my parents are at the store. They're going to cook this whole meal for Wes's family, and I'm supposed to make sure Josh does his homework before then." I chase her up the stairs and step around her trail of chaos.

"Relax, we'll just—" She stops when she swings open my door and finds Wes on the ground. "Oh. Well this is a fun twist."

"Why is she here?" Wes clumsily scrambles to his feet.

Klara scrunches her face. "Miss me?"

"What now? Did you get in trouble with Daddy again?" I'm surprised by the animosity that emanates from his tone.

"No, but this time he practically paid me to get out of the house. He's been throwing money at me ever since the Alex thing." Klara sprawls onto my bed and soaks up the attention. "Apparently it's to fix the fact that I've been 'acting up more than usual.' He did the same thing when he married my stepmom. I guess he thinks that just because he created me, he can control me with money like all his other projects."

Wes clears his throat. He looks toward the window as if he itches to jump out. I wish I had something on the walls to pretend to stare at.

"Anyway," she picks at her nails, "why did I barely see you at school this week? I could never find you."

"Oh, lots of tutoring with Jimmy." I avoid her gaze, sit down at the desk, and fiddle with my pencil. "Hey, I forgot to ask. How did your meeting with the guys from YouTech go?"

Klara glances up, eyebrows raised. "How did yours go?"

I shrug. "Good. Did they say anything weird to you?"

"Nope." She touches her hoop earrings. "You?"

"Nope."

"That's good."

Silence fills up the space until it feels like there isn't even room to breathe.

"I'm gonna go," Wes says. "My parents will notice if I'm not back from the gas station yet. We can talk about that thing later after dinner."

"Ooh, what thing?" Klara sits up.

"Mind your own business." Wes straddles the window.

"It's about Jimmy," I say. "We're trying to figure out what happened with Elliot and Alex in the past, like why they aren't friends anymore. Has Elliot said anything to you?"

Wes gives me an appalled face of disbelief from the sill. He jerks his hand and signals for me to shut up.

"No, honestly he's not the best boyfriend material right now. I've been giving him space to deal with the Alex situation."

"Yeah, Jimmy has been pretty distant too. Lately I'm just so worried about him, but I don't know how to help." *I ignored the signs with Wes and Alex. I can't let it happen again.* "The problem is these boys never want to talk about it. I don't even know his whole history with Elliot and Alex. I wish there was some kind of way to find out what happened."

Klara shrugs. "The school keeps records of all of us."

Now Wes is intrigued. He crawls back into the room, and the fire in his eyes rekindles.

"But there's no way we could get to those. Right? And even then, that would be…" I exchange glances with him. "Breaking and entering."

"Well you could always just go through the boys' locker rooms. They put tape over the door lock so they can go hook up with girls in there after school," Klara says. We both look at her. "At least, that's what I've heard."

My mind reels. I can't help but feel a tight flutter in my chest. *I should leave it be, but I have to figure out what's really going on here.* "Let's go. Right now. We have at least another hour before I have to be back for dinner."

"For real? Omigod I love this side of you!" Klara pops up in a flurry of hair.

"Wait, you're going with her?" Wes scratches his head. "On an investigation? Just the two of you?"

"Well, don't you need to be home? And I just thought that, after everything with Alex and your parents, maybe investigating isn't… the best thing for you. Right now."

"No, I'll go," he says. His face is set with conviction and serious unwavering eyes. With all my concern about Jimmy and Elliot, this is the last thing I need to worry about. But I'm not about to stop him.

"Fine," I nod. "But if Josh gets kidnapped while we're gone, I'm taking you down with me."

* * *

"God, we're like the holy trinity." Klara shivers in excitement.

"Shut up. Is this where the door is?" I point through the trees. We parked in a neighborhood down the road so we could sneak through the back woods on foot. Wes and I both wear dull clothing, but Klara's neon bomber jacket stands out like a beacon in the early evening shadows.

"That's the door!" she exclaims. "Again, heard it from a friend."

The maple trees clear to unveil a sliver of pavement behind the back of the high school. A thrill courses through my veins, and I look up at the sky that stretches its grey gloom in all directions above me. Without any kids here, the building is empty like unscathed ruins.

"Via, are you sure you know what you're talking about? Look." Wes clings to a tree trunk and points around the building at the parking lot. "There are cars here. You said it would be abandoned."

Panic courses through me for a moment because I wasn't expecting people to be here on a Sunday. I shake my head. "It's probably just cleaning staff. But it doesn't matter. This will still work. Trust me."

He and Klara exchange glances, and their shoes crunch on the fallen leaves of the undergrowth as they shift nervously. I settle my focus on the school, watching the lights above the closed doors. I clench my fists in anticipation and hold my breath to wait. *One, two, three, four...*

Klara steps forward. "Via, I—"

Just then, a single alarm cuts through the crisp air. The trees shudder. The school building powers off and goes dormant in a great sweep, and then it's silent. I watch as the lights above the door flicker to black. From the other side of the building, distant sounds of janitors and building staff waft through as they file out of the front entrance.

Klara laughs in disbelief, and Wes just eyes me.

"Power drill." I shrug, relieved. "Principal Conners moved them to five o'clock on weekends so they don't interrupt classes."

We dart out of the safety of the trees, and just as Klara promised the door is taped so it can't close. The boys' locker room reeks of sweat and damp clothes, but we move quickly to reach the gym.

"We only have ten minutes until the staff is let back in," I whisper. Through the dark, I jog across the glinting floor like a shadow.

"I think a life of crime suits me. I've never felt so goddamn sexy in my life." Klara flicks her ponytail.

The school looks like the empty hull of a ship—large and metal so our footsteps echo deeply into the halls. Even though everything is shut off and all the electronic locks are open, I glance around every corner in paranoia to look for secret cameras. Wes still rolls around and slides against the walls as if he's a spy.

"Will you stop that? You're ruining the sexiness," Klara hisses at him when we get to the administration office.

"Guys, listen." I hit Wes so he doesn't retaliate. "There's no guarantee Principal Conners won't be in his office today, so I need you both to be my lookout."

"No!" they protest in unison.

"Shush!" My throat tightens. "One of you watch the front entrance, and the other watch the back hall. Text me when five minutes is up. And no fighting!"

Why are they both so clueless? It's like babysitting. I leave them and navigate through the pitch black until I reach the principal's office. I peer through the blurred glass, but this time the only shadows that move are in my head. *You can do this, Via. You need to do this. You will find something.*

I close the door behind me and scan the room. In the meeting with Mr. Richards I was so nervous I didn't remember what I saw. A tall file cabinet sits behind Principal Conners's desk. I don't know why I didn't think of it until Klara said something. *This whole school was built for the simulation. We are all variables in it, so of course they would keep extensive records of us.* My hand reaches into my pocket and I feel for my pin. As I fiddle with the lock on the top drawer, I can't help but wonder again why this kind of confidential information wouldn't be digitalized. *Maybe these days they're more scared of a hacker with a computer than a kid with a bobby pin.*

It gets easier every time. When I hear the click, I yank the cabinet open. My fingers flit across the names on the folders. The first one I look for is Alex Brockman, but I soon realize it must have been taken out because his file isn't in here. *Stupid, of course they would remove his records.* The next one I go to is Jimmy Andrade. It's right at the top.

With my phone light I scan through the pages. Transcript: perfect. Criminal records: nothing. My foot taps on the carpet anxiously. I try not to picture Jimmy's heartbroken face if he were to see what I was doing right now.

His education history is filled with names of elementary and middle schools in the next district over. The high school that he went to before is called Northwest High, but there's nothing to imply what happened between him, Elliot, and Alex. I read through his demographics, his family. Mom working as a software engineer in their commercial branch, dad in HR, and a brother. *Wait, brother?* I squint closer, and there it is. I flip to the next page, where a printed record from Northwest High School describes a leave of absence his freshman year.

Due to mental health concerns after a suicide in the family, they excused three weeks of absences from class.

My phone buzzes. It's Wes. *Hurry up, Detective. Did you find anything?*

I quickly take pictures of Jimmy's file and return it to the top drawer. It rattles shut, but before I leave the office I pause. There's one more person I want to look up.

My knees ache as I crouch down and unlock the bottom drawer. My fingers slip into the folders in the back, and I pull out Dean Wallace. I can practically hear a clock ticking in my head as I do this, and hairs stand on the nape of my neck.

The pages of his record are chaotic and read very differently from Jimmy's. His school history is one misdemeanor after another ever since seventh grade. Suspensions, absences, even some criminal records of alcohol possession. Under his family there isn't much—only two parents working for YouTech and employee housing provided by the lab. I don't see any connection to Klara or her father. But then I see his financial aid for Park Falls Technical High School. He has a scholarship. *Why would they give a scholarship to such a troubled kid?*

Another text jolts me away from the files, and it's Klara this time. *Wes is leaving. You better come out.*

"Leaving?" I murmur. Hurriedly I slip the folder back into its place and shut the cabinet tightly. With one last glance at the files, I head out of the room and close the door behind me. I can just barely hear sounds of raised voices and arguing, which sends a spike of fear through my chest. *If they don't shut up, we'll be heard.*

In the hall, Wes's blonde hair bounces as he storms in the opposite direction. Klara's eyebrows are deadly sharp, her arms crossed forcefully.

"What happened? You couldn't leave each other alone for five minutes?" I spin on her.

"It's nothing. He's just being a little baby." Klara grabs my arm. "Let's go, okay?"

I rip my arm away from her. "How come every time I find you, you're pissing someone off?"

She turns up her chin, her cheekbones piqued in the darkness. Long nails tap on her phone case.

I ball up my fist and feel a stir in my chest. "You know what? I don't even ask about the Dean thing. Because I know you won't tell me. So don't pretend you're any better than the boys, because you're all the same. Unless you feel like explaining yourself?"

Then suddenly there's clanking from the front entrance. A beam of light shoots from the double doors.

"Shit!" I scrape my heels on the tile floor and take off down the hall. I hear Klara's bomber jacket flap behind me as we run. With as much stealth as I can pull off, I sprint around the corner and grab Klara's hand to drag her with me. We burst into the gym and squeak across the court just as the industrial lights bang on. I duck into the darkness of the locker room, and Klara practically trips over me as we scramble for the door.

The outside world blinds me and I gulp deep breaths of frigid air into my burning lungs. Klara slows down once we hit the trees and gasps for air with her hands clutched to her chest. I scan the woods for Wes's lanky figure. The sun is almost set now. A vibrant orange radiates through the maples and sets the leaves on fire.

"Jesus, that was close." Klara's ponytail dances in the light. "Via?"

I ignore her and race after Wes.

"Hey," I call to him when I'm in earshot. He overtakes the ground in large strides and doesn't turn around. "Hey." I run up and push him from behind.

He keels over, and then whips around with tumultuous waves in his eyes.

"What happened back there? I thought you were supposed to be my partner in crime. Were you really just going to leave me?"

Jaw clamped shut, he shakes his head. "You don't get it. I told you to stay away from Klara and you didn't."

"This has nothing to do with her! You were a shitty friend back there in the school, and you've been a shitty friend these past couple of weeks. I didn't ask you to be perfectly okay with everything after Alex, but you could've at least answered my calls."

"Well if I'm such a horrible friend, maybe you should just replace me with Klara. Because obviously she's the one who's really looking out for you."

"Hey, I didn't ask you to go on this mission." I choke on my own voice. "I was just trying to be sensitive about… I mean, Beth and Lawrence won't even let you leave your house without them."

The trees around us creak and shiver. "Let's just go back to your house for dinner. Okay?"

The sunlight dwindles, and a cold wind replaces it. I'm chilled to the bone. Wes pulls his sleeves down over his wrists and shoves by me, headed for the road. I look down at my hands. Maybe it's the adrenaline, maybe it's the exhaustion, but they subtly tremble.

* * *

Dinner is tense. Beth is already two glasses of wine in, and when Wes and I returned from "picking up milk at the store" we all heard Lawrence scold him out in the driveway. Josh and Danielle are the only ones who don't seem bothered.

"Wes, how are college applications going?" My mom passes the salad to him.

He clears his throat. "Good, for now."

"Via has already applied to a handful. I think she's really excited to get out of here." Mom nudges me.

"I'm sure she is," Wes grumbles. His parents shoot him a glare, and for a moment I feel bad. *Maybe I shouldn't be so hard on him.*

Suddenly the doorbell rings. Everyone around the table drops their silverware, but I jump up to get it. I can't stand the stifling tension of the dining room another second, but when I swing open the door, a shock of fear runs through me.

"Good evening, Olivia." Principal Conners beams from the doorstep.

My parents come up behind me, startled. My dad puts a steady hand on my shoulder. "We weren't expecting a home visit. Is everything alright at school? Is this about Olivia?"

I can hear my heart pound in my ears. The stout man just folds his hands over his round belly. "Actually, this is concerning Wesley. I'm looking to speak with Beth and Lawrence Carmichael about recent events that may be of consequence to them."

At the sound of their names, Wes's parents join us at the entryway. If things were tense before, this is like a nightmare of palpable stares and suffocating silence. I don't even need to look at Wes to know he thinks the same thing I do. *They know.*

Principal Conners smiles cheerfully above his beard. "How would you like the exciting opportunity to enroll at Park Falls Technical High School? I have an offer you simply cannot refuse."

CHAPTER 14

I cup my face in my hands to block out my parents and press my forehead deeper into my palms as they talk. The kitchen table separates us, but not enough. The dishes sit in the dining room, untouched after our interrupted dinner.

"What in the world would compel you to do something like this, Via? And bringing Wes along with you, to make matters worse." My dad bores into me, his contempt is withering.

"It wasn't my idea," I grumble.

Dad purses his lips. "We know you were a part of this, so help us understand why."

"You can't let him go to Park Falls." I shake my head. "Anywhere but that school, please."

"You know his parents don't have a choice." My mom places a warm hand on my arm. "Principal Conners gave them a very fair deal in light of everything."

My fist clenches. *How do I make them understand?* "Listen, this is not a good place for him. Look what happened to Alex. You can't seriously think this is a good idea?"

The kitchen light beams like an interrogation spotlight. "Ultimately, it's not up to us." Mom sighs. "And you should've thought about that before you pulled him into all of this. It's the best arrangement that could be made. Don't you want that for your closest friend?"

"I feel like he's not even… never mind." *They don't care what I have to say.* I push away my chair. "You guys are unbelievable. You don't care about Wes. You don't care about what's best for him. You just don't want to be responsible next time we get a call that he's in the hospital. You don't want to get involved anymore, but that's pathetic. What if it was me?"

Mom just crosses her arms on the polished wood. Dad takes a slow sip of his diet soda.

"This is such bullshit."

"Watch your language," Mom snaps. "Josh is right in the other room."

I roll my eyes and stalk out of the kitchen, feeling a migraine darken the front of my mind. *Park Falls is like a black hole. It sucks everyone and everything in so that nothing can get out.* I stomp up the stairs and slam the door to my room as I rub my fingers against my temples. *One, two, three, four…* The fresh sprinkle of snow outside my window blankets the view.

I cross my legs on my bed and pull out my phone. I scroll through my contacts while chewing on my nails. I stop at Jimmy. *Do I even bother calling if he never picks up?* Then my finger hovers over Klara's name. I shake my head, changing my mind.

The phone rings and fills my vacant room.

"Hey, Elliot."

"Via?"

"Um yeah, hi." *This was a bad idea. Why did I call him?* "I just wanted to call and… ask you how it's going with Klara?"

"It's fine, I guess. We see each other at school." I hear him let out a sigh. "Hey look, I'm not really feeling it right now. Can we talk some other time?"

"Oh, right." I pace in circles around the room. "Is everything okay?"

Silence. For a minute I think I've lost him, and then he says, "Yeah. I'm just in a mood."

My heart sinks. I'm about to hang up, and then I hear him clear his throat.

"You'll be at Chad's party on Friday, though. Right? I mean, you don't have to, but it would be nice to have someone there who… I don't know, understands the whole Alex thing."

I sigh. "You'll have Klara and your teammates. You don't need me. I'll just end up being the designated driver."

"Not true. Listen, I won't even drink!" his voice brightens.

"Such a liar." A smile tugs at my lips.

"How about this. If you go, I'll make it up to you on Saturday. We can go hiking, I know this really great trail—"

"I'm going to stop you right there, for many reasons," I laugh. "Firstly, how is *that* your idea of making it up to me?"

"The gift of nature?"

"Secondly, I know you're one of those boys who considers a hoodie the heaviest jacket you own. But shockingly, some people don't like doing outdoor activities in winter."

"November isn't winter."

"Whatever." I feel my resolve crumble. "Fine. I'll think about it." He sounds like he's having a really hard time, which is the only reason I decide to agree. I don't know how hiking in the snow will help with anything, but I can't just leave him hanging. It's Elliot Kang. You can't say no to that kid. And maybe, just maybe, I'll learn something else about what happened between him and Jimmy.

Besides, it might be nice to spend some time in the woods. No people are watching there.

* * *

This party is even wilder than Halloween. I can sense it before I even step into the house, because a wave of sound hits us on the way up the street to the cabin. The ambiance is louder and reckless, maybe because Elliot and his team won their game tonight. But maybe they always win. I don't really follow sports.

"Hey, thanks for driving me," Klara says. She pulls her jacket tighter around her chest.

"You were walking in the snow with dangerously tall platform sneakers. What was I supposed to do?" I grumble. She gives me a sideways glance, and I walk faster to pull ahead.

"Via," she whines. Her clunky shoes slap on the snowy road. "Don't be mad. Why are you mad? Love me."

"Jesus Christ." I stop. *It's too cold out for this.* "I'm not mad, Klara. Forget it."

"No, I won't. I've been thinking a lot about that night at the school, with your dork friend and everything." She steps closer. "And I'm not saying you're right, and I'm not apologizing, because I don't do either of those things. *But*... I'll admit that I haven't been the best friend to you. I've messed up a lot. I've done a lot of horrible stuff to a lot of people that I regret, but you've really grown on me."

"*I've* grown on *you*? What an honor."

"You're welcome," she says. "So then I thought about it, and I want you to know that I care about you. Which is why I want to tell you that I think you should stop investigating."

I shiver deeper into my coat. "What?"

"Forget all that stuff I said before. I know I was the one who told you to go check the school records, and I wanted you to dig up all this dirt. But maybe that's not the best idea."

Her eyes flit to the ground. "I just think you should be careful. That's all."

"Oh." I rock on my heels. *I was not expecting that.*

"So are we cool again?" Her eyebrows perk. "Because I know this great coffee shop that just opened up downtown. I know, Park Falls is finally becoming somewhat cool. We could go tomorrow morning, and—"

"Actually, I'm going hiking with Elliot."

"Really?" She freezes. Her breath whistles in the cold air. "But you don't even like exercising in gym class. You hate walking. I've seen those racing bots from the robotics club beat you."

"I know. But Elliot sounded really sad."

She touches her gold hoops. "Well that's fun. When did he—"

"What are you guys doing out here? It's freezing!" The door to the cabin swings open and Elliot greets us with a large grin I haven't seen in a while. His dimples shine in the glow of the party, and his cheeks are already red. *Why does he look so... happy?* He ushers the two of us in, and we shimmy off our coats in the entryway. Elliot goes and slaps one of his teammates on the back. Their hoots add to the house's cacophony.

"Now remember what we said?" I whisper to Klara as I take off my shoes.

"Chasers are for losers?" she teases.

"I meant," I look over at Elliot, "go spend some quality time with your boyfriend, without me."

"You're such a fun third wheel though," Klara mumbles.

"Hey, Via!" Elliot shouts. "Chad thinks he can take us in beer pong, but I think we'd be a dream team. Come play with me?"

I see Klara shift out of my periphery. "Maybe another time. I'm not drinking tonight."

Klara looks between me and the boy with piqued eyebrows, but then Elliot throws an arm around her and she seems to soften. He leads her off into the dining room where the table is set up, and I let out a relieved breath. *At least he seems to be doing okay...*

I push past warm bodies into the living room, where I'm met with the intoxicating bitter smell of beer. I settle on the arm of one of the couches and examine people. I watch a girl with terrifyingly long acrylic nails sit on the lap of a blond kid and start pulling at his collar for his attention. I study a group of boys from the hockey team go outside to shotgun beers over the edge of the deck into the woods. I observe a boy with a mop of hair open his mouth to release snaking tendrils of smoke that drift up into the wooden beams of the ceiling. I see Klara and Elliot in the other room; they steal glances and touches in between small bursts of excitement from the game. *How could any of these people be programmed to act this way?*

After a while I stand and make my way toward the kitchen. I squeeze past two girls who are huddled over a phone, and then a hand grabs my shoulder. Max pulls me over to the fridge, causing a couple of kids perched on stools around the island to glance up.

"There she is," he exclaims. "Thought we scared you off on Halloween."

"Nope, I'm back." I try to imitate the casual lean of one of the boys against the cabinets.

"Please tell me you aren't driving tonight." Max holds up a handle of hard liquor.

"Unfortunately, I am. Elliot and Klara need their cupid." I shrug.

"Damn, nobody can ever say no to Mr. Elliot Kang. The man is a saint." Max pours his own shot. After he smacks his lips, he says, "I gotta say, though, I'm glad to see him out at these things again. He looks good. Before he showed up tonight, the rumors were really starting to pile up."

"Rumors?" I lean out toward the doorway, and my gaze follows the trail of kids from the arches of the living room all the way into the dining room. Even from here, I can see Elliot's laugh that makes his eyes squint.

"Oh, come on. Don't pretend like you haven't heard them," a girl I recognize as Laura says. "Ever since Alex… you know, ended things, those YouTech guys have been all over campus. Of course people are going to talk. And it's hard to ignore the fact that Elliot and him were friends from before."

"Yeah, but, none of you knew Alex that well."

"How do you know that?" Max raises his eyebrows and takes a pull from the handle of alcohol.

I stand quietly against the fridge as I feel more and more like I need a drink. *How do I not hear any of these rumors? Are people scared to talk to me because I'm friends with the people the rumors are about?*

"Well one thing's for sure." He slaps his cup on the counter, causing his drink to splash on the granite. "Now that people are all suspecting Alex and Elliot and Jimmy, at least you don't have to worry anymore."

"I'm sorry?" I stand up a little straighter.

"Not here," Laura hits Max.

"No, no, it's nothing personal," he says. "It's not like I thought you were the Agent, Via. I'm just repeating what I heard other kids say. It's not a big deal. It's just that you kinda spooked everyone with that whole ESP incident. And

I mean, you're really good at math, and you also haven't been dating anyone, so..."

My face flushes under the stares of everyone in the kitchen. *I didn't realize I had to date someone to be considered human.* "People say that? People think I'm the Agent?"

"Well, not anymore, not after everyone kind of assumes it was Alex." Max says this as if it's reassuring.

"Don't listen to him. He gets like this when he's drunk." Laura kicks the boy lightly. "He thinks he knows everything about everyone in Park Falls and doesn't know when to shut up."

"It's fine." I tug at my sleeves.

"Exactly, see? Via's a badass. She doesn't care about rumors." Max throws his arm around me.

"Um, I'm going to go see Klara. I'll catch up with you guys later." I wriggle underneath his arm and squeeze past the girls in the doorway. *Did it somehow get more crowded?* Everywhere I go I see clusters of seniors, and I catch myself looking at each of their subtle movements and little gestures, watching how they stand, how they breach personal space, and how they talk so much without really saying anything. *Who teaches them how to flirt?* The incessant noise of drunken teens is deafening. The cesspool of heat from sweating bodies and alcohol makes it suffocating to even be in the same room as them.

I end up on the second floor and look for a bathroom that isn't occupied. The carpet feels springy underneath my feet. I shuffle past Chad's room and then a bathroom that's packed with four girls who roll a joint. I find the next small door and knock on it but hear certain muffled sounds from two kids that I'd rather not hear. I back away, following the maze of log walls until the hallway leads me to the parents' room. There's a small door at the end, with a crudely drawn "keep out" sign taped to the wood. *I thought Max said no rooms in the house were forbidden...*

I wiggle it open and find that it's not a bathroom at all. A large desk with a computer and neatly organized stacks of papers face a screen door that looks out on the view of the moonlit lake. Bookshelves with a printer stand against a wall, and as I wander closer, I find a keycard with the YouTech logo on it. The picture of Chad's mom stares up at me through the dark. I glance around and then tap on the keypad lightly. The monitor turns on with a blinding flash, but there's a password required. *Damn, it couldn't have been that easy.*

And then, in the corner, I see it. I want to laugh. *Why is it always a file cabinet?* Part of me smiles in triumph as I pull out my hairpin, but another part of me worries for the security measures of tech employees.

These folders are less concise and more confusing than school records. I don't really understand what I see. Are they even confidential? Some are blueprints while some are contract agreements, and a few are account balance sheets. They all have to do with development projects for YouTech, outsourcing labs and experiments and data storage, but eventually I stumble on some of the paperwork for Park Falls Technical High School. *Chad's mom must have overseen the project.* The executive summary at the top of one of the reports reads like a pitch as it describes how and why this school needed to be built. It's all a lot of crap, but then a certain phrase catches my eye. "This institution will reduce external risk and control the variables that have threatened the AI testing program."

Control the variables? What variables? They obviously didn't reduce the risk if Alex still self-terminated.

After I go through a number of folders and don't find anything else interesting, I return to the desk. I need an excuse to not go back to the rest of the party, so I open the drawers and shift around the office supplies. Then, in the bottom drawer, my hand comes across something strange. It's a phone—a modern one like mine. I turn it on and almost drop it when I see the lock screen. It's a photo of Alex and Elliot on a hike, framed by trees.

This is Alex's phone.

I glance at the open door to the hall with echoes of chaos from the party and then over at the screen door. I slide it open and duck out onto the balcony with the phone to shut out the noise.

It's dark and quiet out here. The fresh November air bites at my skin at first, but then it feels good because I can finally breathe again. The smell of alcohol is distant. The balcony is a cold awakening, and moonlight bathes the lakeside in a silver glow. I wander to the edge of the small deck and sit down so that my legs dangle over the side, one between each post of the railing. I lean my head against the posts and hold Alex's phone out in front of me. That picture glows in the night.

"I would put that back if I were you."

I flinch at the sound of another voice, and my head whips around in the dark. I search to see where it came from, and it's above me. On the roof.

"That's not yours." From ten feet above me, Dean waves the bottle of vodka in his hand.

"Well it's not hers either." I shiver in the cold.

Dean's eyes glint in the night. "I know the passcode. If you want to unlock it."

"Liar." I flip the phone in my palm. "And I wasn't going to look through it."

He starts to slide down the roof, quickly. My heart beats fast because someone as drunk as him should not be on top of a house. I get this horrible feeling, this dread. It builds up inside of me and sends a shiver through my body. He finally gets to the ledge of the roof and drops down as his long coat flares out like a parachute.

"Sure you weren't." He collapses down next to me and awkwardly throws his long legs through the poles of the railing. "Because you didn't find anything else interesting when you were snooping through her office."

I push myself up to leave. "Always a pleasure, Dean."

"Wait," he says. "Stay for a minute."

I stand, and the cold wood bites through my socks. "What makes you think I want to sit out here and talk with you?"

"So I guess you don't want to know what's up with me and Klara, then?"

I stop. "No. Klara will tell me when she wants to."

He chuckles as his mouth hangs open. "Everyone is hiding something, Via. If they haven't told you yet, they're not going to. I'm the only one willing to be honest with you."

My eyes trace his long coat, the bottle, the mess of hair. "You're lying."

"Oh yeah?" His tongue plays along the inside of his mouth. "And suddenly you can read minds?"

My heart skips a beat. I look away. Behind me is the warm buzz of the party, where Elliot and Klara and Max are all flirting and gossiping in drunken whispers.

"Just for your information, I wasn't snooping." I sit down again on the other side of the balcony. "I don't even care about the program, or the Agent, or any of that. I was just trying to get away from… everyone."

"Fine." He pulls out a flask from inside his coat and fills it with vodka.

"You probably think I'm like everyone else at this school, always needing something new to gossip about, someone new to target. But I'm not. None of this bothers me." I tap my nails on Alex's phone case. "It's just annoying because you can't ever have a normal conversation with anyone here. There's always another secret or another rumor, and I'm tired of feeling like I have something to prove. The only reason I want to know the truth is so I can be done with it."

"You're right. You sound completely unbothered."

"You know what, never mind. You couldn't possibly understand."

"You wanna know what I think about the program? I think it was doomed from the start." He clicks his tongue. "High school is just a bad simulation of the real world for teenagers. An Agent would never learn how to be a functional human being in that building. I mean, how could it? Normal kids don't."

We fall into silence. A chill whips through the air and sends a ripple of motion through the slumbering forest. Skeletal bushes and trees shiver at the touch of the wind and send shadows dancing on the surface of the frozen lake. Dean takes a drink from his flask every now and then, but never glances my way. I look away too and fix my gaze on the frosted woods. I shake a little in the cold, wishing I had brought my jacket with me.

Out of the corner of my eye, I see Dean glance over and hold out the handle of vodka. I roll my eyes.

"What, it'll help with the cold," he says. "I can't handle winter in Park Falls."

"November isn't winter."

His mocking Cheshire grin makes my blood boil. The bottle clinks on the wooden panels as he sets it down. "Listen,

I get it. You saw me and Klara, so there's something going on that you don't know about. It's driving you crazy, all these secrets. You don't want to have to deal with it anymore. You just want someone to be honest with you. Right?"

I gaze down at the forest floor. The pine trees that surround the cabin are frosted with snow.

"I'll tell you the truth. You're not going to like it, but I'll tell you to save you some pain. I don't care, but I'm doing you a favor." I can feel the intensity of his piercing eyes through the dark. "There's more to YouTech than they tell you, more to it than just a robot. See, the truth is..."

I try to seem uninterested, but I hold my breath anyway as I wait for him to finish the sentence. I stare into his eyes, and suddenly that dreaded sensation creeps into my mind that I try to push away.

But he doesn't speak. He just closes his mouth and then opens it again, frowns and shakes his head. I see his eyes fall back into his thoughts. He sighs deeply and takes another swig from his flask.

"I knew it," I grumble. *I can't believe I fell for it.* "You're just like everyone else here. You love your secrets and you love to keep everyone guessing. It's just a game to you."

Through the shadows of the balcony I watch his mouth hang open in that way that I hate. "I know. I'm a coward." He exhales. "I just... I can't..." he bites his tongue and then laughs.

"You think you're so funny. Don't you? Messing with everyone, pretending like you don't give a shit."

"Okay. You want to talk about pretending?" He waves his flask. "You come up to the balcony by yourself. Right? Sit out here all angsty, look at your dead friend's phone, and pretend you don't care about all the rumors inside. Was that the plan? To think profound and existential thoughts until maybe someone finds you and asks you what's wrong? All the while painfully sober, freezing your ass off, and wondering the whole time how much longer you should stay out here until your point is made."

"Well what's your excuse? You were up here on the roof when I got here. I heard you're not even invited to these things."

He rubs the back of his neck. "Do you want Alex's passcode or what?"

I grit my teeth in the cold and look down at the phone. *I've already invaded Jimmy's privacy, why draw the line now?* I hold it out, and Dean's long fingers swipe the device away from me. In a matter of seconds, he hands it back.

"How do you even know his passcode?"

He tilts his head. "Why are you so interested in Alex's phone?"

I ignore him and stare down at the screen to see hundreds of text notifications that will never be read. I check his messages with Elliot first, and my hair stands on end as Dean watches me intently. No texts from Elliot since the day before that weekend, nothing useful. Then I look at Alex's call record, and that's when I see something curious. His last call was from me, the night of the party. It says Via, right there on the screen.

But I never called Alex that night.

"Hey, what is it?" Dean leans forward. I can smell the vodka on his breath.

"Nothing. I'm going back to the party." I take the phone with me and slide through the screen door.

"See, I told you! Everyone's hiding something!" He calls after me. I can practically picture that stupid open-mouthed grin.

CHAPTER 15

I bend down to the faded Subaru window and rub at the bags under my eyes. *It doesn't matter, Via. It's just a hike with a friend. Don't make this an interrogation. Don't make this about Jimmy or Alex. Just chat.*

In my winter getup I resemble a marshmallow. And not the cute kind. While I am in layers of coats and pants as if I'm trying to jump into the ocean and sink to the bottom, Elliot shows up in shorts and a thin jogger with Park Falls's basketball logo plastered across the back of it. The front strands of his long hair peak out from his beanie, and his skin glows in the morning sunlight.

"Hey." He waves. As I get closer, I notice he's not as energetic as the night before, and a tired weight pulls at his smile.

I survey the parking lot, and my jackets swish loudly as I move. "So, which direction are we walking down the road?"

"Nice try. There's the trailhead over there." He points to a break in the trees, lightly dusted with snow. "It does a nice loop through the woods and then circles back to the church. You know, the one with the graveyard."

Graveyard? The only thing that could make winter hiking more psychotic is the trail being littered with rotting bodies.

He clears his throat. "Should we, uh, get started?"

"Lead the way. I'll just wait until you're really far ahead before I turn back and run to the car."

"Don't know how far you'll get in that hazmat suit." Elliot's dimples come to life and he bounds across the frosted road. I laugh and shuffle along behind him. His muscled legs overtake the snowy path beneath us while I just follow in his shadow and pray his hangover kicks in.

The trail weaves through barren vegetation for a while, and heat rises up in my body underneath all my layers. Speckled sunlight filters through the pines. It dapples the soft blanket of snow on the uneven ground. The only thing I hear is my own heartbeat in my ears and the sound of my boots as they crunch on frozen maple leaves.

Breathing gets harder as my muscles quickly wear. *For the love of God, please take a break.* He finally stops when we reach a clearing in the woods that opens up to the sky. I exhale in relief, and bend over to clutch my knees for dear life. Elliot turns around and I straighten up, trying to hide the fact that my chest heaves like it's going through cardiac arrest.

"Thanks for getting up early to come with me." He plants his hands on his hips. "I love this hike."

"No problem," I moan. *I think I have an ulcer.*

"Usually this far up into the woods everything is super green." He scans the scenery around us. "The maples are pretty, too, in the fall and summer. They start to show all their colors. With the birds and animals, it's normally really loud. But now it's so quiet."

"Yeah, it is." I listen for sounds as I catch my breath, but he's right. It's like a vacuum of noise, as if the whole forest has been frozen in time.

"Kind of depressing, actually." He kicks the snow. "I know it should be nice, all the quiet, but it just makes it seem empty. Makes you notice that everything else from before is missing. You know?"

I watch my breath turn into a visible cloud. It billows up into the icy canopy. "Did you used to come here with Alex?"

He nods.

"Is that why you don't want to do it alone?"

He takes off his beanie and runs his hands through his hair. I worry I've made him uncomfortable, but my tongue seems tied in knots.

"We used to do it every week," he finally breaks the silence. "He did cross country, though, so he would kick my ass and then give me crap for being so out of shape. I needed the workout to keep up with all the other guys on the basketball team, but Alex, he just did the hike for fun."

"I must be a disappointing partner after that."

His eyes squint in amusement but only for a brief moment before he fades back into a solemn mask. *If this is how he always feels, it must be exhausting to put on a happy face. Don't his eyes get tired of laughing and his dimples wear from holding up that smile?*

"How are you doing? I mean, like, *really* doing?"

He shoves his hands in his pockets. "I started going to church again."

I don't hide my shock. "You're religious?"

"Lutheran."

"I didn't know that about you."

"Well, I didn't know you were Asian."

I laugh, rolling my eyes. "What gave it away?"

He shrugs. "You're the only other person who takes off their shoes at Chad's house."

"It's the blonde hair and my mom's last name. Throws a lot of people off," I say. "Anyway, now that you're back at church, are you gonna be one of those guys who wears a chain? With a cross on it and everything? And then, like, snort cocaine out of it during bible study when nobody is looking?"

"Yeah, right." I get a rise out of him, which makes my heart swell. "It's been a while since I've done the whole… religion thing. I used to go a lot when I was little, but my dad stopped making me when I said I was busy with sports. And my mom was fine with that. Especially when Alex started having his seizures."

A chill runs up my spine. *I thought his shaking hands were an Agent glitch?* "Seizures?"

"Yeah, epilepsy." He rubs the back of his neck. "I think it was mild but I don't really know. He was diagnosed freshman year. It was hard for him, and not everyone stuck around for the ugly parts."

Something tugs at the back of my mind, an itch. *Don't do it, Via. You can sense he's hurting.* But I can't help myself. "What ugly parts, exactly?"

A flurry of sparkling snow shakes down from a pine tree to our right. Elliot sighs. "I don't know, the serious stuff. He was in and out of the hospital a lot, changing medications. There was this one time our sophomore year, he just disappeared for a couple days. I thought if we never talked about it, it wouldn't be a big deal. And so we didn't. About anything, ever."

My mind drifts to the night when Alex was released from the hospital. "So this year, do you think that was why he was…"

He nods and shuffles his feet. *He doesn't seem like he knows about Alex, unless he's covering it up with the epilepsy story. But how could he be best friends with someone for all these years and not know?*

"Sorry, you probably don't want to hear all this." He pinches the bridge of his nose. "It's just… I think about him all the time. You know? All the things we could've talked about. I even stay up at night and go through things I want to say to him. Like he's still around."

His almond eyes find mine across the frostbitten clearing. This feels intimate, this moment in a pocket of the woods. The way he looks at me makes me feel like I'm exposed despite all these layers of clothes.

"So, church." I clear my throat, continuing to hike along the path. "I mean, I'm not going to ask you if you believe in God and all that. But sometimes they have food at the services. Don't they?"

"I guess. It's kind of boring though." He follows me and picks his footsteps carefully. "But lately it's been good. Everyone there has been really supportive of my family. You know? And it's nice to have someone get up in front of a podium and tell you everything's going to be all right. Things like… it all happens for a reason, let patience do her perfect work, God's plan or whatever." He pauses, and I hear his footsteps slow. "I don't think I'm a very patient person though."

"Is this the part where you show me your favorite passage tattooed on your bicep? Corinthians?"

He stops. "Don't do that."

"Do what?"

A bird chirps in the distance, and it echoes through the frigid trees.

I tug at my sleeves. "Keep going. I'm listening."

He nods, and we tread forward on the packed snow. He gets closer and closer, and soon he's right on my tail. His rhythmic breathing tickles the back of my hair. "The thing is, at my church they tell you to be patient, to trust in God.

And I get all that. But I guess I just keep waiting for things to make sense, and they don't."

"That's why I don't like religion." My chest heaves. "It's all so… unanswered."

"Sure," he says. "But so is everything else."

After a few more minutes we overtake a small hill. I see a thin tower rise up through the skeletal branches. The hill drops into a discreet glade as dark tombs protrude from the ground like fingers that claw for air. Beyond the burials, the church hugs an unassuming road that leads back into town. The tranquil building is modest but strangely divine in the midst of these dark towering woods.

Elliot leads me down to the opening. We weave through gravestones, and something in my chest stirs as I absorb each name. The graveyard is so quiet. It's almost as if I can hear the snow trickle down from the headstones as it melts in the sun.

"Did you know they're not even doing a funeral for him?"

I glance up from two rows over. I don't know what to say, but the air feels heavy, and a lump forms in my throat from being around so much death. It's like I'm in one of my dreams.

"I know it shouldn't matter, but I don't know. It feels wrong." He shoves his hands in the pockets of his jogger. As he studies each tombstone, he pushes aside long strands of hair. "You know who *is* buried here though?" He stops at a grave, one with sharp edges and dark stone as if it was cut yesterday.

I wander up next to him, slowly. My heart that already palpitates from the exercise skips a beat when I see the name. Oscar Andrade. The weight of Jimmy's silence these past two weeks hits me like a wave, and I can almost sense his grief like it happened to me.

"Did you know him?" I breathe.

"Not really. He died right when I was getting to know Jimmy. Beginning of our freshman year."

Amidst the sickening grief, something about what he says makes me stop. "Wait, our freshman year?"

"Yeah. Did you hear about it in Lakeland?"

My mind reels as I look at the stone in front of us, and my eyes trace every carved detail. "They have the wrong year," I murmur.

"I'm sorry?"

"The year it says he died. It must be wrong, you said it happened when we were freshman."

"No, that can't be right. I clearly remember..." He runs his hands through his hair while he studies the tomb. The sunlight glints off the sweat on his neck. I look back at the church behind us and feel a shiver in my chest. *Either Elliot is wrong, or the people who buried Oscar made a mistake.*

How could his own family make that kind of mistake?

* * *

I didn't think Wes and his family would be coming for dinner on Sunday, but there they are. Beth and Lawrence clamor up the driveway and hug both of my parents. Danielle sports a bright fluffy jacket and immediately cuts down Josh for his hat-hair. As they all make their way into the house, Wes lingers with an embarrassed shrug.

I shiver in the evening chill and cross my arms.

"I'm sorry. I should have told you sooner," he says. He plays with his hands and intertwines them as he sways on his feet.

"What happened to no secrets between us? Since day one, remember?"

He stares at the pavement. "Yup. Day one."

"I don't care that you were expelled, Wes. I won't ask." I sigh. "But if you don't want to do any of the investigating or digging into YouTech anymore, that's fine. You could have told me if you were having a hard time. You could have told me if this whole Agent thing was too much for you."

"No, I can handle it." His eyes flit up to mine. "We have to figure out the truth. I'm part of this now."

"So, it's official then?" I bite the inside of my cheek. "You're going to Park Falls?"

He steps up to the doorway. "I've got your back. Don't worry."

"Same here." I smile curtly and nudge him as he rolls his eyes under waves of blond hair. As we enter this box of a house, his smile radiates the kind of comfort and empathy that makes me forget all my anxiety about Alex, my concerns about my friends, my fear about my dreams, my eerie sensations, and all the other unanswered things in my life.

Wes's lanky figure stretches out on the carpet in front of the living room TV, and he grabs pillows to construct our nest. "It sucks to have to move schools and everything, but I have to say, I am very excited to meet all of your boyfriends."

I hit him, and the familiar thump of the pillow brings me joy. "I think you'll get along with Jimmy. I actually figured out he's into comic books, just like you. His computer password is even The Balancer."

"Oh, no way!" Wes crosses his legs and snatches up a controller. "You really are replacing me with a carbon copy."

"What is it with teenage boys and The Balancer, anyway? Isn't he just a superhero? I mean, what's his whole deal?" I lean over to turn on Immortal Soldiers.

"Do you know what he does?"

I tug at my sleeves as the game starts. "Doesn't he, like, balance things in the universe?"

"Yes, but he wields a ridiculous amount of power." He wiggles his controller violently. "Besides just the time control and mind abilities, he chooses what to create and what to take away in the world. He makes sacrifices for the betterment of time and space, not just for humans. He collects souls and all that dark stuff just to balance the scales. It's like being an all-powerful master of death."

"So, like, a grim reaper or something? He sounds more like a villain than one of the good guys."

"No, he's a badass." The sounds of firing guns mix with distant clatter of dinner being prepared. "And you know why he's a hero? Because he's the one who makes those sacrifices when no one else will. He can see the truth when no one else does."

"I guess I see why Jimmy is into that." My mind begins to wander and my game avatar pays the price. When I'm killed, I take out my phone to distract myself while I wait for Wes. On my music app, I search for Jimmy's account and see what he's downloaded recently. To my surprise I see he's online right now. I recognize the song he listens to from my playlist. I see him skip around and watch him dance between moods. I can almost hear each song, as if I feel what he feels in each moment. Almost like I can read his thoughts through the phone, like I'm there with him, in his head. Like the day we sat on the couch after Alex died, splitting earbuds.

"You're worried about him. Aren't you?"

I didn't even realize Wes had died in the level, and he stares at me as I'm lost on my phone. "It doesn't matter. He doesn't want my help."

"How do you know?"

"He won't tell me anything. In fact, nobody will. So what choice do I have? If he needs space until he's ready to talk, fine. I have my own problems to deal with."

"Can I give you some advice? On the subject of constant smothering and concern?" He faces me and pulls his sleeves down over his scars. "People don't need space. People need people. Because, look, as much as you're hurting, the truth is that they're probably hurting more."

I stare at my friend with his bright childish shirt, his video game controller in hand, and I can't believe this is the same boy who tried to end his life after the Incident.

"Wes, Via, get in here for dinner! You still need to set the table!" my mom calls. Wes huffs and climbs to his feet, and I get up to follow. But just then I feel my phone buzz in my pocket.

Like a distant dream, a face I can't quite remember, the anonymous number pops up on my screen. I haven't gotten a text in so long, I almost thought it was all in my head. But something about this message is different. It chills me to the bone and drains the blood from my face.

You are in danger. Don't go digging up graves that aren't yours.

CHAPTER 16

"Are you good?" I turn to Wes.

"Of course," he brushes his hair out of his face. "Why wouldn't I be?"

I shrug and go back to my phone. I scroll through social media, trying not to go back and look at the anonymous text for the hundredth time. Wes sits next to me in the stiff chairs of the administration office. He leans his head against the wall while we wait for Principal Conners to come out of his office as the receptionist clicks away at her keyboard.

In a sudden commotion, the door down the hall bangs and two voices ring out in mid-conversation.

"But, sir, if I could just speak with Mr. Richards..." I recognize with a shock that it's Jimmy.

"Nonsense! Anything you need from him can also be answered by me and my staff." Principal Conners's sprightly tone jolts even Wes out of his morning daze. "We're here to help with anything we can, Agent-related or not." The man beams as they round the corner.

"Yes, thank you." I see Jimmy shrivel into his collar as he comes into sight. He twitches and adjusts his glasses—all the familiar signs of his discomfort that I missed so much.

He doesn't see me and continues to speak rapidly at Principal Conners. "But you never answered me. Regarding my questions on other forms of AI and technological advancement, I believe Stephen Richards is best suited to respond. I'm curious about other machine learning functions that You-Tech is investing in, not just robots but specifically androids, cyborgs, and possibly systems that advance cognitive functions such as—"

Then he sees me and closes his mouth with a clenched jaw.

"That's all very well, Jimmy, but this was a meeting about your attendance and solely that. Now take those curious thoughts and bring them with you to class!" Principal Conners slaps his backpack, and the boy's whole body sways.

I stand to catch a word with him, but he's already two feet out the door. He avoids my eyes and disappears into the crowded morning rush of the front halls.

"Was that Jimmy?" Wes whispers to me. "Not much of an intro. What happened to us getting along?"

"Wesley Carmichael!" Principal Conners claps his pudgy hands. "Welcome to our esteemed institution. You are the first transfer we've ever had! I read your transcript just now, very impressive. I knew immediately that your mind was ready for great things."

"Um, thank you?" He stands and gives a firm handshake. I look down and press my nails into my palm. *I can't believe this is happening. I thought my greatest fear was getting punished by Mr. Richards for breaking into records... somehow, this feels worse.*

"You're here for your student passcode. Correct? I have that right here." That rounded belly jostles as he fishes though his pocket. "Oh, that reminds me!" He turns to his receptionist. "Can you call today about changing the lock on my file cabinet? I worry it's gotten a little loose."

Wes gulps and exchanges glances with me. My heart hammers.

"Alrighty then, here's your login!" Principal Conners cheerfully hands over a slip of paper. "Any more questions before I send you off to begin your hunt for the Agent?"

"I have a question," I say. "What were you talking to Jimmy about earlier? Is he okay?"

His cheeks bulge as he grins. "Why wouldn't he be?"

"Has he been seeing the school counselors? If he's missing classes, don't you think it has something to do with Alex's suicide affecting him because of his brother?"

"It's not my job to pry into students' personal lives."

"Then how did you know Wes and his family were having dinner at my house that one night?"

He just smiles, his bushy beard unrelenting and perked. "I just encourage all of you to reach your full potential."

"And what *is* our full potential?" I clench my fist.

"Exploring the abilities of your brain and contributing to this historical simulation, of course."

My face flushes with anger at the helplessness of it all. "What is the point of all these games and exercises if you have kids who are struggling with mental health? What is the point of a wild goose chase for the Agent when there are other real issues in your school? Alex killed himself and you're not doing anything!"

His blank cheerful stare doesn't waver. "What would you have us do?"

"Via." Wes grabs my arm gently. My heart quickens but I choke down the agitation and take a deep breath. I turn and stalk out of the office as the receptionist's typing clicks in my head.

We charge into the moving masses of kids, but very quickly I notice we won't have to squeeze and push our way through. The clamoring hallway slows when each pair of eyes lands on Wes and stops to register a new face. Groups of students make room for us, and they stare Wes down like vultures assessing their next meal. I can practically hear my name on the lips of every whisper. I watch my friend out of my periphery as he attempts to be nonchalant about it all. But I notice him rub the back of his neck and pull his sleeves down over his wrists.

Meanwhile, the vacant hull of my locker gapes at me as I dread what comes next. *English class, where we don't actually do any English.* I'm scared of what will happen. If I'm honest, I don't trust myself.

"I saw Jimmy on the way to English." Klara's voice jars me from my thoughts. "Man, he looks upset. I can't believe you and your boyfriend are going through such a rough patch."

I sigh. "Don't call it a rough patch. We're not dating."

"Fine. A couple's spat."

"Stop."

"A lover's quarrel."

"I hate you." I push away from her, but she just laughs and throws an arm around me. Her eyebrows perk when she sees something down the hall.

"Speaking of boyfriends." Klara fixes her ponytail as Elliot makes his way toward us with Ben and Cole in tow. "He looks so cute in his jersey." She waves.

Elliot's head snaps up above the crowd. "Hey! Via, I was just going to text you. You left one of your jackets at the trailhead."

"Oh, thanks," I say. Klara pulls her arm down from my shoulder. For a minute, I think I see something fire up in her eyes.

"Hey, Via, do you know where this physics class is?" Wes comes up to my locker, which is now a social gathering. All the boys study him in confusion, and even Cole looks up from his phone. Klara crosses her arms and I can practically feel the intensity of her attacking eyebrows on the boy.

"Um, who is this?" Ben points blatantly.

"Hey, can you do this really quick test—"

"No CAPTCHA test," Elliot holds back Cole. He reaches out a hand to Wes. "I'm Elliot."

Wes shakes his hand curtly. Silence settles in the group as nobody talks. We just hear the sound of banging lockers and fresh gossip. He clears his throat. "Do any of you read comic books?"

"Haven't you heard? We're basically living in one." Cole is glued back to his screen. "But yes, of course."

"Really? That's the first thing you ask? This school is going to eat you alive." Klara shakes her head. Wes returns her glare with a steady loathing. "Elliot, walk me to class?"

"Yeah, sure." Elliot turns to me. "I'll call you later. We should talk."

I nod, but my skin crawls as I feel the slice of Klara's sharp expression and cunning eyes. *He doesn't want me to tell her about what we discussed on the hike. I'm not telling her about Alex, yet this feels like a worse secret.*

"Welp, good luck with the rumor mill." Ben does a little hop away from us, and although it's playful, I watch the warning sink into Wes like a bitter pill.

"I have physics too. Follow me. I want to hear all of your opinions on The Balancer even if they're wrong and I have to correct you." Cole leads Wes away. I feel a pang in my chest as I watch him go, wondering if he misses any of his other friends at Lakeland.

I show up to English class late, but the exercise is already set up and I haven't missed anything. To my dismay, desks are set up with pairs of students facing each other. There's one empty spot, and it's right across from Jimmy. He sees this and immediately shifts in his seat. I stride over with determination and throw my backpack down.

"Great, let's get started then!" Ms. Xavier waves her arms. "In front of all of you is a small computing machine that acts as a polygraph of sorts. But not only will it detect lies, it will detect all the subconscious thoughts and sensations in between. The sixth sense is all about receiving information through different channels than your basic physical perceptions. So ask some questions and really try to tap into your partner's conscious."

It's consciousness. She knows it's consciousness. Right?

Jimmy raises his hand politely. "Excuse me. Can I switch—"

"No time to waste! Begin attaching the wires to your temples and your wrists, then the back of your neck..." As she rattles off instructions, I try to get Jimmy's attention. He focuses intently on hooking up all the wires, and the machine glows in front of us.

Finally, he can't avoid my gaze anymore.

"How are you?" I tug at my sleeves. There's so much I want to tell him, to ask him, and I feel like I could explode.

"Great," he says. The dome-shaped machine in front of us glows, the signal that he's lying.

"You know you can talk to me about anything. Right? Not just schoolwork?"

He fidgets. "I know."

I scan the classroom, making sure nobody listens. "I never asked, how did your meeting with Mr. Richards go? And just now with Principal Conners?"

"We're not... we're not supposed to talk about that." His brown eyes glance around nervously.

Suddenly the door to the room bursts open and all eyes snap up. Dean saunters in with his long coat and pulls at the collar of his turtleneck as he looks for an open seat.

"Dean, nice of you to finally join us for class." Ms. Xavier's mousy nose wiggles. *She must hate that he's on a scholarship as much as I do.* "We don't really have a partner for you unless we switch some people around..."

"I'll switch." Jimmy shakes the desk as he jumps up.

I feel a pang in my chest as I blurt out, "No. You can't change now. We're not done."

"That's perfectly fine! Dean, why don't you go with Via then, and Jimmy can come do the exercise with me. Remember, guys, really ask your partner questions that will get the brain activity going. You want to try and tune into each other's conscious."

If she says that one more time, I swear to God—

"Swell." Dean alights into the chair across from me. His open-mouthed grin triggers a deep irritation in my gut as I notice everyone in the room doesn't even pay attention to their own machines. They watch us with eager eyes, hungry for something abnormal to happen between this odd pairing. *As if I wanted to draw more attention to myself...*

"Since when do you show up at school?" I cross my arms, and my knee bounces under the table.

"Well, after our little chat on the balcony this weekend, I decided you're absolutely right. I am a coward." He ruffles his hair to attach the wires on his temple. "But no more. I am going to be *very* involved from now on. I am going to pour my heart and soul into this whole Agent thing and really dive into uncovering the truth. It's what Alex would have wanted."

"Screw you." My teeth grind together to fight down a swell of rage. A sick, dreadful ache rises up in my throat at the sound of Alex's name along with the devilish glint on Dean's face.

"So," he leans forward on the desk and clasps his long hands together. "Do you want to go first, or should I just fire away?"

The dome-shaped machine in front of us begins to glow, but I can't tell from whom. The whole class watches on the outskirts with hushed murmurs and curious stares.

"Alright, let's jump right in. Who's your new friend that showed up today? Is he the Agent?"

This asshole. My skin prickles under all the attention. "No." The dome still radiates a bright luminescence. I feel a warm buzz where the wires stick to my neck and wrists.

"Do you know who the Agent is?"

I can't swallow as my mouth dries up. "No."

"But you want to find out?" His piercing eyes bore into me. "Do you trust your friends? Do you trust this school?"

"Stop trying to mess with me, Dean." My fingers drum on the desk. *One, two, three, four...* That horrible sensation grips my mind, a chilling fear of what's going to happen. I feel like I'm in one of my nightmares with all of my peers as witnesses.

"Oh, come on. That's the point of the game. Isn't it?" He scrunches his nose. "Really tap into my brainwaves, Via. What am I thinking about?"

The machine in between us surges with energy, a blinding light that sends a warm hum through the room. *I'm not even saying anything. Why is it doing this? Come on, Via, pull it together.* I can't help it, though. In the wake of the device's pulsing luminescence, my thoughts go back to the flickering desk lamp.

The lamp turns into a streetlight on the night road, heavy snowflakes falling through the milky fluorescence like ash.

I'm back on the wet asphalt in January, heart racing as I hear the sound of Wes's desperate cry. Then I'm blinded from oncoming headlights, my whole body racked with a paralyzing fear as I brace for the shattering impact.

The sound of screeching tires turns into the high-pitched beeping of a heart-rate monitor. Now the stark lights of a hospital fill my vision, and my throat gags at the bitter smell of sanitizer. Then I look down at my hands as they shake violently, sending a ripple of helplessness and panic through my veins until I lose all control. I rip at my wires and my hospital gown, tearing at my flesh, but nothing stops the convulsing from bringing me to my knees.

As I fall to the floor, it suddenly turns to ice, and with a wicked crack it gives out underneath my feet. My fingers claw at the jagged and unforgiving edges, but an inescapable gravity pulls me under. I can just make out a glint of sunlight above me as I sink to the bottom of the lake, but soon I'm dragged under its crushing weight. My lungs scream and pump for air, but all that rushes into my throat is freezing water.

That's when the suffocating flood of water turns to smoke, and it invades my throat until I choke on my own coughing. Dark fumes and stinging heat press down on me, and bright flames lick at my skin in a rapturous fury. With a deafening boom, a section of the burning house collapses, and I'm consumed by roaring fire in a flash of terror.

"Via, snap out of it!" The wires are ripped from my body, and Jimmy's deep brown eyes fill my vision.

A cold sweat clings to my skin as my hands grip the edge of the desk. The whole classroom is stunned into silence, wide-eyed shock and blatant disbelief plastered across the face of every kid. I can practically hear the rumors already.

Across from me, Dean leans back in his seat with a twisted expression. Almost one of… fear.

"You never know when to stop. Do you? Not everything is a joke," Jimmy snaps at Dean and then swings his backpack over his shoulder to leave. Dean just seems spooked, as if all the blood was drained from his face. *I did this to him, a kid who didn't give a shit about anything. And now he looks like he's seen a ghost.*

"Um, I'm gonna…" I rise to my feet and wobble unsteadily on my way out. I have the most intense migraine, and I can't even hear myself count over the pounding in my head. I stumble out into the hallway as a queasy feeling overtakes my stomach. My organs turn in knots. I push open the doors to the stairwell and throw myself down the flights, but just then I collide into Wes.

"Hey!" He laughs and then switches instantly and grabs my shoulders. "Hey. Whoa there, what's up? Talk to me."

"Wes, I…" My vision blurs, and I can't breathe as my lungs convulse in ragged shallow breaths. "I think I can see things."

* * *

Heavy sheets of wind tear through the thickets of forest. They buffet the suburbs in an incessant chill. My teeth chatter as I lean against my car, my hands shoved into the pockets of my jacket with force. In another blast of wind, a wall of cold rips across the road and makes the whole bus stop shudder. *Come on. It can't be running that late.*

A moment later the bus roars up the street. When it putters to stop, I see the doors swing open and Jimmy hops out. He has headphones on, but when he sees me with my Subaru parked on the shoulder of the road, he lowers them. He stops a whole length away from me, as if afraid to get closer.

"I told you, I don't need rides anymore."

"I'm not here to give you a ride." I hug my jacket tighter around me.

"Oh." He shifts. "I'm sorry about what happened in class. Why didn't you go home?"

A gust of wind howls through the December air.

"Did I do something to you?"

His face contorts with confusion. "Why would you say that?"

"I don't know, maybe because you haven't talked to me in weeks."

"I talk to you. We say hi in the halls. We text sometimes."

"That's not talking." The gravel hardened with snow crunches as I approach him. "I don't mind that you don't come over anymore. I don't mind that my grades in English are dropping, and my college essay sucks. What I mind is that you're going back to how you were before."

"How I was before?"

"Yes. You don't talk to anyone. You don't see anyone outside of school. You don't even sit with me in the library. You say you're okay, but you can't even pretend to want to be around me? And the worst part is, you won't even tell me why."

"You don't need to know everything about everyone, Via." Jimmy turns away from me and flees toward the bus stop.

"Why won't you tell me why you and Elliot stopped being friends?" I pace after him.

He plants himself on the cold bench and shrugs into his backpack. "It doesn't matter. It's nothing."

"What happened with you and Alex?" I stand over him. "Why were you looking into Klara and YouTech on your own? Do you know something I don't?"

"Just leave me alone." He squeezes by me and stalks away, as if he's going to walk home.

"Were you ever going to tell me about your brother?"

He freezes. I see his fists clench around the straps of his backpack, but he doesn't turn around.

"Is it because he died the same way Alex did?"

The shaky frame of the bus stop rattles against the wind. A single strand of hair falls out of place, and I can barely hear him when he says, "You don't know what you're talking about."

"Then explain it to me. Otherwise I'm just going to make assumptions about your brother."

He ignores me and continues along the shoulder of the road. "You don't know anything about my brother, so don't pretend like you do."

I chase after him. "I'm not trying to push you away by talking about your brother. I just want to know why you're upset."

"No, you don't."

"Yes, I do. I'm trying to figure out the truth."

Jimmy whips around, and a single strand of dark hair falls out of place. "You want the truth?" he says dejectedly. His backpack slips off his shoulder in defeat. "You want to know why I'm upset? Why I sit in the library like some weirdo?"

I watch his brown eyes waver.

"My brother was my best friend. Even when we were little kids, he always had my back. There's this lake behind my house that I used to walk on when it froze over, and one time I got too far out and it started cracking. I was so scared I couldn't move. It was like I was paralyzed. And Oscar went out there to get me, no fear at all, and he fell through the ice. He fell into the water and almost got hypothermia, but he never held it against me. He just laughed and said it would have been an epic way to go."

He doesn't fidget. I've never seen him so still.

"When I first came to high school, I was terrified. I didn't know anybody. I didn't feel like I could talk with any other kids in my class. I walked in on my first day thinking that was it. I was going to be alone, but Oscar didn't let me. He made me sit with him at lunch, with all his older friends, and if it bothered him that his little brother was there, I didn't know. Then he helped me try out for the basketball team with him, and we would practice every day after school. I wanted to be like him so bad. So, anyway, there was this park behind our house, right next to the lake, and we would play there until it got dark. And when I finally made it on the team freshman year, god, he was so proud. He bought me a bunch of beers and we drank them with his friends. I hate beer, but that night I felt so cool. I felt like we were invincible. A month later, they found his body in the lake. It was the same lake, the one right behind our house."

My heart lurches, and I look away.

"Apparently he drove his car right off the road into the water. It was across from the YouTech headquarters at that little spot on the bank, no signs of a crash or an accident. My parents didn't let me see the body. And after that I couldn't sit with his friends anymore at lunch, so I sat in the library. I quit basketball because I couldn't really play without thinking of him and feeling sick. And I never went to that lake again."

The wind howls through the pines with a soft cry.

"So if you're going to tell me my brother was an Agent, don't," he says. "Don't tell me that I don't know who he really was, because I knew who he was. He was my brother, and he made sure I was never alone. And now he's gone."

Jimmy's brown eyes tremble, and he clenches his jaw so hard it looks like it's going to shatter. I can hear the exhaust of the next bus as it pulls up behind me.

My voice cracks, "I'm sorry."

He picks up his backpack from the soiled snow, throws it over his shoulder, and pushes past me. Another billowing gust of wind sweeps through the trees, but it can't move me from where I stand rooted on the shoulder of the road, haunted by the ghosts of Alex Brockman and Oscar Andrade.

CHAPTER 17

The coffee shop brims with life, packed with buzzing high schoolers who are ready for winter break to start. It's cold and wet in Park Falls, so everyone wants to huddle inside a cafe and drink coffee to cure the insatiable chill. And considering it's the only cafe in the area, it feels like the whole town is here.

"Wait, so how do you know this Wes kid?" Elliot asks me for a second time.

I'm dragged out of my deep thoughts. "Oh, um, he's just my friend from childhood." I don't mean to ignore Elliot, but I've been distracted since yesterday. The dreams of drowning haunt me in full force, and the conversation with Jimmy at the bus stop weighs heavy on my mind. *It's too much of a coincidence. Alex I understand, Jimmy I understand, Dean I understand... But how can I see the memories of someone who's been long dead? Someone I've never even met?*

"And, Klara, you hate him because..."

She doesn't pay attention to Elliot either, busy with pictures of her latte and finding the right angles. Klara and half of these other kids probably only come here because it makes them feel artsy, like they're one of those people in cities who spend their lives at cafes reading poetry or something. Klara hates reading, and people.

Finally, she flicks her hair and puts away her phone. "Because he hates me."

Elliot tilts his head. "I'm confused. Did he hate you before you hated him?"

"I think I hated him because I knew he hated me for apparently hating him."

"Wow, that clears things up." My sarcasm evokes a chuckle from Elliot but nothing from Klara. She knows how I feel about her picking on Wes, and it's not funny to me.

"Anyway, are we good for hiking over break?" Elliot lifts his mug. "There's a longer loop that takes you past the church—"

"Can I come?" Klara asks.

We both set down our coffee. I exchange glances with Elliot, and he scratches at his ear. "I don't really think it would be your thing," I say.

Her eyebrows attack me, with more ferocity than normal. "Well, it's just walking and talking, right? I'm great at talking."

"We know," I laugh lightly but shift under her intensity.

"What do you guys talk about?"

Out of my periphery, Elliot's eyes beg me not to say anything. I see the fear and vulnerability from under his long strands of hair.

"Nothing." I gulp. *Why is it suddenly so hard to breathe? Why do my lungs feel compressed?*

Klara resets her jaw. "I have to go." She throws her bag over her shoulder and swipes up her phone.

"Wait, but it was your idea to come here." Elliot frowns.

"My dad is bugging me. He can be such an ass after work." She puts on her coat and strides out of the cafe without a second glance. I exhale into my drink and stand to follow her.

"Klara!" I push open the door with a rattling chime. "Don't be so dramatic. You're going to hurt Elliot's feelings."

"Really? Well I guess you'll have more to talk about on your hike then." Her shoes splash on the wet sidewalk.

"It's just a hike," I groan. "Have a little faith. Okay? I'm his friend too."

"He's not your *best* friend, though. That's me," she snaps. "I'm the one who always goes to your house, and who takes you to parties, and who protects you. Plus, I say I love you all the time. Do any of your guy friends do that?"

I throw up my arms. "You say you love everyone! If you say it to everyone, it doesn't mean a damn thing. You can be so fake sometimes. I swear, half of what you say is just bullshit. How is Elliot supposed to invite you to things and talk to you about real stuff if he doesn't know what you're really like?"

"Oh, so this is my fault?" she reels. "Classic Olivia."

"Don't act like I'm starting this. Ever since I got close to Elliot, you've been picking fights with me. Just because you don't get attention from your dad doesn't mean you have to be a bitch to everyone all the time."

"Screw you," she flips me off.

"And don't act like *I'm* the one who needs *you*," I yell after her. "I was the one who picked you up on the side of the road when all your other friends ditched you. Remember?"

She ignores me, and her ponytail cuts through the wet air as she disappears around the block. My pulse fills my ears so I can't even think. I reach up and pull back at my scalp. *What is wrong with me? Why do I feel so agitated all the time?* Cars whir down Main Street as I retreat back inside the cafe.

I slump back down in my seat at the table. Elliot doesn't say anything. Something uneasy stirs in my chest. I know why Klara has been upset with me. I know what it looks like from her perspective, but I can't help it that I always end up in this situation. *What am I supposed to do? Abandon Wes and Jimmy and Elliot just because of her feelings?* I feel like I'm drowning in secrets.

We sit in silence for a while as Elliot plays with the strings of his hoodie. I suddenly long for the dead silence and isolation of the woods. That's the only place it's so quiet I can talk to him because I can practically read his thoughts and sense his emotions. Here in this coffee shop, surrounded by chatter and commotion, I don't even know what I would begin to say. *I can't find the words to describe what I'm feeling right now. How do I explain that I'm dreaming about memories that aren't mine?*

"I think there's something wrong with me," Elliot says. He pokes around at Klara's untouched coffee mug.

"What do you mean?"

I can tell he wants to say something, but he can't find the words. I take another sip of my latte as I look up from the foam and try to read his expression.

"I think I'm missing something." He runs his fingers through his hair. "With Klara, I mean. How do you know if you're, like, feeling the things you're supposed to be feeling? I don't know if I'm supposed to be in love or something, or if I'm even doing it right."

"It's high school. I'm sure it doesn't matter."

"But it does." His eyes meet mine. "You know why it does."

I set down my mug. He doesn't even have to say it, but I know it's on everyone's minds, all the time. Mine too. *I wonder if Alex could feel emotions. I wonder if he knew they weren't real. I wonder how you would even know.*

I shake my head. "Aren't you going to take a picture of your drink?"

His dimples flex above a small grin. "You're right, what a waste."

"Did it even happen if you didn't take a picture of it?"

He taps on Klara's mug, pensive for a moment. "Do you think if you didn't take pictures of things, you wouldn't remember them?"

The drink churns in my stomach. I push away a dark image that presses on the back of my mind. "I mean, how could you forget? It's your own memories."

"I don't know." He shrugs. "I'm starting to think you can remember things wrong."

Elliot continues to tap on Klara's mug. The latte art melts and sinks below the surface of the untouched drink.

* * *

The gym floor squeaks with wet shoes and soaked bodies. All the students itch to be released from the school assembly, but Principal Conners keeps us halted where we stand. Wes fidgets next to me, and I swear I hear our names in a conversation behind us. The murmurs and whispers prick at my nerves, that ever-broiling agitation under the surface bubbling up.

Wes glances around us at the knots of kids. "Do you ever think Alex killed himself because he found out?"

My heart lurches at his name. "Found out what?"

He lowers his voice to a barely audible whisper. "That he was an Agent."

I tug at my sleeves. "Maybe. I think I would probably do the same thing if I found out."

"Why?"

The hair on the back of my neck stands from the stares of kids who watched me break the ESP machine in English, kids who tell stories about Wes's expulsion like they were there. "I don't think I could handle it. Knowing I was different than everyone else."

"I think I would want to know," Wes says.

I'm shocked by his response. "Really?"

"Yeah. I think it would explain a lot."

"Now before I let you go," Principal Conners's voice booms from his microphone. "Always know that our doors are open if you have any burning questions. Don't stop using those brilliant minds just because it's winter break! I want you questioning *everything* you see. We're going to have lots of fun activities with the Agent and AI technology when you get back. Happy vacation!"

Like open floodgates, students pour out of the gymnasium and jostle each other in a buzz of anticipation. Principal Conners's dancing eyes jump from face to face, and I avoid them desperately. But he doesn't grab me at the exit.

"Mr. Carmichael!" His pudgy fingers reach out for Wes's figure. I leave them but hover by the edge of the bleachers to eavesdrop on the conversation. "I wanted to speak to you about how your first couple weeks went. I've heard from quite a few of your peers that you're finding it hard to acclimate."

Wes brushes aside his blond waves. "No, I'm doing great. I don't know why people say that."

"Are you sure? Because I am more than happy to recommend you to a few facilities that could help you… adjust. In fact, our counselor has spoken with your parents and suggested it might be helpful to get away before the spring semester begins."

"I'm fine, thank you." I see the veins in his arms bulge.

"We'll discuss it again soon. We took you out of your last school for your own good, so we want to make sure your transition to Park Falls is smooth." Principal Conners speaks with a lilt as if he shares good news. *How can Conners keep smiling and laughing with that stupid round belly when he's trying to send my friend away? After he practically blackmailed him to enroll?*

Wes diverts into the hallway and mixes into the crowd. I follow and quicken my pace.

"Hey, what was that about? They wouldn't actually send you away—"

"I don't want to talk about it," he cuts me off. "I'll see you on Sunday. Okay?"

I stop at my section of lockers, taken aback, and he strides on. *Maybe Principal Conners is right? Maybe he isn't doing so well?*

With a troubled sigh I fiddle with the padlock and swing open the metal door. I clean out all my textbooks and school devices, and suddenly a small envelope falls out. *People still send things on paper?* I rip open the seal and unfold the note, and with a surprise I notice it's from Jimmy.

Hi. I've notice you're stressed out. I can tell because you do that counting thing when you're anxious. Sometimes you do it out loud when you're stuck on a problem or an essay. Or sometimes you just mouth it when your dad comes in and talks to you. When you're in class you tug at your sleeves instead. You should sleep more.

All the frustration with Wes and agitation toward Klara slips away. *How does he know all this about me, and I know nothing about him?* I exhale shakily and feel my resolve wilt. Some people say they love you without meaning it, and then some people love you without ever meaning to say it.

Sorry to act like a stalker. Again. But I thought this could give you something else to play with when you're nervous.

It was my brother's. He always said it helped. Have a good winter break.

Out of the envelope falls a tiny button. For a second I don't know why a button would do anything, but as I run my finger along its curve I notice small grooves in the material. Four of them. *One, two, three, four.*

My locker gapes back at me as I stand there, holding the last remaining possession of Oscar Andrade in my palm, and feel a solemn sensation swallow me. That hum in the back of my head comes to the forefront. I can feel the hurt, the helplessness, a weight that crushes on top of me like a body of water.

Suddenly, my phone starts buzzing in my pocket. I glance down at the contact ID, and it's Elliot.

"Hey, what's up?" I say. "Have you gone home yet?"

"Um, yes. I just wanted to check in."

"Oh. Great. Well, I'm leaving the school right now. We can call later if my dad isn't on me about college applications."

"Alright. Are we still set for hiking at eight in the morning on Saturday?"

"That's way too early. It's winter break. I want to sleep in until at least twelve." I pull up the online calendar on my phone, where I had our original plan scheduled.

"Let me check my schedule. Let me see… um, how about nine?"

"A real compromiser. Fine." My knuckles tap on the aluminum door of my locker. I watch the appointment on my screen immediately shift to 9 a.m. "Hey, uh, while you called, I've been meaning to ask. Did you know how Jimmy's brother died, like what happened? I know it's none of my business, and I think I made him really upset when I confronted him the other day, but I feel like there's something weird going on. I was wondering if you might know anything else."

"Sure. That's a good idea, we should talk. I have something to tell you anyway."

"Really?" I wander down the hall, the only sound in the student-less school a thudding and rattling from the weight room next to the gym. "Because everything with Jimmy seemed like a sensitive subject. I mean, I'm glad you want to share. I wasn't going to ask, but—"

I pass by in front of the window to the weight room and stop in my tracks. The punching bag in the center of the room is pounded and assaulted by a rapid stream of fists, all of which make contact with the leather in violent thrusts. The source of it all is a shirtless boy with rippling muscles and a bobbing head of black hair.

Still on the phone, I swing open the door noisily and step in. "Elliot?"

He turns and pulls out earbuds to acknowledge me. His eyes blink away moisture through long strands of hair, and his entire body glistens with sweat. "Via," he breathes heavily, his chest rising and falling.

"How are you..." I feel a lump in my throat. "I mean, weren't you just..."

"I know, I missed the assembly just now. I just had a lot on my mind." His eyes flick up to mine. "Why haven't you left yet?"

"Wait, if you're here," I hold up my phone with a trembling hand. "Then who is this?"

"Hello? You still there?" Elliot's voice rings out from the speaker on my phone. I hang up so fast that my phone drops to the ground and hits the vinyl with a crack like a whip. My hands fly up to my mouth.

"Are you okay?" the Elliot who stands in front of me asks. "What happened?"

The corners of my vision blur, and I rush out of the weight room as fast as my feet will carry me. I gasp for air and clutch my neck, feeling like I'm drowning.

"Wait!" Elliot's voice calls after me. "Via!"

I don't turn around.

CHAPTER 18

My breath curls out in front of me like tendrils of smoke as the cold cuts through my bones. I crouch in the driver's seat of my beaten-down car and hug my knees. The doors are so skeletal and frail that they let all the winter chill inside. Despite the shivers that rack my body, my eyes are dead set on the trailhead. *The texts said nine. But I don't know which version of Elliot sent them.*

There he is. He pulls up and climbs out of a nondescript silver car with his jogger and shorts. He adjusts his beanie over that hair that's so familiar and glances around with his eyes squinted so I can practically imagine his laugh. His dimples flex as he checks his phone. Those dimples I know so well. After a minute he seems to give up and heads for the trail, and only after he disappears into the pines do I climb out of my car.

I don't hike along the path. Instead, I pick through the frosted undergrowth and weave through skeletal trees. I skirt the trail at a good distance from Elliot, watching him meander through the woods deep in thought. I pull out my phone with numb fingers and shakily redial the contact "Elliot" that called me. It rings as I watch him, watch as he stops and fumbles into his jogger. I hide behind a thick pine branch and hold my breath.

"Hello?"

The whole forest is silent.

"Via?" He stalks along the path. "Hey, where are you? I waited for you at the trailhead."

I feel my voice tremor as I walk. "Is this... is this really you?"

"Who else would it be?" I see him glance around. "Is this about the thing at the gym the other day? Why did you run off like that?"

My boots treading carefully through the snow, I shadow him. "If you're messing with me, it's not funny. Is this part of the simulation?"

"Via, is everything okay? It's just me. You can trust me."

I rake my hands through my hair and bite my lip. *I want to believe him. I do.* But I can't get that other voice of his out of my head. In my pocket I reach for the button and feel the four grooves on its smooth face.

"Jimmy told me about his brother, and something's not right. I can sense it. Okay? You need to tell me the truth. I don't care. I just need to know."

"And what, you trust Jimmy, but you can't even go on a hike with me?"

An unforgiving breeze slithers through the canopy. I step faster, trying to stay silent as I follow him. "I trust Jimmy because he told me the truth."

"Don't trust him, Via. He's just going to stab you in the back." His pace picks up as his vexation builds. "He's lying to you like he's lied to everyone else. You don't know anything about that kid. He's a rat. I'm the one who has your best interest at heart. Okay?"

"If you did, you would tell me the truth." I stagger on the uneven ground, and my heart quickens.

"Stop digging into things you don't know about. You did the same thing with Alex!" His tone bites, cold and mean.

"Don't talk to me about Alex. You don't know—" I stop myself, swallowing bitterly. "I don't even know who you are. This is not you. The real Elliot would share things with me."

"Maybe this is the real Elliot then!" His angry cry echoes through the silent air. "You're acting insane!"

He hangs up on me and I can't bring myself to follow him any further. My lungs scream in the bitter air, and for a moment I wonder if the whole thing was just in my head. *First you're seeing things. Now you're hearing things. Get your shit together, Via.*

I rush back to my car, trudging through snow while the cold stings my cheeks. My phone buzzes in my hand, and I look down to see it's Elliot. I decline with a lurch in my chest and grip the device tighter. I stumble out onto the road. The voices from my calls with Elliot echo in the cavities of my mind. That's when I get the buzz of a notification.

It's from the anonymous number: *Don't trust anyone.*

"Leave me alone!" a scream rips from my throat and I hurl my phone away from me. It shatters on the asphalt and birds erupt from a neighboring tree at the ear-splitting sound. My whole body shudders as I take my head in both hands.

A looming sensation of fear grips me—fear of all the things I don't know. It's like I'm back to square one.

* * *

"Where do you think you're going?"

My dad stops me right before I reach the end of the hallway, and I jump in surprise. Everything scares me these days, but I'm especially spooked by my reflection in the dark windows of this strange house.

He stands up, illuminated by his reading light in the living room, and I take my time to turn around. "I'm going to Chad's. Same place I always go."

He sets down the book he was reading. "You've been going there a lot lately."

I glance at the doorknob. "It's winter break, Dad. I don't have any work to do." The real reason I need to go, the reason that is impossible to explain to him, is that I need answers. Ever since I got to Park Falls, something different has been happening with me, something beyond the physical. I need to figure out if YouTech has other experiments besides the Agent.

"This is that house on the lake? The one the parents are never at?"

"Dad, I'm really responsible at these things. I never drink, I've always made it home before curfew, and I'm the designated driver every time I go out."

"What did I tell you about driving other people? Especially after the Incident?"

I sigh, "I know."

His eyes bore into me. "Say it, please."

"A person in the passenger seat is just as dangerous—"

"Just as dangerous as a drunk driver," he finishes for me. I bite my tongue. "I trust you. I'm just making sure you're thinking about your actions."

"Can I go now?" I say. "Or is this you trying to stop me from going out because you're worried I'll get drunk and end up on the road again?" I grip the button inside my jacket pocket and pinch it between my fingers with force.

He purses his lips. "Aren't you going to take your phone?"

I feel a lump form in my throat. I didn't tell him about smashing mine, but he's probably noticed I don't constantly have it with me.

"You haven't touched it for days. How else are you supposed to contact me if something happens or if you need something from me?"

I don't need anything from you. "Here." I grab Alex's phone that was hidden underneath the other devices. "I'll be home before twelve."

He settles back down into his reading without saying a word.

* * *

The Subaru door slams shut behind me. The shouting and muffled bass of music echoes through the dark forest. *I wonder if there's anyone around to hear? I wonder if YouTech Labs down the road can hear?*

Next to me, I see Wes shiver. He shifts in discomfort, and I say, "You didn't have to come."

"No, I did. My parents are *this* close to sending me away to some psychiatric ward." He shakes his head. "I need to prove to them I'm a normal teenager. Doesn't mean I like the idea of being hotboxed in with a bunch of kids who think I'm an Agent, but I guess I need to prove it to them too."

"That's right, normal." I put on a smile as my boots crunch on the snow matted to the gravel driveway.

Wes's discomfort inside the cabin radiates. We sidle through groups of kids who don't even hide their stares, and I'm so distracted by the whispers I stumble right into Elliot and Klara. They stand under a huge maple beam that stretches into the living room, and I watch them both shift miserably.

"Hi," Klara says to me while she shoots a glare at Wes.

"Hi." I glance over at Elliot.

He ignores me and only addresses Wes. "Hey, man, can I get you a drink?"

Wes tucks a wave of hair behind his ear. "Yes. Alcohol. My favorite."

As the two boys beeline for the dining room, I shimmy past Klara. But she grabs my arm and her eyebrows dig into me. "You're okay. Right?"

I groan. "If Elliot told you anything—"

"No, I mean like… you're good?" She touches her earrings. "It's just that I've been really impulsive lately, and I messed up big time. But it was just a thing in the moment and it's over now. So is everything fine with you?"

"Yeah…" I pull back my arm hesitantly. *That was the weirdest apology ever.* "Hey, I know you have a problem with him, but can you and Elliot just watch Wes for me? Just make sure he isn't being awkward or, God forbid, starts dancing. Don't let him outdrink you."

She smiles faintly, one of the genuine ones. "He won't outdrink me. I've been refilling my mom's vodka with water since seventh grade."

Then suddenly we hear an uproar from the kitchen, and I'm drawn in by the chaos. When I walk through the log archways, I find kids packed in like sardines. They lean and sprawl against every square inch of cabinet and countertop. There are handles of alcohol and beer cans on the center island. It piles up like a bar shelf. Instead of a variety of conversations and incoherent drinking, the focal point of all the attention is on one person.

Dean stands in the middle, right up to the edge of the island, and all eyes are glued on him. It's a strangely intense focus for a mess of intoxicated kids. *Why is he wearing that stupid long coat indoors?*

I squeeze through the doorway toward the corner of the room to see what's going on. Dean seems to notice my entrance, and his mouth dangles open in a grin. "Look who it is."

"Shouldn't you be kicked out of here already by Chad?"

"He's not here right now. Shouldn't you be up on the deck, puzzling your existence?"

My face flushes with the sudden attention from the whole room. *I just wanted to be invisible tonight and slip into Chad's mom's office.* "What is this, a cult initiation?"

"Even better," he says, and then louder to everyone. "We're playing a game! It's called…" his eyes narrow, "I don't know what it's called actually, I made it up just now."

There are slurred giggles and shouts from everyone in the kitchen. Dean speaks to the whole audience as he holds their attention, which seems melodramatic. I cross my arms. Something about all of this is getting under my skin. *I thought Dean's whole thing was avoiding people. What changed?*

"Okay, I got it." Dean sways. "It's called: Never Have I Ever… Been a Robot."

More laughs. Not from me.

"Hang with me here." He stumbles a little, and I think for a moment that he could be pretending. "It's a really easy game. I just spin this bottle," he sets a beer bottle on its side, "and if it lands on you, you have to—"

"Kiss!" a girl exclaims. Dean just smirks.

"You can get mono another night, Laura. No, if it lands on you, all you have to do is give us one reason why you're definitely human. And then everyone else in the room, if you can't relate, you have to put down a finger and drink. First person to lose all their fingers is the Agent!"

"Don't you think this is a little… insensitive?" Klara speaks up from behind me. I didn't even notice her presence, but she seethes at Dean. "Remember *Alex*?"

"This game is *in memory* of Alex," he says with a sweeping gesture. "The real disrespect to him would be to pretend like nothing ever happened. Which is what you are doing," he points directly at me, "if you don't play."

I feel my blood broil and fists clench as I turn around to leave the kitchen.

"Wait, where are you going?" He stretches over the island and grabs me. I whip around and glare at his hand on my wrist. In that moment I am hit by a wall of emotion, engulfed in flames. A horrible darkness fills every pore and sets my nerve endings on fire. It's like I can feel his heartbeat, his thoughts, his deep loathing.

I yank my arm away from him. The entire room's eyes are locked on me. They eat up every one of my movements. He pulls back his hand and says gently, "Via, as my *very* close friend, I want you to be the first person to go."

"I'm not playing your stupid game."

"Well that's suspicious. Don't you think?" Dean glances around at the rest of the room.

What is he doing? Does he know I saw something when he touched me? Kids in the room whisper and judge, so I reach over to the bottle and spin it. The sounds in the kitchen lower to a hush, and eager anxiety pulses in the air. I don't even think they care about the game. Just the act of spinning a bottle and not knowing who it will land on excites them. So primal.

It points right at Sydney, whose cheeks glow red above a loose smile. A shout of excitement erupts, and all the kids around her nudge her in playful anticipation.

"Alright, Syd, let's hear it. Why are you not the Agent?"

"Easy," she laughs. "I've had sex."

Drunken cheers. Lots of kids throw back their drinks, shout at their friends, and put down fingers. I don't put down a finger, and I see Dean glance my way. I hide my hand quickly and look down.

"Hold on, hold on. I'm not sure that's a valid reason," Dean commands attention again. "You don't think Agents can have sex? Even dogs have sex; just look at Laura and Chris."

The crowd erupts into a chorus of "oohs" and laughter, and Laura flips Dean off. Kids take shots anyway, and I realize they don't even care about what's happening in the game. They just want an excuse to drink.

His devilish piercing gaze lands on me again, and I find myself unable to move. "Spin the bottle, Syd. I'll let this one go." As the bottle turns in mesmerizing circles, Elliot enters the kitchen with Wes close behind him. I notice Klara and Wes scoot a little farther away from each other.

The bottle lands on Max, who immediately looks up at me. "Never have I ever..." then something changes in his expression. "You know what, I'm drunk. I'll just show you guys." He pulls up the sleeve of his sweatshirt all the way to his shoulder, and a gasp fills the room. For a second his arm just looks like normal skin and flesh, but then he bends it and the joints reveal the gaps in between. It's advanced robotics, a prosthetic.

"He's the Agent!" Chris exclaims.

"No, no. YouTech does a lot more than just build robots." Max thrives under the attention of entranced girls. "I had this accident with a wood saw a while back and they agreed to install this if my parents started working for them. It's like a part of me now, I don't even notice it."

I glance over at Klara to see a twinge of annoyance cross her face. *Does she know about all these deals YouTech makes through her father?*

"Can it feel things?" Sydney gapes.

"Totally, every little thing. It can feel pain, feel heat. It gets goosebumps, even when I don't know I'm cold. Like it has a mind of its own." Max pulls down his shirt.

"How is that possible?" Laura asks incredulously. The whole room is still perplexed.

Dean takes a swig of his flask. "Pain is just the brain sending signals, firing neurons. A computer can do the exact same thing. It's essentially like texting. It's the same for feeling drunk, feeling sad, or getting off. But instead of thoughts, it's feelings."

Just like texting. A shiver goes down my spine.

"Let's go, people. I don't see any shots being taken! This room reeks of sobriety, you're all too sober," Dean riles up the crowd. "*I'm* too sober, damnit." He takes another swig and wipes his mouth. "This is fun! Let's keep going. Come on, Chris. You're not throwing up yet."

I can't take any more of this. I turn around to head for the door and notice more people have come in. The whole party seems to be gathered in the kitchen to see what the commotion is all about. As I struggle to get through, I hear my name.

"Via, it's you."

I whirl to see the bottle pointing right at my spot around the island.

Dean scrunches his nose. "I love irony." All the kids packed into the kitchen feed into his energy. I see Wes and Elliot exchange glances across the room, and Klara is already gone.

"No thanks. I'll pass."

"Well, then you'll have to accept your consequence." Dean holds up a bottle of vodka that's almost done.

"I'm driving tonight, sorry."

"I'll drive you home."

"You're more hammered than most people here."

"I could just be great at pretending. You don't know that." He stumbles drunkenly for show. "Okay here, I'll play devil's advocate *and* I'll give you a reason. You have a house and a family. Right? You've been with them your whole life. Haven't you? There's no way that could all be a setup."

I meet his eyes with a cold stare.

"What about your brother? You've had some great memories with that kid. I'm sure that couldn't all be fake."

I can't believe him. My mind immediately goes to the phone call with Elliot, the anonymous texts, Jimmy's strange behavior, my dreams. I feel the button's presence in my pocket and feel the stares of everyone in the room.

"What, no response?" He leans across the counter. "For Alex?"

"You're such an asshole." *Does he know about Alex? Does Klara tell him things about me?*

"There has to be something. Think really hard."

"This is an impossible game. You can never prove it." I glance back at Elliot, and he glares at Dean with an icy stare that could take all the warmth out of the stuffed room.

"Sure you can," Dean says. He lifts his hand into the air and it wanders in a circle around the kitchen, searching for something. He finds what he's looking for and shuffles between people briskly. A moment later he's back to the island with a kitchen knife in his hand.

I jump back when I see him swing the blade. "What the hell!"

"You're the one who asked." His tongue plays along the inside of his cheek, and he sets it down between us. "There's an obvious way to prove it."

My stomach churns just at the sight of the blade. "Are you saying..."

Dean's eyes level with mine.

"No way. You've got to be kidding. You," I step back, "you are something else. You're psychotic."

"Oh, come on, don't tell me nobody here hasn't thought of this before..." he turns to survey the room. "The idea has crossed all of our minds at least once. Right?"

Nobody responds. I see Wes wither in the background and pull his sleeves down further. The glinting blade on the granite countertop has killed the buzz in the room.

Dean plants his hands on the counter. "If you really want to prove to everyone that you're not an Agent, all you have to do is let us see for ourselves. Just a little cut. Sure it might hurt, and you might see blood, and you won't spot anything at first. But if you go deep enough, and I'm talking *really* deep, you're going to start feeling some adrenaline. That'll really make you feel alive. And then eventually you'll hit something. And maybe it will be real bone, or maybe it'll look like Max's arm, but we'll have our answer either way."

I search his eyes for some kind of sincerity and try to calm my heart that pounds like a drum. "You're sick."

He tilts his head. "I'm giving you a way out, but you just don't have the guts."

"Hey!" Elliot pushes through the crowd suddenly, right to my side. "This is some seriously messed-up shit, Dean, even for you."

"I'm so honored. The star of the basketball team playing *my* game."

Elliot turns to me. "Come on, Via. Let's get outta here."

"And what about you, Elliot Kang?" Dean snatches up the knife from the island. "There's no way Mr. Perfect could be an Agent. Right? He's got his basketball scholarship, all those abs, his perfect girlfriend..."

"Nobody wants you here. You're just that kid everyone feels bad for because he's an alcoholic."

"*High-functioning* alcoholic." Dean scrunches his nose.

"Let's go." Elliot puts his hand on my back and leads me away.

"You look pretty upset, man. Might not want to drive tonight. You don't want another accident happening."

When Dean says this, he stops in his tracks. I feel his hand squeeze like he's trying to dig his nails into my back. For a moment I think he'll snap, and I picture him pounding on Dean like the punching bag in the weight room. *Is this the Elliot I know or another version entirely?* But then he lets go of my hand and disappears from the room.

"Elliot!" I chase after him, glancing back at Dean's insufferable open-mouthed grin one last time. I catch him in the entryway and slam my hand on the door. "What did he mean back there?"

"Nothing. He's just trying to piss me off."

"Well, it worked." I block his way. "What did he mean, accident?"

"I don't want to talk about it."

Just then, Alex's phone slips from my jacket pocket. In that moment I remember the call history, the fact that I never called him but my name shows up as the last person he spoke to. The lock-screen photo of Elliot and Alex stares up at us, and I can already feel his explosive rage.

"What the hell is this?" His neck bulges. "Via, what the hell is this? You're accusing me of hiding things, and you have my dead best friend's phone in your goddamn pocket!"

My breath chokes in panic. "Elliot, listen. I was just trying to protect you. There are things you don't know."

"You sound crazy! What does that even mean? Why do you have to suddenly know everything about everyone's life?"

"I wouldn't have to pry if you would just explain what happened with Alex and Jimmy. Or at least tell me what Dean meant when he said 'accident.' I don't need to know everything, but—"

"It was a stupid crash last January, okay? It was nothing. I wasn't even driving!" Elliot shouts.

The room spins, and my brain goes fuzzy. "Wait, did you say last January?"

"Alex and I were in the car, and I knew he wasn't supposed to drive because of his seizures, but it wasn't snowing hard and I thought it would be okay. And then he just freaked out, for no reason. He saw something out his window and froze up. I tried to take the wheel but we swerved into the other lane and I don't even know what we hit. It was an animal or something, but Alex was unconscious and I didn't know what to do, so I drove away. I drove away, okay?"

I grab his shoulder. "This was a car crash? In January?"

"And now that asshole wants to bring it up at a party like he was there, like he even gives a shit. Nobody gives a shit, especially not about Alex," Elliot fumes. "You wanna know why I don't talk to Jimmy? Because he cut Alex out of his life the second things got hard, the second he didn't want to deal with it. He doesn't give a shit about Alex, or about anyone. He just ditched his best friend when he was in the hospital. When he needed him most. So don't treat me like I'm the one who can't be trusted. Okay?"

He pushes past me and the darkness swallows him up. I watch him storm off as blood pounds in my ears. The sounds of the party echo behind me, like some kind of distant memory. And right then in the doorway, I am taken back to the Incident.

CHAPTER 19

"Did you hear me, Via?"

I look up at my mom. "Sorry, what?"

"I was asking how the party went, the one you took Wes to."

Across the table, Wes stabs at his noodles and grumbles. "I'm wondering the same thing."

"Can we not talk about the party?" I set down my chopsticks. "Please." I shoot him a look. *I said I would tell you later.* Both nights since the party have been plagued with dreams of dying in a burning house, and I can still feel the heat closing in on me. Even now.

"Awkward." Josh makes a face. The only sound at the table for a while is the clattering of dishes and Wes's dad grating his fork on his plate. My dad stares at Lawrence with loathing as he eats the Japanese noodles with a fork.

My mom nudges my brother. "How is your girlfriend Annie? Are you still talking with her?"

"I broke up with her last week." Josh lifts his chin. "I think it was for the best. We were starting to grow apart."

"What is going on with eighth graders these days?" Beth chuckles into her wine. Wes's eyes lock onto me from across the table, and they sear into my scalp.

Josh continues. "I got her friends to tell her we were over at lunch, but I sent a text just in case. Then I unfollowed her on all my accounts and posted a mirror selfie to make her jealous."

"She did like your chub," Danielle says. "She said you were huggable."

"I am. So now I'm going back to school after break. I'll ignore her for a couple of weeks. I continue to like all of her pictures, and then probably ask her friend Kim to the dance."

"Dope." Danielle fist bumps him. All I can hear is the grating sound of Lawrence's fork against the plate. My ears ring.

"Via, the last time I heard you update us about your love life was before your Incident," Beth chuckles into her wine.

I drop my chopsticks. "I'm sorry, I need to… I'm going to the bathroom."

"Via, sit down. Your father made these noodles from scratch. We're trying to have dinner as a family," Mom says.

"We're not even the same family! This is two families!"

I stomp out into the hallway, past cheesy Christmas decorations, and slam the bathroom door behind me. I turn on the sink and let the stream of water drown out the thoughts in my head.

"Hey," Wes knocks lightly. "You all good in there? You're missing the best part of the story. Apparently there's a love triangle. I'm going to draw out a whole tree."

When I don't respond, he cracks open the door.

My voice shakes. "I just… I can't listen to middle school drama or talk about my dad's noodles like everything is normal. I can't do it. I'm sorry."

"Look, I know you've had a rough year, but you only have one more semester with your family."

"Did you hear them in there? It's like nothing about me *after* the Incident even counts."

"At least they remember your time in the hospital. My mom drinks three glasses of wine so she doesn't have to remember mine."

I glance down at his wrists. "I know we agreed we were never going to talk about the Incident. But I need to tell you, Wes. I need to talk to someone. Everything is getting so mixed up in my head. I swear I didn't call Alex. I know I didn't call him, but it's right there on his phone. And now with Elliot..."

He steps into the bathroom and closes the door behind him. "Via, what happened at the party?"

"It was them, Wes."

He scratches his head, "You mean, in January—"

"Elliot was in the car and Alex was driving. He had some kind of weird panic attack and swerved into the other lane. Then they drove off, and I don't think they saw us, but I also think Dean might have been involved somehow." My heart pounds. Wes leans back against the door. "Say something, please."

"You didn't tell Elliot anything about us. Right?"

"No."

"And you still haven't said anything to your parents?"

"Have you?"

"No, of course not."

I pause. "Oscar Andrade drove off the road into a lake. That's how he killed himself. And knowing Alex was the Agent, and he had this moment while he was driving... it's all too much of a coincidence."

"Are you saying what I think you're saying?"

I nod and wipe my face. "It's fine. We can just look into it some more. I'll ask Jimmy some questions, I'll get to the bottom of these phone calls, and we can go to the lab and—"

"Hey, no, stop it." Wes grabs my shoulders. "No more investigations. No more digging."

"What? But you were the one who—"

"I changed my mind. It was fine when we were just looking for the Agent, but this is getting too deep."

I tug at my sleeves. *Where is the button when I need it? Did I leave it in my room?* "Wes, I can't stop. I know things. I can see things now, things I shouldn't be seeing. I might be the only person who can figure out how everything is connected."

I look into my friend's eyes. He sets his jaw and shadows darken his face.

"Then you're on your own. I'm out."

I feel a sharp pang of betrayal. "What happened to day one?"

"I have to go. I need to be somewhere." He reaches by me and turns off the sink. "Tell your dad thanks for dinner."

* * *

The new year starts off with a dreadful twist. Instead of snowfall and crisp winter air, everything becomes wet and damp and miserable. Thick sheets of slushy downpour splash my roof and drench my neighborhood. I've only been outside once today, but the feeling was enough to make me retreat back into my house with the rest of the paintings on the walls. That kind of cold goes right through your clothes, to your core, and I hate it.

"That's your resolution? Are you serious?" I hold my new phone up to my cheek and swallow down the irrational fear that builds in my chest. I had to gather all of my courage to even pick up her call. *It's her. You know it's her. Don't be that crazy person who doesn't use a phone.*

Klara's voice rings through the speaker. "Damn right I'm serious. No cussing this year."

"You realize you just cussed."

"Guidelines, Via, guidelines," she sighs. "Anyway, why did you leave the New Year's party so early? You left before midnight, which makes me think you don't really understand the holiday."

Last night was a blur, like another dream. I had barely walked into Chad's cabin before I walked right out. I couldn't see Dean, couldn't look Elliot in the eyes, couldn't face the whispers and the reek of alcohol. "I don't know. I didn't want some random drunk kid coming up and trying to kiss me."

"Come on," she groans. "There isn't anyone you would've wanted to kiss? Not a single person? What about Max? You're always talking to him at parties. I need you to stop being single. You're too hot for this. I'm done with your shit."

"You just did it again."

Suddenly, the doorbell rings from downstairs. I jolt up from my bed. My parents are out, Josh is already asleep, and I'm practically home alone. A shiver goes down my spine at the sound of someone outside my house this late in the pouring rain.

"I think someone's at my door." My heart pounds. "Klara, I swear to God..."

"It's not me."

There's another ring from my doorbell. I stay on the phone, and with my eyes on the dark staircase, I descend down to the front hall.

Nothing is scarier than being in an empty house at night, especially with these paintings that gawk at me. I keep all the Christmas lights on, but still this house doesn't feel like home. My dad will probably scold me for the electricity bill when he gets home. *I kind of hope it's my dad at the door.*

Cautiously, I gather the willpower to twist the doorknob.

A boy is standing on my front step. I can't help but feel relieved it's not another Klara. "I gotta go." I hang up on her quickly.

Jimmy takes shelter from the heavy downpour under the small roof that juts out from my door. His slick black hair is plastered to his head from the rain. His shirt, sopping wet, clings to his body as his chest rises and falls. With one hand he wipes water from his brown eyes.

"What the hell are you doing?"

He opens his mouth to respond but closes it again. I've never seen his hair like this, far from its usual groomed perfection and stuck up in wet clumps. Without his glasses he looks like a completely different person.

"Where are your glasses? Your coat?" I cross my arms. "Why are you out here like this?"

"I don't…" his forehead wrinkles. "I don't know."

I recall a distant memory of Alex in the middle of the road and feel my mouth dry up. "How did you get here?"

"I…" he trails off and turns to look back at the road. "I just came."

"Why?"

Still out of breath, he says, "I'm sorry."

I just stare at him in awe. This idiot, out here in the middle of the worst January weather imaginable, in nothing but a t-shirt. The nerve of this boy. The nerve for him to show up like this.

"I'm sorry I…" he wipes his face. "Can I come in?"

"No," I say.

"Oh. Why not?"

"Because," I stammer. "You can't just do that. You can't just cancel our tutoring sessions, ignore me at school, send me notes in my locker, and then act like everything is normal.

You hide things from me for months and then think you can just show up at my door and I'll let you in?"

He fidgets for a second and then nods. "Yes."

"It's late, Jimmy. Go home." I shake my head and close the door.

"Via!" He stops it with his hand. "If you're not going to let me in, just hear what I have to say out here."

"I'm cold."

"I don't care," he says between gritted teeth with a kind of ferocity I've never heard from him before. "Look," he says. "I can't lie to you. You know that. Which is why I had to avoid you."

"You and Elliot both. I don't know who's worse," I huff. "He told me you pushed him and Alex away after the seizures, that you cut them out of your life."

"I didn't have a choice." His brown eyes beg. "Please, you have to know there was nothing I could do. They said they would terminate him if I said anything."

I freeze. "Wait, what are you talking about?"

"I know you know." He clenches his jaw. My heart stops, and my mind reels with the cold memory of the road. "That's why you were asking about Oscar and why you were digging around in school records."

"How did you—"

"Before Alex was your friend, he was mine. I went down that spiral a long time ago, a lot earlier than you did. I saw something in the hospital after his seizure, something I shouldn't have, and I'm paying the price. Do you understand?"

I stare at him in disbelief, words caught in my throat. "No, I don't understand. Who are you afraid of?"

"I can't… I can't tell you anything else." He twitches and glances around nervously as if we're being watched from the street.

"Then why did you even come here?"

He looks at me with large wavering eyes but doesn't say anything. He just stands there out in the cold slush. "I'm sorry for coming. Goodnight, Via." He turns to leave, and I trace the shape of the button in my pocket.

"Jimmy," I say and hold it up in the porch-light. "Why did you give this to me?"

He looks from me to my hand. "I don't know. You invited me to sit with your friends at lunch, and you always text me even when I don't respond. I guess it reminded me of Oscar. You're the only other person who doesn't leave me alone."

The weight of what he says sinks into my skin deeper than the cold. I watch him take a couple of steps down the driveway as his sneakers splash in the slush. I'm suddenly taken back to the Incident in January. The memory plays out in my head so clearly, the lone figure of Wes under a streetlamp, his sneakers wet from running through the snow.

And just then, Jimmy stops. He turns around, and with conviction, marches back up to the porch.

"Seriously, I don't think—"

He grabs the side of my neck with one hand and pulls my face into his, and suddenly, his cold lips seek warmth from mine. His face drips with water, and his fingers tangle in my hair. I inhale sharply and push him away from me back out into the rain.

"You just..." I backtrack to my doorway. "What the hell?"

"Would you believe me if I said I was in love with you?"

"No." I shake my head. "Trust me. You're not in love with me."

"How do you know?" he persists. "How do you know what I feel if you're not the one going through it? What's next? Are you going to tell me my anxiety is all pretend too? Or that

I don't get to grieve for my brother? And if it is fake, who cares? I still have a right to feel it, even if none of it is real."

The more I squeeze the button in my palm, the more I feel that foreboding sensation swell up in my chest. "You don't know what I see. Okay? I know what people are going through. I can see it in my head, so much that I can't even tell which memories and emotions are mine anymore."

He just shakes his head and backs down the driveway toward the pools of water.

Irritation bites, and the urge to throw this button at him is overwhelming. "What do you want from me?"

His soft brown eyes look back at me like moonlight. "Nothing, Via, that's the point. That's what it means. I would do anything for nothing."

He slips down the driveway and into the shadows, this boy I don't even recognize. It's scary how quickly someone so close to you can become a complete stranger again. The heavy icy rain swallows him up. I watch him go, lost for words. *How am I supposed to know what I feel when almost everything in my head is from other people?* It's scary how quickly I've become a stranger to myself.

CHAPTER 20

I find myself on the road again. I can't seem to stay away. Dark trees stretch above my head, and snow falls down around me like ash from a volcano. One foot in front of the other, I follow the lines down the middle of the pavement. I look for something, search for someone. In this trance I lift my hands up to the moon. They shake, covered in blood, and glass shards protrude from the flesh. Suddenly I'm in a car. I drive down that same winding road while my hands grip the steering wheel. I turn a corner and that's when I see myself, Via, a silhouette in the headlights. I hit her, I hit me, and the car flips. I drag myself out of the crushed metal, one arm in front of the other, through shattered glass on the ice. I crawl on my knees. Snow drifts down onto the wreckage. My own body is there, mangled on the road. Blood pools from her head, my head. I kneel over her, over me, take her head in my hands and hold it up to mine.

And then I get a phone call. Through the pitch black I answer it, and fear grips every muscle in my body like a biting cold.

"Alex?"

"Via," the sound of his voice makes my heart break. It's so real I can almost see him. Like seeing a photo of a distant memory I'd forgotten about. "I need to find him. I need to find my brother."

"You don't have a brother," I choke.

"You can't tell Elliot, okay? I'm scared, please. Don't tell anyone."

"You're dead." My voice trembles under the weight of those words. "You died. You can't talk to me anymore. Leave me alone."

"I'm a line of code, Via. I can't die."

"Via?" My dad's voice shatters my thoughts and rips me out of my head as I realize where I am. I turn around and see him in the driveway, his sleeping robe wrapped tightly around his form. Cheeks stained wet with tears, I look down at my pajamas and at the phone in my hand. My bare feet are numb in the icy puddles of the street.

"Dad, I don't..." My mind reels, the freezing night finally sets in, and I can't discern what was a dream and what was real. On the glowing screen of my phone, Alex's name is still there. Like a ghost.

"It's okay." Dad's expression hardens. It's the same one I saw when I woke up in the hospital. The same face he gave me after the Incident. He reaches out to me. "Come back inside."

I nod and let him guide me inside. Only then, as I see it from the road in the moonlight, do I realize why I dislike this house so much. It's too rigid, too boxy, too straight and untouched to ever be lived in. It looks like a doll's house.

* * *

"Alright, scholars, this way. Follow Mr. Richards into the lab over here." Principal Conners ushers our group of students through the slick halls of the YouTech headquarters. When the teachers said we were going on a field trip our first day back, I didn't think I would end up here. This is the last place I would ever want to be. Not to mention that I linger in the back of the crowd with Wes so as not to see Jimmy.

The main lobby of the colossal building is just tall concrete walls with a large YouTech logo above a security desk. But the further back you go, winding through the maze of halls and glass laboratories like fishbowls, it gets busier. *How many kids' parents are in here? How many hidden projects are happening inside these walls? Do they know what they're doing?*

"What if we see your dad? Do you think he could get us into special locked rooms? What if there's a secret basement where they're doing tests on people?" Wes murmurs to me as we file through the glass door into a small lab. I just shrug, not in the mood to entertain him after he left so abruptly at Christmas and has been acting strangely since. The walls of computer monitors glow and hum, and that's when I realize the jarring image of a human head on the table. After a moment I realize it's not a human head, but a robotic frame of one, aluminum and wires in the shape of a skull.

Across the lab, Elliot has his arm around Klara. Her eyebrows attack elsewhere though, and for a minute I think she stares at Wes.

Mr. Richards swoops in like a hawk suddenly and descends upon the center table. "I'm sorry I can't show you one of our many advanced robotics labs today, but it's highly confidential. However, I did agree with your principal to give you a little demonstration." He pulls out a tablet with his claw-like hands and the robotic skull animates. A little shock ripples through the room, and I see Max fidget with his arm out of the corner of my eye.

The lights in the lab dim so that only the luminescent glow from the animatronic eyes reflects in the glass. And then I see a glint from somewhere else—thick-rimmed glasses on the face of Jimmy.

"The fascinating thing about our work with the human brain is that it's fairly simple, in the end." Mr. Richards pulls up his tablet screen on one of the monitors, and we can see him scroll through a programming system. As the lines of code fly across the screen, he continues. "Here at YouTech we've been able to mimic the part of the brain that stores memories. A computer stores memory the same way a brain does, short term, long term, and episodic memory. But the trick is how to associate sensory, nostalgia, and sentiment with these memories. That part is emotional intelligence."

Between the panels and wires of the robotic skull, small lights like fireflies bounce from one side to the other. Almost like a hundred small streams that trickle through the air, veins of light fire off signals. It's alive.

"So you can create memories?" Jimmy speaks up in the dark.

Mr. Richards stalks around the table, "More like… recreate. You quickly learn in this field that nothing can be created from scratch, the same way matter can't be created or destroyed. Building a human being without a foundation is like trying to teach a child to speak without letting them hear language. Everything has to come from imitation of something else. It has to be built from something real."

Something about what he says takes me back to the phone calls. The voices sound so real—the voice of someone who's dead.

"That's the thing about humans. It's fairly easy to fool our brains," he says. "When we see someone displaying behaviors a lot like ours, displaying things like intentionality and understanding, we assume they actually have those things. From a philosophical standpoint, that's what puts our Agents in the threshold of personhood. That's what makes our program such a success."

Again, that word success. I wince when he says it.

"Do you know what else tricks the human brain?" He changes something in the code and suddenly the features on the robotic face begin to move. "Mannerisms. Little gestures and ticks are the key to fooling someone into thinking they're seeing a living thing. Once we unlocked that coding in our lab, it changed the game. The mannerisms can be something as small as tapping its foot, or touching its hair. It can even be a detail in someone's eyebrows."

Next to me, Wes rubs the back of his neck. Across the room I see Klara step away and slip out of the lab.

"It's funny, though, how similar humans are to Agents. All it means for something to think like us is for it to be able to convince us it's thinking like us." Mr. Richards takes a hooked finger and strokes the metal cranium in front of us. "If we can't tell the difference, there really is no difference. Sometimes it makes you wonder if there's anything special about our personhood at all."

"I have a question, Stephen." Dean steps out from the back of the audience, his long coat in hand. The whole room buzzes as he calls the man by his first name, and the disrespect paints contempt over Mr. Richards's face. "Are there ever limits to what an Agent can do? I mean, sure it can imitate and learn, but can it ever break the rules of its programming?"

Mr. Richards taps on the screen of his tablet. "No, I'm afraid not."

"So there is a difference then. It doesn't actually have free will. Does it?" Dean's piercing eyes challenge the man.

"It can act like all of its choices are its own, but really it's just following a script within certain bounds."

"Yeah, but that's everyone," Wes says, and the whole crowd shifts their attention to him. "I mean, are we any different? In our classes they feed us information, give us exercises to train our brain, but isn't that just programming us?"

"Ooh, fantastic!" Principal Conners bubbles with excitement in the corner.

Dean's mouth just hangs open, and he turns to Mr. Richards. "While we're at it, let's just say the whole world is a simulation. Nothing is real. It's all just a mind game. Right? Hell, there might not even be an Agent. Is that the kind of exemplary thinking you were looking for, Principal Conners?" With an edge in his tone, he swishes his coat and strides out of the lab. Everyone falls into an uncomfortable tension.

"Well, onto the next part of our tour." Principal Conners claps his hands together. "Now we're going to visit the energy department that works with some very exciting initiatives in..."

I pull Elliot aside the second we're out of the glass doors and duck into a side hallway. Wes is swept up into the crowd so he doesn't even notice.

"Look, I know you're probably still mad at me, and you have every right to be, but something happened and I don't know who else to tell." I lower my voice and see his almond eyes narrow in concern. "Alex called me last night."

He shakes his head. "What are you saying? Do you hear yourself?"

"I'm serious. It was him. The same way I was sure it was you. Something is going on, Elliot."

His lips pout into a deep frown, and gears turn behind his expression. From just around the corner, the sound of two people arguing catches our attention.

"Is that..." I peek out of the hall and, sure enough, Dean and Klara are up in arms in the nook of a doorway.

"For the last time, I didn't call you, Dean!" she snaps. "Do you want me to show you my call history?"

"Just because your dad pays for me to go to this school doesn't mean you have any right to my life," the boy hisses. "When I said I wanted you to leave me alone, I meant it. No more calls. Stop trying to get in my head."

"Hey, back off, man!" Elliot charges over and puts himself between Dean and Klara. Dean just laughs and shakes his unruly hair. "She isn't calling you, okay?"

"Oh yeah? Then what's this," he pulls out his phone and shows them the screen. Four missed calls from Klara.

Klara fumes. "That's not me. He's just trying to have some kind of dirt on me so he can—"

"Wait. Everyone, stop," I say. They look at me, and the hall goes silent. "These calls aren't from us. Klara, you swear you're not calling Dean. Elliot, you swear you're not calling me. And last night, I got a call from Alex."

"Alex?" Klara gulps. "But he's—"

"Dead, I know." I reach for Alex's phone in my backpack. "None of these calls are actually us, right? Here, look at this." I show them the screen of the boy's call history. "It says his last call was from me, the night before he died. There's another one from me the night he was admitted into the hospital. But I never called him, either of those times."

"Someone else is. Or something," Elliot murmurs.

"Well, fine. We can just track the calls. Right?" Klara fiddles with her earring. "I mean, even if it's under our names, if we talk to a phone company or something—"

"You realize how crazy that will sound. Right?" Dean leans back against one of the stark walls. "No, we need someone who could hack and trace the calls to their origin under the radar. Someone good with computers."

With a sudden twinge of dread, I sigh. "I might know someone like that."

* * *

"Wow, Jimmy, this is actually kind of creepy." Klara leans over the boy as he types. The four of us stand over him with an intense focus in the tiny computer lab and watch the door for employees. It's only a matter of time before someone from the tour realizes we're missing, but ironically that's not what gives me anxiety. The elephant in the room, the kiss that hangs in the air between us, makes my stomach churn.

"Yeah, um, good job. I guess." Elliot scratches his head, unsure how to interact with him.

Jimmy adjusts his glasses and murmurs to me. "Anything for nothing."

Heat rises up in my cheeks and I turn away. "Just trace the calls. Okay?"

Klara makes a face. "What's gotten into you two?"

"Nothing," we both respond synchronously.

"So," Dean breaks the tension and pulls out his flask from his coat. "They're all coming from the same source. Right?" He takes a swig, and everyone in the room stares.

"You're kidding me. Right? Literally all of our parents work in this building. Jesus Christ." Klara rolls her eyes.

"Hey, do not use the Lord's name in vain." He stashes his flask. "Have some respect for your boyfriend."

Before Elliot can pick a fight, Jimmy holds up a hand and his face lights up. He smiles to himself, that thin smile, and points to the screen. "I got it!" We all huddle in closer. I can smell the alcohol on Dean's breath and practically hear Elliot's heartbeat. "It looks like they're from the same location. It's up pretty far in the woods. Not the lab, though, it's from..." Then suddenly he frowns. "Klara, the calls are coming from your house."

We all turn to her, and the color drains from her face. And I don't even need to ask her because immediately I know what it is. The computer room in her house. I look around at the people who surround me, realizing we all have secrets and we all know different amounts of the truth. Together we're like some dysfunctional puzzle, too stubborn to be put together. Someone just needs to be the first to break.

"It's not... it can't be. That computer is just AI used for storing data. It doesn't even have any functions." Klara's cunning eyes spark, and I see her sift through her own mind for an explanation.

"What kind of information does it store? And why does your dad have it?" Jimmy asks.

Klara gets defensive as she senses an accusatory edge to our stares. "I don't know. It's not like I ever wanted to learn more about this messed-up Agent program. I think YouTech moves the equipment around to keep data in other locations, for security."

Elliot turns to his girlfriend. "If these calls are coming from that AI system, it's doing a lot more than just storing information. We have to shut it down, Klara."

"No way. My dad almost disowned me for messing with it that one time."

"Then we'll go together." I reach for the smooth edge of the button in my pocket. "We'll go to your house and shut it down. No more calls, no more YouTech machines screwing with us."

"As much as I hate to say it... she's right." Dean's mouth hangs open in a devilish grin. "Looks like our little team is taking another field trip."

CHAPTER 21

The car hums as it races through the woods and shudders with the weight of five bodies crammed inside.

"Right." Klara claps her hands from the backseat. "I'm just going to take this silence to, once again, express my unhappiness in this situation."

"If you wanted shotgun, you should have called it earlier." Dean shrugs. "It's not your fault your boyfriend wanted to be up front with Via so badly."

Elliot snarls, "Dean, if you don't shut up—"

"Not about that." Klara's eyebrows cut like knives. "Besides the fact that I'm stuck back here with your vodka breath, I'm now helping you all break into my home and destroy thousands of dollars of AI equipment. For which I will be blamed."

"It's not vodka, by the way. It's gin," Dean says. Klara groans and shoves him into the door.

"I want to go home," Jimmy whines on the other side of her.

"I don't care how much that computer costs. I'd love to take a baseball bat to the piece of shit." Elliot presses his forehead to the cold glass and stares out at the blur of trees with a troubled shadow behind his eyes. "If this AI really was calling Alex and messed with him before he died, I'll destroy it. If it's the reason he killed himself, I'll burn the whole lab to the ground."

My heart tears in two for the boy who doesn't know. I don't even have to look back at Jimmy to tell what he thinks. I can read his mind from here, and I feel the knowledge about Alex's true identity burn like a festering wound.

I pull off to the side of the gates to Klara's property, and the Subaru putters to a stop. I turn around, and with a deep breath I say, "Shut up. All of you. Elliot and Klara are going to distract her family while Jimmy and Dean go with me to sneak in through her bedroom. Jimmy will watch the security footage and tamper with it so there's no evidence of us being here. Dean and I will go and see if we can shut this thing down, and then we meet back at the car. Clearly none of us want to be here with each other, so let's just get this over with."

We pile out like a reluctant band and Klara unlocks the gates with a code. As they rattle and squeak open automatically, I feel Jimmy's stare on the back of my neck. I push away memories of the rain and the kiss, memories that take me back to Alex on the wet road and then to Wes's fearful eyes in the snowy headlights. Three different nights. They all blend together like one dreadful nightmare.

I stalk across the grass as Elliot jogs toward me. "Can I go with you? I want to talk about that call with Alex. Can you tell me what he said?"

Klara glances between Elliot and me, and I say, "No, go with your girlfriend. We can talk later."

"You heard her." Dean throws his arm around me. "She's already got company."

I see Elliot's neck bulge, and Jimmy clenches his jaw tight. I shove off Dean's arm, grab him by the collar of his long coat, and drag him away from them. "You. Just because we're doing this together doesn't mean we're friends. I'm still mad at you for that disgusting knife game."

"You know, this collar thing is really aggressive." He narrows his eyes. "I could be into it."

I let go of him with a huff and continue. I sneak along the edge of the gardens and maple trees, watching Elliot and Klara disappear around front. When I check the door to Klara's bedroom, it's unlocked like she promised. *No lock-picking this time. But there could still be a file cabinet somewhere.*

The last time I was in this bedroom, breaking in with Wes, seems like ages ago. I miss him deeply and suddenly, the way you listen to a song and it takes you back to a moment you forgot about until just then. I try to shake the feeling of last night's dream as I creep around the dark halls, listening to the sounds of Klara and Elliot talking to her father in a distant part of the sprawling house. Dean doesn't even try to be subtle. He saunters over each rug with his long coat flared out and taps on the walls and the decor that we pass.

Jimmy texts my phone. *I'm in the security closet. Going through all the camera footage now.*

I know the way to this room, the one at the end of the hall with the big double doors. I remember when I stumbled upon it, seeing the glowing lights of the computer in the dark and wondering what massive amounts of data that machine must've contained.

But when I crack open the doors and slip inside, it's empty. The whole room, everything except for a single small monitor.

"That's not possible," I breathe. "It was right here. I know it was."

"Klara's lying. I knew it." Dean swings in a circle and curses.

"No, she isn't. They must have moved it. Her dad must have moved it." I fumble with my phone and text Jimmy and

Klara rapidly. From another part of the house, I can hear voices drifting closer. Our distraction is almost up.

"Well, what now?" he breathes down on me as his piercing eyes search mine. "Use those superpowers, huh?"

Before I can snap at him for making a joke out of everything, I get a response from Jimmy. *Come to the security closet. Now.*

"I have to go get Jimmy. Wait here for Klara and Elliot and then meet us by the car." I leave a confounded Dean behind. He groans dramatically and I close the door on him. *What a diva. It's like he's trying to get me to snap.* My palms sweat and I have to hold a hand to my chest just to slow my breath. Someone could come around the corner any minute. I picture the intimidating image of Klara's father on the YouTech website.

Finally, I find the security closet, a small door off the main hall. It's away from all the bedrooms, so I don't risk running into any of Klara's brothers. Jimmy is inside the dark room, and in front of him spans countless monitors of live camera footage.

"Of course they have a security room. This place explains so much about Klara," I murmur and lean down over him. Then I realize how close we are and take a step back immediately.

"Um, here." He fidgets and gestures to the screen in front of him. "I erased the footage of us tonight, but look what I found from a couple days ago. It shows a bunch of YouTech guys coming in to move all the equipment. And right there. Do you see that?"

I squint, and sure enough there's that round belly and lumberjack beard I could never mistake. He stands in the room with Klara's father, directing people with his sausage fingers.

"Principal Conners," I breathe. "Does that mean YouTech is keeping it at the school?"

"There's also something else." He pulls up another camera footage. I don't recognize the date, it's some night right before Christmas. It's the camera footage of Klara's back door and the gardens, and out of it sneaks a lanky boy with waves of blonde highlighted hair. "That's Wes. Right?"

"That's the night he left my house. Why would he be… they hate each other." My pulse pounds in my ears, and too many thoughts swirl in my brain. "None of this makes any sense. What if they know something we don't? What if they're investigating something together behind my back? Do they have something to do with the AI being moved?"

Jimmy stands and faces me with serious eyes. "You know what else they could've been doing?"

I swallow with a rock in my throat and shake my head. "No, Klara is dating Elliot. And I know Wes. They would never."

"Strong emotions make you do crazy things, Via. Why is it so impossible for you to think people our age can't feel that way? Not everything has to be rational and logical."

"Some things do, Jimmy. Some things have to be explained, like why your brother was an Agent and yet you knew him your whole life. Don't you think that's strange?"

"Via, don't talk about my brother," he warns.

"And what about Alex? You saw what happened to him, and after everything with these phone calls and the glitch, you know it's more than just suicide. You did it before and you're doing it again. You let your emotions take over, and you had a chance to save Alex but you didn't. You knew he was an Agent and you did nothing. And neither did I, but this time we have a chance to do something!"

Right when I say this, I see Jimmy retreat into his collar. I turn around and there, at the doorway to the security closet, is Elliot. He stares at both of us with vacant eyes, a look of numb disbelief from under long strands of hair.

"Elliot, wait—" but he's already gone. He storms out and I feel panic rise in my gut so fast I could puke. I whip around the corner to follow him, but as soon as I'm out in the hall, I hear the sound of Klara's stepmom. I freeze up and my feet trip over each other to scramble in the other direction. Jimmy sprints after me with a terrified whimper. Shouts of surprise erupt behind us.

We take refuge back in what used to be the computer room, and Dean is startled to see us.

"We're gonna get caught. We're gonna get sent to jail." Jimmy hyperventilates. "Oh man, what if we get expelled?"

Dean glances around and then chuckles with a devilish glint in his eyes. "I got this. Get out of here." Then to himself, "Let's see how much I can get away with."

Before I can question what his plan is, he busts out of the double doors and calls the name "Charles Brooks!" at the top of his lungs. *He must have a death wish.* I push Jimmy ahead of me and we slip out the back exit. I take one last glance at the door and then run off through the gardens while every muscle and organ in my body scream at me that I'm alive.

* * *

It's a Friday night—the first basketball game of the new year to kick off the season—and nobody has seen Elliot anywhere.

"This is ridiculous. Mr. Perfect has never missed a game." Ben kicks one of the lockers in the hall dejectedly. "I made a sign for him and everything."

"It's true. We need him to keep his reputation. He brings up our group average." Cole trails us while he games.

"I'm sure he's fine. You saw him after the field trip. Right? Didn't you guys and Klara bail together?" Wes glances over at me. All I can think about is him sneaking out of Klara's room. Words get tangled in my throat, and I don't know how to explain the bomb I dropped on Elliot the other day.

"Ah yes, Olivia Prescott, everybody. The ultimate third wheel," Ben teases. I don't laugh. My eyes scan the bustle of students in the halls as we wander toward the gymnasium.

Just when we pass the double doors into the game, a deafening roar sounds like the belly of a beast. Right inside I see Klara with Sydney and some of the girls, and I swear her eyebrows look even darker than they've ever been.

"Hold on, guys. I'll catch up with you in a minute." Wes splits off, and my heart sinks. He and Klara disappear behind the bleachers, but right before they do, she looks back at me with a bitter glare. *Wait, is she getting close with Wes just to spite me?*

That's when I hear the jolly chime of Principal Conners's voice from behind me, and something triggers. Ben and Cole go into the game, but I spin around and chase that stout man with ferocity.

"Principal Conners. Principal!" I stop him. He greets me with an exuberant, warm smile. "That AI system at Charles Brooks's house. It's dangerous. I know you moved it, but you need to know that something is wrong with its programming. I think YouTech Labs is working on something else, not just Agents, and they're not telling anyone."

"I'm sorry, I don't know what you're talking about." He laces his fingers over his bulging belly.

"The computer, the one with all that data from YouTech. It's been calling some of your students with other people's voices. I think it may have something to do with Alex's death.

You need to shut it down. It could seriously psychologically damage someone else."

"I love your imagination, Olivia. Does this have to do with research for your ESP project?" He blinks at me.

It's like my mind blows a fuse. *I can't believe him.* "You know what I'm talking about. People are in danger. I'm serious. I'll go straight to YouTech if I have to."

"I wouldn't waste your time with that," his voice lilts. "You see, the computer you're referring to holds information on all our students. That data is very important to the simulation. We need it to track all of our variables and possible risks to the program." He strokes his beard, and in that instant, I see something in his eyes I've never seen before. "It's one thing to watch you blossom in our school environment, but it wouldn't be an effective test if we didn't monitor everything that goes on outside of these walls. Just like in your science labs in class, we need a controlled experiment. That's all. And we would hate for that information to end up in the wrong hands. Now wouldn't we?"

A terrifying, icy fear grips my spine. It wraps its claws around my chest and squeezes so hard I lose my breath.

"It would be hard for you to continue your studies here if the wrong information got out. I would hate to imagine what your peers would think if they saw what happened with you and Alex out on the road. Or for your parents to lose their jobs because of your affinity for breaking and entering. But that's our priority at this school. We bring in students like you and Wes because we're controlling our variables. I would hate for all that to go to waste. Do you understand what I'm saying?"

I nod, my blood gone cold. "Yes."

"Now, go enjoy the game! I just saw your friend Elliot run out onto the court." Principal Conners winks and strolls away, humming a happy tune to himself.

I head into the gym with a sick wrench in my stomach, like I'm about to throw up. The clanging bleachers and blare of the buzzer drown out all my thoughts. In a dizzying haze, I snake along the side of the court with the game in full force. But then it takes a sudden turn and moves right under the basket next to me. I stumble back a few steps into the wall as the bodies of the players wrestle toward the hoop. And before I recognize what happens with my own eyes, I hear the crowd. Both sides gasp, as if the air was suddenly vacuumed out of the gym. The movement stops with a whistle. A small clump of players gathers around one boy who's collapsed on the ground.

Elliot clutches his arm and the whole world watches.

I press my back against the wall as a coach and trainer run out onto the court. The trainer kneels down and inspects Elliot, and I don't breathe. They ask him a series of questions.

"Where does it hurt?"

"Can you move it?"

Elliot doesn't respond. He just stares down at his arm and holds it with his eyebrows furrowed and lips pouted. The trainer reaches over and touches it a little, moves it, rotates it. That same numb expression fills his eyes, the same as when he found out his best friend was an Agent.

"It's not broken. Maybe slight bruising but nothing serious," the trainer says.

And then, I see it. His hand starts to shake. He grabs his wrist with his opposite hand as if to try and stop it. *Oh no,* my blood pounds in my ears. *Not this.*

The coach bends down to talk to him, but Elliot doesn't seem to hear anything. He gets up slowly, still holding his arm to stop it from betraying him. He looks around at the crowd, the other players, and then back down. That's when he rushes off the court. He heads for the locker rooms and disappears while the whole gym observes. Without hesitation, I follow him.

"Elliot!" I burst into the hall, frantically chasing him down the linoleum tiles. I hear the door to the locker room slam. Around the sharp corner I whip it back open and stride into the boys' locker room as if I'm trying to keep up with him on our hike in the woods.

"Elliot, what the hell!" My chest heaves. "Why did you—"

I stop when my eyes settle on him. He's hunched over one of the sinks. His sweat glistens in the bathroom light. His long hair hangs down in front of his face, and through the long strands he stares at the mirror. He breathes in slowly, deep gulps of the sweat-drenched air. With white knuckles he clutches the sides of the sink.

"Are you okay?" I step forward hesitantly.

He rises from the sink, and I notice that his hand trembles again. He looks up at me with scared eyes.

"Elliot, listen, it's okay. You just hurt your arm. You fell pretty badly on it. Of course it's going to be shaking. It's just going through some shock."

"No," he growls. "No, you're lying. Stop lying to me."

"I'm not lying to you. I'm just trying to help."

"You knew about Alex. You watched me talk about him and you lied to my—" he curses and slaps his hand. "This isn't happening. This isn't real." Then louder, "Why won't it stop shaking?"

"I'm sorry, just—"

Suddenly, he roars and slams his fist into the locker on his right. I flinch. He does it again, and again, like the metal is just another punching bag in the weight room.

"Elliot, stop!" I scream, but the whole locker room bangs as he smashes his fist against the doors. I get a hold of one of his shoulders and try to rip him away.

"Let go of me!" I see his next few punches change from rage into desperation until he's just like a broken machine. He falls against the metal. "It won't... I can't..." He stumbles back from the lockers and stares at his hand. Blood paints his deformed knuckles and drips slowly to his elbows. His whole body shudders now.

"Hey." I step closer to him. "You're okay." With one hand I hold onto his shoulder, and with the other I gently grab his bleeding, shaking arm. As I do this he falls onto the lockers and presses his head into the dented metal.

"Something is wrong with me," he says through tear-stained cheeks. "I'm like Alex. It's just like Alex."

"Hey, nothing's wrong with you." My head spins. "Remember your church? Everything's going to be alright. All of this is happening for a reason. You just have to be patient. Right? You have to trust. You have to have faith."

"I can't." He gasps for air every time he inhales. His exhales are just as heavy, suffocating almost.

"You can. Do you trust me?"

He cries, his whole body racked with sobs. "I trusted Alex."

Just then, the door to the locker room swings open.

"Elliot?" Klara walks in and freezes. I let go of Elliot and slide away from him. Klara sees the blood on the lockers and then the blood that stains his white basketball jersey. She sees my hands, now covered in his blood as well. Before she can say anything, Elliot climbs to his feet. He runs a bloody hand through his hair and then walks out. His cheeks are still wet with tears.

Now it's just me and Klara. My eyes search hers, but I can't tell what she thinks.

"I was just trying to help."

After a few seconds of silence, she just lets out an exasperated laugh. "Yeah, well, you always are."

"Klara, wait—" but she's already gone.

CHAPTER 22

My car pulls up to the YouTech headquarters while the sun is high. The building looks out of place against all the frozen maple trees and the dense forest, just a wet concrete block with glass slits for eyes. My fingers drum on the dashboard. *Dad will kill me when he finds out I skipped school on a Tuesday. And here I am, at his workplace.*

I pull out my new phone and stare at its screen as if I dare the AI to call me again. When I open up social media, it's filled with pictures of Friday night's game, rumors and jokes about Elliot being the Agent. This has been a hellish week for him already, made worse by the fact that Klara dumped him. Neither of them will talk to me, and I don't blame them.

I almost slip as I cross the road. My heart races as I approach the glass doors. I don't even know if Mr. Richards will be here today, but I just hope I don't run into my dad in the lab where he does software development proofs. *Or at least, I think that's what he does.*

I notice a keycard scanner on the side wall, but the heavy door is unlocked when I try it. I step inside, my cheeks still tingling from the cold. The woman at the security desk glances up as I approach.

"Hi, can I help you?"

"Um, yes." I'm unnerved by this whole place, but I need answers. "I'm looking for Stephen Richards?"

"He may still be in his office. Let me check." She picks up a phone and dials for him. "Name?"

"Olivia Prescott."

As she calls, I flip the button in my pocket between my fingers. I'm calmed by the rhythm. It's the only thing that keeps me sane during waking hours. It keeps away the other memories and sensations.

"You're in luck. He's still here." The woman stands up. "He seemed a little surprised to hear from you. I'm guessing you don't have an appointment?"

"No, but it's important." I follow her down the left hall as our footsteps echo on the floor.

As we pass too many doors to count, I notice something I didn't catch on the school tour. Some doors have keycard scanners just like the front door. *It makes sense if you have something to hide.* Finally, we stop at a framed glass panel and the woman knocks. Mr. Richards opens up, and his beady eyes assess me as I enter.

"I'm surprised to see you here, Olivia. I was not expecting this. Welcome to my real office, although I don't usually hold meetings in here." He gestures to the cramped space, which is rather scarce with only a few devices and a single framed photo on the wall. The photo evokes a smile from me.

"The Balancer?" I point.

"I'm afraid so," he grunts, slightly embarrassed. "You know him?"

"Sort of. I kind of relate to him these days." My foot taps on the floor as I sit down.

"Well, yes. So do I, interestingly enough. When I was in college, I discovered these comic books, and something about The Balancer's whole mantra resonated with me. The sacrifices he makes for the greater good, blurring the line between life and death."

I pinch the button in my pocket and gather the courage to look him dead in the eyes. "Is that what you're doing with the Agents? With Oscar and Alex? Are their deaths worth it?"

The man folds his hands together and studies me with an expression I can't read.

I flip the button in my hand a few more times. "I'm not as easy to fool as everyone else."

"I am fully aware." Mr. Richards nods with a faint laugh.

"Did you know about the AI in Charles Brooks's house? Did you know it keeps information and data on all of us?" I swallow hard. "I'm sure you know this already, but something is wrong with it. It's been calling people, using my friends' voices. Using Alex's voice."

"Hmm," he raises an eyebrow. "Someone must have tampered with it. That's probably why Brooks moved it to the school."

"So you admit you're watching us? You admit you're collecting information on all of us, without our knowledge, and using it for other projects? What else do you experiment on besides the Agents? Where do you draw the line?"

Under my attack, he doesn't flinch. "That's the point of YouTech. We're trying to blur the lines between technology and our lives so there is no difference anymore. Why do you care so much if we have information about you when your information is already everywhere?"

"Because," even though I don't want it to, my voice cracks, "I am so sick and tired of being treated like an experiment. Not just by you, but by my parents, and my teachers, and the whole world. It feels like everything I do is being watched and judged by people who have some kind of stake in what I become. And I'm doing my best. I really am. But I don't know what you want from me. I'm trying so hard to pass everyone's test, but I don't know what I'm even trying to prove anymore."

Mr. Richards just stares at me with his deep-set eyes.

I laugh and tug at my sleeves. "I know. High school must seem dumb to you. This all probably seems trivial—the relationship drama, the fights at parties, and the angst you have to watch us go through. And it definitely is just a lot of bullshit. We'll probably go to college and we'll grow out of it." I run my finger along the four notches. "But for now, can you just… let us have it? Please? It's how we process the world, and it doesn't help when you mess with us when we're already confused. What we preoccupy ourselves with may seem superficial and pointless, but we're trying to make sense of things on our own here. It's not like any of you tell us anything important. You just give us the rules of the game, set these ridiculously high standards, and then it's our fault if we can't handle them. If Alex killed himself because he didn't like who he was as an Agent, is that his fault?"

"No, it's not," he says after a long pause. *Maybe he wonders how I know about all this. Or maybe he's not surprised but wanted me to know the whole time.* "It's my fault for letting the glitch get out of hand. I didn't account for all the variables. If it were up to me, nobody would even know about the simulation."

"But that's just hiding the truth from everyone. That's not right. We deserve to know."

"Can you handle it? The truth? Because in my experience most people can't." He leans forward. "And after what you've told me, I don't think you can."

"I didn't expect you to tell me anything when I came here. I know I'm just another insignificant variable in your simulation." I stand from the chair. "It's just that lately there are all these patterns. I like math. I'm good at spotting patterns. And I keep seeing things like they're repeating themselves over and over in my head, but I can't figure out how they're all related. I don't know. Maybe it's all just unrelated."

"I'm sorry I can't tell you more. It's for your own good. But I will tell you one thing." He stands up so he towers above me. "I believe there is no such thing as coincidence."

When I leave the office, his words echo in my head. I hurry down the monochrome hallway, and like the buzz of the fluorescent lights, something buzzes in my head like a migraine. A sensation, a strong swell of images, pushes to the forefront. I pass the security woman in haste and dive back out into the cold air of the parking lot. My vision is blurred with images of my body bleeding out on the asphalt and someone kneeling over me as I lie on the ground. A feeling of cold, lonely depths. I can't remember if any of this is from my memory of the Incident or just a dream.

Suddenly as I drift out onto the road from the parking lot, I hear a voice call my name. I'm jolted out of my head, only to find Dean wander out in the snow.

"What are you doing out here?" His tongue plays on the inside of his cheek. "At my house, really? Shouldn't you be at school?"

"I forgot you live on this road." Only now do I realize the quaint cottage tucked away in the forest. I shake my head and push away images of hospitals and my parents' faces.

He clicks his tongue. "Can I just make an observation?"

"Nobody asked."

"Okay, then a question."

"No."

He steps closer to me, and the cold wind buffets his unkempt hair. "What's your role in all of this? I mean, are you for real with the whole mind powers thing, your holier-than-thou truth mission? I can't figure you out."

"Why do you need to figure me out? I'm not playing some role."

"Sure you are." He takes out his flask and drinks from it. "Everyone is. It's not a bad thing. It's just a fact."

"Oh, is it?"

"Yes, it is. That's what I realized when I so bravely sacrificed myself for all of you at Klara's house. Hence, why I'm on probation with the school." He points his flask to me. "You're welcome, by the way."

"So what did you realize? Nothing is real and it's all pointless?" I cross my arms and feel the chill ebb away.

"Think about it this way." He clicks his tongue. "We've all been to an art museum. Right? But be honest. Do you ever go because you appreciate fine art? Do you really go in there to be enlightened by the paintings, to understand the deeper meanings behind each stroke? No, you just end up standing in front of each painting like an idiot, wondering how long you should stand there before it's considered fully appreciated. Most of the time you're not even looking at the art. It just provides a backdrop for you to think about other stuff."

"But you still go because you want to try."

"Exactly. You go because you want to be that sophisticated person who appreciates fine art. Even though that's not actually you, and it's not real, you still try. So it doesn't matter if everything is fake."

I think about my parents and all the art in our house. "So there's nothing real about your life?"

He sits there for a moment and thinks. Then he turns back to the small cottage next to the parking lot and tilts his head up to stare at it.

"My house burnt down in a fire when I was twelve," he says. "That was real."

Suddenly the whole world seems sober. The pale woods, his cottage without any lights on, it's all so empty. I try to think about my old house. About Josh. About our old rooms. But all I see is my dreams of fire and death. I want to tell him, *I know. I've seen it. I've lived it.*

"Nothing after that seems quite as real. You know?" He brings his flask up to his lips, and it lingers there.

I have never understood Dean, but in this moment, I feel like we share the same brain. Because nothing seems real after the Incident in January, not really. This could all be one weird dream, the program, the Agents, all of it. And one day I'll wake up from it, for real.

"So, these visions of yours." He shoves his hands in the pockets of his coat. "When did they start?"

"Why?" I ask, but then I press my mind and think back. *When did I have that first dream? That first sensation that I was seeing something that had already happened?*

"I guess it doesn't matter. But if you know what triggered it, you may understand it better." He shrugs. Then he wanders back into his cottage and sways a little as he walks.

And that's when something clicks. I do remember. I was playing Immortal Soldiers with Wes before I even got to Park Falls Technical High School, and that's when I remembered the dream. The video game triggered my memory.

Then a cold chill shivers down my spine, and I hear Mr. Richards's words echo in my head. *There is no such thing as coincidence.* With a start, I turn back down the road to my car.

I have to go see someone.

* * *

"Via, what are you doing here?" Wes looks confused as he meets me out in his front lawn.

"The game, Immortal Soldiers." I approach him. Memories of his face illuminated by headlights flood my head, and I can barely focus on him in this moment. "When did we start playing that game?"

"Is this why you drove all the way out here?"

"Wes. Where did we get that game from?"

"I got it for you when you were in the hospital." He shifts on his feet. "We started it when you came out of surgery."

My mind whirls, and my heartbeat quickens. "Why did we start playing? Every Sunday, the same thing, for almost a year. We never did anything else but play that game. Did you set that up on purpose?"

He scratches his head. "What is this about, Via? I don't understand."

"And Klara. She's been there from the beginning. I know you guys are secretly meeting up. I know there's something going on. Are you two part of the test?"

Wes laughs and rolls his head back at the sound of her name. "Is an elaborate conspiracy theory the only explanation for her wanting to hang out with me? What if we're hooking up? You don't know that."

"If that was true, it would be even more disturbing. She would just be doing it to get back at me because she thinks I stole Elliot from her or something. You said it yourself all the time. You can't trust her."

Wes shakes his head. "This is so typical. Not everything is about you, Via. This whole world wasn't made to revolve around you."

"Revolve around me?" I scoff. "Come on, Wes. Our entire childhood was dealing with you and your problems. Everything was always about being careful around you, making sure you were okay, making sure you didn't relapse. Why do you think I followed you onto the road last January?"

Wes glances back at his house. "Can you lower your voice, please?"

"What? Are you scared your parents are going to hear? That they're going to find out that you were the reason I was put in the hospital for a week?"

"Via, I don't understand. Why is this coming out now?" He comes closer to me with a concerned shadow. "Let's go for a drive or something. Okay? Clear your head a little."

"My head is perfectly fine."

"Well it's obviously not, because you don't seem to remember what actually happened that night."

"I know what happened, Wes. You did the same thing you always do. You tell everyone you're fine, and that you're done with all that, and then you end up in therapy. Or worse. All I've ever done is worry about you, and you just keep telling me you're fine. This is why both our parents are constantly worried and smothering us, because of you."

"Oh my god. That's it. I'm done with this," he snaps. "They were never worried about me. They were worried about you! You're so busy trying to find out what's wrong with everyone else, you're so convinced that everyone else needs fixing. You're fooling yourself, Via. It's just you."

I'm surprised by the sound of his voice, like a tidal wave of emotion he's been holding back.

"You were the one who went onto the road that night, Via. You were never happy in school. You never let yourself get close to anyone else besides me. And when you were having an episode, I was the one who had to go find you and talk you down. You want to know why I see a shrink, why I started cutting? Because of the trauma of seeing my best friend get hit by a car and almost die. For God's sake, you're the reason my family comes over to dinner every Sunday night!"

"What?" My brain can't process what he says. Not after everything with Mr. Richards, not with all the images in my head.

"Those Sundays *are* my therapy, Via. Playing Immortal Soldiers with you is what my psychologist prescribed so I could keep you in my life. That month after the Incident, I couldn't even look at you. I even tried to end things because I couldn't handle it anymore."

I stare blankly at my friend. "You're lying. I don't believe you."

"And this whole superpowers thing? You're not saving anyone, Via. You're just hurting them. People just end up in hospitals because of you. Look at Elliot. Look what he did to his hand in that locker room." Wes kicks the dirt. "But obviously your memories are warped, and it's easier to blame me than accept the fact that there's something wrong with you."

He sets his jaw and stalks back toward his house. My whole world shakes, and I'm left with nothing but fear in my whole body. I'm scared and suddenly so alone. That's real.

CHAPTER 23

"What are you reading?"

My mom approaches me in the kitchen, and I close my laptop screen. I don't want her to see all the news headlines I have pulled up on my browser: the car crash in January, Oscar Andrade's body found in a lake, Alex Brockman's suicide. And most recently, the Wallace family's house fire.

"Nothing, just schoolwork."

"On a Friday night? Well, Josh was telling me about all the homework he has on the drive to hockey. Apparently, he disagrees with everything the school is teaching him. He says it's all pointless, which you know, is great for a mother to hear." She sits down at the kitchen table next to me.

"If you're going to ask me to tutor him again—"

"I'm not," she says. "You seem really stressed lately. Want to take a break and watch something with me?"

"No, I'm fine."

"I haven't seen any of your friends around here in a while, like Wes and Klara. I was just curious." I don't respond. "Are you hanging out with the boys more, like Jimmy? Or how about Elliot?"

"Wes has more important things to do recently," I say. I didn't even recognize him the last time we fought. I couldn't stand to see Elliot the way he was in the locker rooms. Klara's face of betrayal was more terrifying than any attack of her eyebrows. And now I can't even look at Jimmy without feeling crushing guilt.

"It's second semester senior year. You can't expect him to be at every family dinner like Josh and Danielle. It could just be a very busy time for him. For everyone."

"But it's like I don't even know him anymore." I tug at my sleeves.

"People are allowed to change, honey. You've certainly changed a lot this year."

"If you bring up the hospital, I think I might scream."

"That's not what I meant." My mom gives me a sympathetic look, which makes me even more angry for some reason. "You're so defensive lately."

"Maybe it's because dad won't leave me alone. He grounded me for missing one day of school. It's like he's still trying to punish me for the Incident."

Her voice wilts like a rose. "He doesn't want to punish you. He wants to protect you. He just has a very controlling way of doing it. You know your father. He doesn't even listen to the radio because he doesn't like other people choosing music for him."

This makes me laugh a little, but it's a tired laugh.

She walks around the table and faces me, so close I can smell her scent of honey. "You may not remember this, but when you were little, you used to come home from school every day and read with him on the couch."

"I know. He loves to remind me."

"He brings it up because you loved reading, and you loved when he would read to you. He thought that would be your guys' thing forever. But then you got older, and things changed. Now you want to spend time with your friends and go to parties, be in your room on your computer, and you don't want to sit and read with your dad anymore. You're choosing your colleges based on greek life instead of academic programs, and you would rather watch reality TV instead of documentaries."

I look down at my hands and turn the button in my palm.

"Just because you're a different person than he expected you to be doesn't mean he doesn't like who you are. As hard as parents try to raise their kids in a certain way, you always take on a life of your own. We can't control who you turn out to be. And that frustrates your father because he's always used to being in control of everything."

I picture his glasses that sit on the coffee table by the reading lamp. Vividly I picture his stern expression set in stone, the hardened lines of his face.

"I know you don't want me to bring it up, and I can't make you go to therapy anymore. But you can't just ignore what happened last January. You don't want to admit it, but being in the hospital did change you." My mom with her beautiful golden hair holds my hand. "It's okay that you're not who you thought you'd be."

My chest tightens, and I pull my hand away from hers. "I need to go somewhere, actually."

* * *

Why am I here? What am I doing?

I stand in front of the lake house, my feet rooted in the snow. I go over in my head for the millionth time why I should turn around and get back in my car. I tried to fight it. I tried to stay away, but I keep finding myself back here.

After everything my mom said, maybe I just feel lost. *Maybe I can get back to myself somehow.*

I take a deep breath and step up to the door. The frozen air bites the back of my throat.

"Oh, Via. You're here." Sydney is surprised to see me when I walk in, but not the good kind of surprised. She steps away from her group of drunken friends in the entryway and glances around nervously.

"I want to get drunk."

She almost spits out her drink. "I'm sorry, what?"

"I want to drink," I say with conviction. I'm about to crouch down and take off my shoes, but then I stop. *You know what? Maybe I won't this time.*

"Um, okay. Are you sure?" She leads me through the maze of log walls. I notice people's eyes follow me where I go, and the hush of my name leaves the lips of every whispering circle. "Let's go to the kitchen, though, you might not want to—"

Suddenly, I halt. Sydney tries to usher me into the kitchen hastily, but it's too late. I've already seen it. Klara leans against the makeshift pong table, and Wes stands beside her.

"You've got to be kidding me," I breathe.

Klara's eyes flicker up to mine, and her eyebrows attack me from across the entire house. My blood boils, and although Sydney tries to stop me, I march through the party over to where they stand.

"Hi, Via. Funny seeing you here." She gives me a small wave.

I ignore her and turn to Wes. "What the hell?"

"Klara invited me. I don't always have to follow you around." He shrugs.

"So what? Are you two together now?" I snap.

"Wait, who's together?" a voice says from behind us, and I spin around to see Elliot. His features darken with shadows, and I can't help but drop my gaze to his swollen and bandaged right hand. Around us, I hear kids whisper, "That's the new kid," and "...the Agent."

"Maybe we are together. It's none of your business." Klara flicks her ponytail.

"Oh boy, this is going to be fun," another voice chimes in from above. I realize that it's Dean, who hovers at the top of the staircase and looks down from the wooden beams of the rafters.

I can't believe this is happening. Sweat builds on the back of my neck. Wes ignores me even though I try to get his attention, and I remember everything he said to me like a knife in my gut. *This can't be happening. I'm too sober for this.*

As if reading my mind, Sydney pipes up from the corner. "Shots?"

"Please." I glance up and see Dean watch me with intensity.

"Same," Klara says.

"I'll do shots." Wes shoves by me.

Sydney is shocked. "New kid too?"

"That makes five of us." Elliot steps in and faces Wes with a fiery rage. My head whirls, and I push back a flood of images that I can't make sense of anymore. *I need something to drown it all out.* I can still feel Dean's stare locked onto me. As Sydney goes to get alcohol from the table, the whole party moves in closer to watch the drama unfold. I pull Wes to the side so it's just us.

"You're unbelievable. You know that?" I hiss.

"Oh yeah?"

"You don't even like shots!"

"You don't know that."

"You threw up taking apple vinegar shots at our Thanksgiving party," I whisper. "I know you."

"You don't know anything about me, Via. Worry about yourself."

I gesture to Klara, who fills up her shot. "You know she's just using you. She doesn't even like you. If she did, she would do something to stop all the rumors."

"I don't see you trying to stop them."

"I hope Elliot beats the crap out of you."

"What is wrong with you, Via?" he lowers his voice. "You seriously need help. You're completely delusional!"

Someone hands each of us a solo cup, and I move away from Wes. Sydney hesitantly raises her cup to the group. "Cheers?"

"Cheers." Klara shoots me a glare. "To friends who always have your back."

My face flushes, and I throw back the alcohol. Out of the corner of my eye, I see Dean disappear up the staircase. Next to me Klara pounds her shot. Then as the whole party watches, she puts her arm around Wes in one swift, purposeful movement. That does it for Elliot. The boy doesn't hesitate to throw his shot of alcohol on Wes, and everyone in the entire cabin erupts into chaos.

"Elliot, stop!" I pull him back before he does anything else to Wes.

"Don't touch me." He pushes me away. "You've done enough, Via."

I recoil from him. The insult stings like a cut.

"Hey, what's all this about?" Max breaks up the commotion, and the noise dies down. His friendly drunk disposition turns to disappointment as he takes in the scene. He points at Elliot. "You. Don't go around starting fights, not when your hand is in a cast, you moron." He turns to Wes. "I'm gonna be real. I don't even know who you are. Aren't you the Agent or something?"

"I'm Wes. I'm new."

"Don't care. And Dean." He points up at the boy on the staircase. "Chad will murder you if he sees you. You're not even invited to these things. Make yourself useful and go get more cups."

Dean shakes his head and locks eyes with me one more time before he disappears into the house.

That's when Max turns to me. "Via, you should probably go home."

I'm shocked by this insult from the guy who was always trying to get me to come to these parties. "Me?"

"Everyone kind of knows this is your fault." He shrugs. "I think it would be better if you left."

I can't believe this. Am I really delusional? Is this actually all my fault? My eyes search the faces of everyone in the house, looking for some kind of explanation, but they all just stare at me like I'm some kind of science experiment. The same kids who are always here. The same exact group of people every week. Now they soak up my every movement and every word with hungry eyes. The same house, with its soaring wooden beams and walls of polished cedar. It holds in all the heat and the tension like a suffocating trap. The same party every week, nothing ever changes, but now I seem to be the one variable. *Am I being tested?*

I laugh suddenly. "Oh my god, I get it."

"Via, I'm sorry, just—"

"Don't you get it? They're watching us." I laugh. "Has anyone actually seen Chad at these things? Where is he? Where are his parents?"

"Via," Wes gives me a warning look.

"This is all a test. Everything is part of the simulation." I shake my head. "I don't know why I didn't see it before, but it's obvious. This is just another experiment, another way to watch us and test us. And we fell for it."

"Please, you sound insane," Elliot says as he holds his damaged hand.

I look around at my friends, and none of them do anything. They just stare at me, unblinking, like the rest of them. I feel as alone as I was on the road that night, the night of the Incident, blinded by the oncoming headlights.

And then, out of nowhere, a hulking boy steps in front of me. A hush falls over the cabin.

Max scratches his head sheepishly. "Chad, don't—"

Chad stops his friend. His cool intimidation holds the whole room captive. With one swift motion, he points to the door.

"Get out."

I'm rooted in my spot, and my mind spins in circles as I try to find some way to explain. *They don't believe me. Why can't everyone see it?* Nobody does anything. My cheeks burn red from embarrassment and shame.

"Whoa, big guy. Why don't we take a step back?" Dean swoops down from the staircase suddenly and inserts himself between me and Chad with a drunken stumble. "Let's not do anything reckless."

"Give me one reason," Chad challenges.

"Well, let me think..." Dean pauses and waits for something. And there it is. Blinding blue and red lights flash through the windows of the cabin followed by the wail of sirens.

Chad's eyes widen. "You called the cops?"

"Oh, my bad. Max, did you say get more cups? I swear I heard call the cops." His mouth hangs open in a devilish grin. "Whoops."

Kids disperse all over the cabin, leaving cups and friends behind to jump ship as fast as they can. I watch as people scramble for the exits and plunge out into the frigid air. The night swallows them up without jackets, some of them from the bedrooms without clothes. Drunk bodies disappear over the outside porch as the sirens get louder. In the panic of the moment I'm rooted to my spot.

The blue and red lights take me back to January. A distinct memory. Those same lights flickering on the cold pavement as I'm lying there amidst broken glass. The blur of paramedics around me, my shuddering eyes watching the ice melt underneath the warm touch of dark blood.

"Let's go!" Dean grabs my hand suddenly, and I'm snapped back to the present. Now we run. He pulls me outside into the night, and together we hurtle the wooden railing of the porch. Under the pale glow of the moonlight, my heart beats wildly. We leave the cabin behind and fling ourselves through mounds of uneven snow. Dozens of kids are scattered to the woods and bounce like shadows in the flashing police lights. We split through the trees like a flock of sheep being chased by wolves, kept in motion only by the fiery buzz of the party that lingers in our chests.

Ah, the joys of underage drinking.

Only when the cabin is a faint glow behind us do my legs scream for rest, and I fall against a tree. My hands press into the bark. Right in front of me stretches the frozen lake, the glow of the party a mere reflection on the ice.

"Come on, one-shot-wonder. I know you're not that drunk." Dean's silhouette stands out against the glossy surface of the lake.

"You think I'm crazy. Don't you?"

Sirens echo from the road in the distance. "I just called the cops to bust a party I'm drunk at, when I'm already on probation with the school. Crazy is relative."

I catch my breath for a moment and let the cold sink into my bones. "You know, you say everything is fake and you don't care, that you've given up. But I don't believe you," I say. "Why else would you keep coming back to these parties?"

He steps away from the edge of the lake and picks his footsteps carefully. "Why do you keep coming?"

"I don't know. Still searching for something, I guess."

He's so close now, I can see the moonlight glint off of his eyes. I hear shouts in the distance, the sound of officers prowling the woods.

"I envy you," Dean says. "You're a better me."

"What does that mean?"

He opens his mouth to say something, but his voice catches and he stops. He chuckles to himself and shakes his head. "Never mind." He glances up at the sky, and his neck cranes to see the stars. "I don't need to say it. I'll just think it."

My eyes trace his silhouette. From his mouth, to his collarbone, to his fingers and back. *I'm tired of thinking.*

I close the distance between us in two slow steps. He takes me in with piercing eyes and I pull down the collar of that stupid long coat. I push away the cold and I kiss him. His hands find my arms, then my neck, and then my hair. He kisses me the way that he talks. I can feel his height in his arched back. I can taste the words on his tongue. I inhale the sincerity in each breath he takes.

And then, he lets go. Gently. He lets go and takes a step back so he floats on the glass of the lake.

"What was that for?" he breathes.

The image of him, balanced on the ghostly ice in the wake of the moon, is surreal. But my heart races like I just plummeted into frigid water, and the taste of him is still warm on my lips. That's real.

A swarm of crisscrossing flashlight beams cut through the forest suddenly, and the officers are close behind. They tear through the snow and soak the trees with pale light, but Dean doesn't move. He just looks at me like he would his own reflection.

So there we stay, frozen in time, and let the wolves descend.

CHAPTER 24

The police station in Park Falls is small, and honestly, I never thought I would end up here with only a few months left of high school. The hours tick by under the sobering fluorescent lights of the station. The events of the night start to feel more and more like a fever dream. *As does most of my life at this point.* We await our verdict from the officers who discuss it in an office on the other side of the station.

I know I should be worried about how my father will kill me for never coming home last night, or what's going to happen if the police decide to file charges for drinking, but all I can think about is the irony of the situation. The only kids taken into custody from the party were me, Elliot, Klara, Wes, and Dean.

Klara breaks the silence. "I guess I'll be the one to say it. Dean, you're a douchebag."

"Thanks, but I'm sure Daddy will bail you out on this one." He scrunches his nose. Then he looks over to me for a reaction, but I avoid eye contact. I concentrate on a crack in the tile floor instead.

"What is wrong with you, Dean?" she presses. "For once in your life, can you just take responsibility and admit that this is all your fault?"

"Oh, we're admitting things now? How about the fact that Via and Jimmy knew about Alex and lied to my face about it." Elliot turns on me. "Jimmy I don't care about, but you? What was all that about me trusting you?"

I'm at a loss for words. "Elliot, not here. I'm sorry. I just—"

"Hold on, even better," Dean's mouth dangles open in a challenge. "If we're going to do this, Klara should start with how she messed up the AI computer system in her house. Stephen Richards says the only way the AI could be making phone calls is if it was tampered with. Right? So, in fact, your incessant need to ruin your dad's work might be why Alex killed himself."

"You don't get to talk about Alex." Elliot growls to him but then turns to Klara. "And speak for yourself, because none of that would've happened last night if you didn't bring *this kid* with you."

"Hey, don't drag me into this," Wes gulps.

"You wanted this to happen, Klara. You love being the dramatic one. You love being the center of attention everywhere you go," Elliot says. "You brought him because you wanted to stir the pot."

"Grow up, Elliot. We're not together." Klara rolls her eyes.

Wes shifts in his chair, and Elliot rips at the bandages on his hand. We fall into silence again with nothing but the tap of shoes and sounds of officers at their desks behind us. I watch the clock tick away, trying not to notice Dean's unwavering stare into the side of my head. But part of me wants to hold onto that memory, the woods and the lakeside and the moonlight, just to keep out everything else.

"And you know what?" Elliot isn't done. "Don't pretend like you're the victim here, like you always do. Dean probably won't graduate. Wes has already been expelled once, your dad practically bought the school, and Via's smart enough to be fine. I'm the one who's going to lose a scholarship if we get charged with underage drinking."

"And he brings it back to sports," Dean clicks his tongue. "How metaphorical."

"Shut up, Dean."

"What are you going to do, big guy? Hit me?" Dean motions to Elliot's cast. "Is it hard to jerk off with your left hand now, or..."

"Shocking, you can't even go a minute without being an asshole." Elliot runs his fingers through his hair. "You must really hate yourself. You can't stand it when you live right down the street from these parties but you're never invited, so you have to make sure everyone else is miserable with you. You have to bring everyone down to your level, just like that stupid knife game. Nobody even wants you around."

"I can maybe think of one person." Dean turns to me. "Via, I'm curious what you think. You've been awfully quiet this whole time."

My eyes wander around the room, everywhere else, anywhere else. "Whatever. I don't care."

"There it is. I knew it was coming." Klara flicks her ponytail. "Olivia Prescott, the girl who's too cool to care about anything. Nothing is ever her fault. She's only trying to help."

I bite my tongue. Wes leans over to me. "You know, originally I thought you guys were a friend group. But now I see you all just hate each other."

Suddenly, the doors to the police station swing open and shatter the quiet tension of the morning. In walks the last person I would ever expect to see in this aftermath—Jimmy.

"Oh Jesus." I bury my head.

"What are you doing here?" Elliot asks.

"Um, Via's mom called me. She's really worried, said she called everyone she could, but I was the only person who picked up. I went to Chad's, and now I'm here." Jimmy glances around at all of us. "What happened? Are you guys being arrested?"

"Jimmy, go home." I cross over to him. "You don't need to keep showing up everywhere unannounced. You're not my mom's pet, and I don't need you looking after me."

"That's not what I was doing. I just… are you mad at me? Is this about New Years?"

Dean perks. "New Years? What happened New Years?"

"Nothing, Dean."

"What if something did happen? Why do you care?" Jimmy threatens.

"Why don't you just do what Via says and go home." Dean stands so he towers over Jimmy. He puts himself between me and the boy. Other people in the station notice the commotion in the waiting area.

Jimmy stands his ground. "Why don't you step away from Via?"

"Why don't you let her speak for herself?" Dean says. "She can tell you what's going on."

"What does that mean?" Jimmy stammers. "Is there… there isn't… is there something going on?"

"I don't know, Via. Is there something going on?" Dean levels his stare.

"Hold on. Is there?" Elliot frowns.

"Everyone, shut up and let me think." Gravity pulls me back down into my chair. I press my fingers into my temple and hold my head like the world closes in around me.

"Oh, I see what's happening," Klara laughs and leans back against the wall.

"I don't," Wes says. "Am I missing something?"

Exactly, I'm missing something. My mind reels and I have to fight back a wave of memories, some of which must be dreams of other people's lives. *Why is it always this group, these people? Why do we always go in circles? Everything is like déjà vu, even my memories.* We're all in each other's lives because of coincidence. We all know things about the Agents, pieces of the puzzle nobody else knows. It's too ironic that we all have some direct connection to the program.

"There is no such thing as coincidence," I murmur.

Just then, a young officer in the station weaves between desks toward us. With his slightly balding head, I remember him as the officer who took us into custody and got our statements. Underneath a thin mustache, he addresses all of us.

"No charges are being filed. You're free to go," he says. "Everything was cleared up by a Stephen Richards. We're sorry for the misunderstanding."

A sound of disbelief escapes my throat. I gasp, and then it turns into a laugh, and soon it bubbles over into full body, chest-heaving amusement. *Of course, the program is everywhere.* He's *everywhere. How did I think I could do anything and go unnoticed?* The puppeteer just reminds me of his strings and tells me to smile for the cameras. I can't believe I was so naive.

"Via, are you… okay?" Jimmy asks. Everyone else watches me.

"Am I okay? You want to know if I'm okay?" I bring myself to my feet. "All of you act as if you don't know, as if you're not a part of it."

"What are you talking about?" Klara says.

"One year ago was the night I got hit by a car and ended up in the hospital. Until recently I thought I was out there saving Wes, but it turns out Wes was saving me. And not only did I convince myself that I was okay after nearly dying, but then I convinced myself that the people who hit me with their car are my best friends."

"Wait, back up. You were there that night?" Elliot stands.

"And then I start seeing things, all because of this video game that *you* introduced to me." I point to Wes. "I'm being tested. Aren't I? Everything, all of this, all of you even. It's the perfect experiment. It's the perfect setup."

Wes shifts. "Via, let's go home. You just—"

"Home? The place I moved to after the crash?" I turn to Wes. "You said it yourself, at home my parents are watching me. Just like Mr. Richards. It's like I'm still in the hospital."

"What are you even talking about, Via?" Jimmy adjusts his glasses. "If this is because we were hiding things from you, I'm sorry. It was for your own—"

"For my own good, yeah." I squeeze the button in my pocket. *That's exactly what Mr. Richards said. That's exactly what my parents always say. This can't just be in my head.* Gears turn, and I strain to remember how I became friends with all of them. "Why did you even get close to me anyway? Wes, I know you say it's therapy every Sunday. But why the game? Klara, you kept showing up at my car and my house. Why? To get back at your dad and use me to bring down the program? And Jimmy, why did you do all those investigations on your own and keep slipping me notes? Were you trying to get in my head?" I study their faces, watching for a reaction, anything. "Even Elliot. You took me on hikes to talk about Alex. You took me to that graveyard. Why?"

"Don't you dare." Elliot's fists clench. "You know why. You know what Alex meant to me."

"No, I don't. I don't know anything. I don't know any of you." My heart beats out of my chest as my organs twist and turn inside me. "Alex was a plant in the school, that's all. I mean, none of it makes sense, unless you're all lying to me and this is all part of the test."

"Wes was right," Klara raises her dark eyebrows. "You really can't stand having other people in your life. Can you?" With a flick of her ponytail, she leaves the station. Wes follows after a long, hesitant moment. Elliot runs his fingers through his hair and then smacks the door on his way out.

Jimmy faces me and fidgets with his hands. It breaks my heart to think he's lying to me.

"Why did you give me this?" I hold up the button.

"I can't give you an answer you want." His soft brown eyes waver.

I toss the button over to him, and he catches it clumsily. Crestfallen, he retreats into his collar and leaves. Now it's just Dean, who ruffles his hair like he doesn't even know what to do. *I know I'm missing something. It's not all just a coincidence. I need to separate myself from it all. I can't let* them *get in my head.*

"And then there were two." Dean sways on his feet.

"No, I'm not buying it. You mess with me for months. You tease and pry and won't leave me alone. You talk about everything being fake and nobody being real, but you're the worst one. I know you were there at the crash, at the Incident. You know things you're not telling me, you're hiding things from me like everyone else."

"Maybe I am. Is that so bad? Maybe I don't want you to know." He takes my hands, and I flinch. "You're so desperate not to be tricked, Via, and it's driving you crazy. Can't you see that?"

"I know I'm being paranoid, but what am I supposed to do? Give up like you?" I shy away from him. "You're just okay with everything being fake. You're fine with it."

"I'm not."

"Then you're just one big walking contradiction! You keep saying you'll tell me everything, the truth, but you never do."

"I've been trying. I have," he urges. "But it's impossible, and I can't tell you why."

I feel sick to my stomach. I don't want to look into his piercing eyes anymore. "Listen, I don't care. You could be an Agent or just an asshole, but I don't believe you either way."

His face goes cold, and his tongue presses against the inside of his cheek. All the moving parts of the station go on around us, and his eyes wander through all of it. Then he leaves. With a swish of his long coat, he strides out the doors away from me.

I'm suddenly alone. For a moment I'm relieved because there's quiet. But then I see snow through headlights as the image flashes in my mind. I take a step. An image of peeling flesh from my forearm. I take another step. Flashes of drowning and a flood of icy water. One more step. Dark flames and the smell of burning flesh. I take another step and another until my hands shake violently and I rush out of the station. I push through the doors and chase down the stairs after Dean. He's already halfway across the parking lot.

"Wait," I gasp. He turns around slowly. I pull at my sleeves relentlessly, desperate to hide the shaking and scared to be left alone.

"You know, you actually had me fooled," he says. "For a minute there last night, I actually believed you." And then he leaves, and this time I know I've lost him. This time, I've pushed them all so far that they started walking away on their own.

* * *

My dad doesn't say a single word on the car ride home. He keeps his eyes ahead, and every few seconds he changes the radio station. He taps the top of the steering wheel with his finger, which is the same thing I do when I drive. Then he reaches over to change the channel again. Frosted trees whip by and the road winds back out of town to the suburbs. Finally, he just turns the radio off.

When we get into the house, he sets down the keys and meticulously unties his shoes at the door. He places them on the mat and then shuffles into the living room. I watch him go through his routine. He turns on the reading lamp, takes out the bookmark in his paperback, and settles into his chair.

I stand in the hallway alone, the art on the walls mocking me.

And then, my dad speaks. Out of all the things that could come to mind, he says, "This is not a very good book."

I hesitate and then step into the living room as if I walk on eggshells. "What are you reading?"

"The author is actually horrible. But he's writing about a very important topic, so it's okay. At least, I think it's important." He lowers his reading glasses and turns the cover in his hands. "Maybe it's not even about what he says. It's just the fact that he's saying something, really."

I lower myself onto the opposite side of the couch. "Hey, can I… read something with you?"

From under bushy eyebrows, his eyes light up. "Anything in particular?"

"No. I'll just try something new."

"Okay," he says. Then he's absorbed back into his book. I take a random hardcover from the side table, one that he's already finished, and open it up. I can't remember the last time I read, just to read.

CHAPTER 25

The living room is quiet for a Sunday night. It's the kind of tranquility I got used to in the northern woods with Elliot, the kind of silence I haven't had in my brain for a while. Nothing much has changed, still the evening lull after dinner and the clinking of my parents' wine glasses in the other room. But without Wes and his family, it seems empty.

"Why couldn't Dani come tonight? You guys are so boring," Josh whines as he clears his plate.

"Danielle and Wes won't be coming back for a little while. Okay? Sometimes it's good to have a break and spend time with just your own family." Mom gives him a sympathetic smile.

I stack my own dishes absentmindedly, picturing Wes at Chad's party tonight. It's a long weekend, and I guess drinking feels even more rebellious and exciting now that his house is on the cops' radar. *I don't have a single reason to go there, but why do I still long to be invited?*

"Via, will you play Immortal Soldiers with me?" Josh begs when he returns from the kitchen. "You used to play games with me all the time before the hospital."

I flinch at his mention of the hospital. *Even he knows it changed me.* I glance into the living room at the pillow nest, the one I made for Wes and me tonight. Something about sitting there with someone else feels alien. But my brother's eyes plead, and his cute round cheeks squish up his whole face.

"Fine." I roll my eyes. He waddles excitedly to the front of the coffee table, and his dark hair bounces.

I hook up Wes's game, our game, to the TV. It doesn't sit right in my stomach. But after a minute I feel the tension in my head release, and I settle into a smile as Josh violently assaults the controller with his pudgy hands. I don't know what it is. It's not even about playing the game, or not being able to pass this stupid level. It's something about sitting in front of the coffee table in this nest of pillows that makes me feel like myself for the first time in a while.

"So, how's hockey going?" I ask. Just to talk about something, anything.

"Great." His mouth lulls open as he concentrates.

"Do you think they'll take you off the bench soon?" It's no secret that Josh hasn't been put in for a single minute of a real game. I vividly remember the day he came home from school last year and told my parents he wanted to start hockey. The look on my dad's face was priceless, and I'd never seen my mom shut him up so fast.

"Probably not." He shrugs. "Coach says I'm not as 'agile' as the other players. He says I should be a goalie and just stand in front of the net. But I could never do that. My body is a temple."

I laugh. "You're damn right."

"It's okay though. Danielle says I'm the heart and soul of the team. They need those too."

"I think she's right." A warmth fills my chest. But just then my avatar is gunned down, and Josh leaves me behind. "Hey, you traitor!" I hit him with one of the smaller pillows.

He squirms and giggles. "Fool. This is every man for themselves."

My character's mangled body on the streets of the level slowly disappears. The blood goes away, and then my body reappears shiny and new at the checkpoint. I only make it a few blocks through the pixelated ruins before I'm hit with a blast and have to start again. I watch myself die over and over, and then come back to life and continue the same pursuit once more.

"Oh my god," I breathe.

"What? Just re-spawn already and help me."

"Oh my god." The controller drops to the ground as my mind whirls. *Of course, that's what I've been missing this whole time.*

The glitch, the patterns between Alex and Oscar and my own life, even the car crash last year. The reason none of it seemed to make sense. How all the Agents had families and a home and a past. The reason the phone calls affected them so much, the reason they committed suicide.

Mr. Richards said that nothing can be created from scratch. Everything has to come from imitation of something else. It has to be built from something real. Nobody in the field of machine learning could create strong AI, because no computer could have the capacity to think outside of its own programming. So they had to base it in something real. They had to give it memories, like a distant echo of humanity.

"I have to go." I jump to my feet.

"Wait, right now?" Josh whines.

I throw on my shoes and a jacket as I grab my new phone and the keys to the Subaru from the charging station. My gaze lingers on my dad's YouTech keycard. *He would kill me.* I shake my head and pick it up anyway, stuffing it in my pocket.

Only when I reach for the door do I see the shadow of my father. He stands in the archway to the kitchen with a book in hand, the lines of his face rigid underneath his reading glasses. He looks from the door, to me, and then to my pocket. My throat closes up. I can't even begin to come up with an excuse.

And then, against all reason, he just nods. That's it. A single nod, without any words. Just a glint in his eyes that says... *Okay.* Then he silently goes back to his book and walks away. As I rush out of the house, I catch him say something to my mom so she doesn't hear the front door close behind me.

* * *

This far up the road, with hills hugged by wind-torn lakes, the cold is all-consuming. I blow hot air into my frozen hands and rub them as I stare at Dean's small cottage. Next to it, the dark edifice belonging to YouTech Labs sends a haunting chill down my spine. It looms like a sinister shadow in the trees, and I head away from Dean's sleeping house.

I know what I have to do.

I pack down snow beneath my feet as I frantically move through the night toward the entrance to the laboratory. There are no cars in the parking lot. I approach the front door with a cautious stealth and notice the security cameras around me. Hopefully hidden by shadows, I face the keycard scanner.

I pull out my father's employee card from my jacket pocket. With a heavy click the glass doors are unlocked, and part of me can't believe that worked. I duck inside the building, gripping the card in my palm with shaking hands as a familiar dark omen creeps up. *Why am I doing this if I know how it's going to end?*

Nerves on fire, my muscles seized with tension, I sneak through the dark building to the hallway on my left. The only lights are the ominous red glow of the emergency exit signs. I can hear footsteps from deep within the concrete maze, most likely from a guard on night duty. Anxiety pulses through me every time one of my feet touches the ground because it's impossible to move in this building without every sound echoing across the slick walls. I pass each door and read the labels through the pitch black, but I don't find what I'm looking for.

My eyes spot Mr. Richards's office with a stab of fear. I get to the end of the stretching corridor, and that's when I see what I was looking for—the entrance to the AI lab.

Its large glass windows don't leave much to speculation, but the shapes and shadows of the machinery inside look like skeletons in the dark. *This was a bad idea.* With the keycard in hand, I swipe into the lab that opens up to a vast chamber of desks and machine parts and computers. Automatic lights flick on when I enter. They spook me as I'm pulled out of the darkness. And then, the sudden clarity of what I'm surrounded by takes my breath away.

What I thought only looked like skeletons in the pitch black of the windows are now revealed to be actual skeletons, shells of what can only be described as humans. This is not like the animatronic skull in Mr. Richards's demonstration. This is life. No flesh yet, but intricate vessels of wires and advanced robotics lay on these tables like hollowed-out corpses. And there's a countless number of them, littered around the laboratory like the aftermath of a battlefield without bloodshed. My breath shortens, heart pounds, and I back away from the operating tables of these human-like chassis.

I feel like a lone heartbeat standing in a graveyard.

I look for a way out and stumble into a door that doesn't have a window. It looks like a side-room for the lab, maybe a closet for holding parts or tools. *Remember why you came here. They're wrong. You can handle the truth.* I unlock the door and step inside, but what I find is much more haunting than spare parts.

It faces me with a blank, unmoving stare. It's Dean. A young Dean, not nearly as tall and lanky as the one that I know, but it's Dean nonetheless. My heart lurches, and I notice on his still, bare chest that something is written on the flesh. It's crudely drawn with a sharpie as if it was one of the signs on Chad's bedroom door telling kids at a party to stay out.

Model 1.0.

And next to the terrifying, unblinking time capsule of a young Dean is a file cabinet. *It's always a file cabinet.* On top of it are stacks of folders. Before I can even make the decision not to read them, my eyes fall onto the top page. It's a certificate of death for Dean Wallace, age thirteen.

With a sharp inhale, it all clicks together. *No, no, no.* I can't even feel my own heartbeat anymore as the realization swells up into my entire body. The edges of my vision blur just as my hands find the bottom folder. The sickening dread that I've been cursed with all year, that horrible sensation I naively labeled as a supernatural gift, comes to a crescendo. In my weakened clutches I hold another death certificate.

Olivia Prescott, age sixteen.

The program isn't building people. They're bringing dead people back to life.

CHAPTER 26

I can't ever remember feeling this alive.

"Dean?" My knuckles sting as they urgently rap on the door of the small cottage. My frozen hands knock again, but it's midnight and I didn't expect anyone to answer anyway.

Where is he?

With restless reluctance I glance up the road, and the glow of a drunken aura radiates from Chad's cabin in the night. It illuminates the trees like a wildfire and spreads closer to me with its intoxicating draw. I always knew I was going to have to go back.

"Oh God." Max winces and immediately closes the door.

"Come on, I know he's in there." I pound on the wooden panel. "We've been friends for two semesters now, Max. You can't say no to me."

He opens it a crack. "Chad said you're not allowed in this house."

"What are you, his crony?" I thrust my arm through the opening and barge inside.

"No, no, no." He waves me away. "Out. Turn around."

"Hi, Max. Great talk, as usual." I march down the hall to the incandescent living room. I see everyone there, all the faces that live in my head.

"Don't 'Hi Max' me." He draws attention to us from everyone at the party. "It's one thing having Elliot here. But then Klara shows up and starts harassing underclassmen, Jimmy came for some bizarre reason, and the new kid had to make an appearance—"

"I'm actually not new," Wes raises a finger. "My name is—"

"Jimmy?" I stop in my tracks. The boy leans stiffly against the fireplace and straightens up when he sees me.

"We used to just play beer pong at these things…" Max mutters.

I scoff at Jimmy. "You don't even like the *idea* of parties. You don't drink."

"Neither do you." He looks around and cowers under the attention of the whole house. "Just because I don't go doesn't mean I don't want to be invited."

"Why is it always you guys? Every time something happens." Max throws his hands up. "Are you all even friends?"

"No." Klara comes out of the kitchen, drink in hand. I see kids creep out from every corner of the cabin and line the log walls to wait for a repeat of last week. Elliot hovers over by the dining room, and we make eye contact.

"I know Dean is here. I need to see him." I scour the crowd for his mess of brown hair.

"He isn't here because he's not invited. Just like you," Max points out. "Don't make me be the bad guy here."

"He must be on the balcony." I head for the stairs, but he blocks my path. "What are you going to do? Use your robot arm on me?"

He falters for a moment, and then his eyes flit behind me. *You've got to be kidding.* I turn around to face Chad, in all his brutish glory.

"Don't make me throw you out." He twists as if to grab my arm.

Jimmy crosses the floor. "Don't touch her."

Chad spins on him. "Who the hell are you?"

Jimmy fidgets. "Right. Well first of all, I appreciate you having me at your—"

"You can leave with her," he menaces. "Unless you want to end up like your brother."

The threat hits Jimmy like a bullet, and he shatters. But before Chad can go through with his word, Elliot strides in from out of nowhere and throws a punch directly at his head. His left hand connects with bone, and a painful smack sends a ripple of shock across the room. Chad drops to the floor with a stunned yelp. It resonates through the wooden beams of the cabin.

Elliot doesn't even flinch. He just stands over him with a stony expression under curtains of long hair. He has two broken hands now—one bandaged while the other bleeds red. After a moment, he and Jimmy exchange glances. With a pang it reminds me of the young photo of the two boys playing basketball together.

Meanwhile the party has escalated to full-on madness as the owner of the house lies moaning on the carpet. Amidst the chaos, Klara rushes over to Elliot. "What were you thinking? You're not going to have any functioning hands left! You need to go to the hospital."

His eyes fall. "Why do you care?"

"Of course I care, moron." Klara hits his arm, and he winces. "Sorry."

"I have to find Dean, but Wes is still sober." I turn to my friend. "Wes, you can drive him to the ER. Right?"

"No, I'll drive him," Jimmy says. "He broke his hand for me. It's the least I can do."

"I knew I liked this kid," Wes says. "He was always my favorite of your friends, no offense." Elliot and Klara give him a look, and he stammers, "I totally would've punched him too, by the way. For Jimmy. You just got to him first. I was right there behind you."

"Sure." Elliot nods, but his dimples flex like he might laugh.

Reassured that my friends will be okay, I scale the stairs and head down the hallway of the second floor. Around every corner I think I'll be faced with the haunting image of young Dean that I saw in the lab. But when I climb out onto the balcony, the figure that faces me is Dean. The real Dean.

"I knew you'd be here," I breathe. In the darkness he looks nothing more than a cloaked figure.

He looks up at me, and immediately he knows.

"I'm sorry," I say.

"Never apologize. For anything." He takes the flask out of his long coat and brings it up to his lips.

"No, I mean it. I didn't listen. You tried to tell me so many times but I thought you were just messing with me. You were the only one who was honest with me."

"Yeah, well." There's a bitter scowl on his face. "Welcome to the life of a living, breathing corpse."

My heart breaks for him, and I don't even know how it's possible. "You were their very first Agent."

His mouth hangs open in a hollow laugh. "You know, the funny thing about Dean is that he never really goes away. I'm stuck with his life, his body, his memories, all the time. And it's like I'm fighting every goddamn second to shut him up, but it's just me."

"You won't commit suicide. Will you? Like the others?"

"No, that was the glitch. See, YouTech made the mistake of giving me self-awareness." His eyes glint in the dark. "Did you know I can't say anything about it? Physically? They programmed me so I can't spill the truth, not a single word.

It's like I have this noose around my neck, and every time I try to say something real, it cinches."

A flood of desperation spills out of me. "Well why didn't you find other ways? You could have saved everyone. You could've stopped it. Why didn't you write it down or—" And that's when it dawns on me, and I feel my heart skip a beat. "The unknown number. The texts."

He gazes out past the cabin, over the frozen lake and the swathes of pines. His disheveled hair blows in the cold wind.

"You knew about the counting in my head, you knew about the crash. You tried to warn me. That was all you. You were trying to save me from ending up like..." I stop myself.

He stares into the void darkly, dejectedly. "It didn't make a difference, anyway. The glitch is going to get you in the end. It always does." He takes another gulp from his flask with tremendous effort. "And I'll just watch from the side, like I always do, and wait to bring your body back."

A cavernous fear clenches at my soul, but it's not from the prospect of my own impending death. It's the fear of reliving *their* deaths, *their* pain, as vivid dreams and memories for the rest of my life. The sheer loneliness of it all, sharing that intimacy with them and then having to walk away, fills my whole body with a panic that's unmatched by anything I've ever felt.

He clicks his tongue. "I kind of had hope for you too. You're the perfected version of me, you know. You're their masterpiece. And you play the game so well, better than any of us."

"I'm not playing their game."

"Sure you are," he says. "You don't have a choice. None of us do. We go on pretending, and we play by their rules. And if the glitch gets us, oh well, they make a new one. And if we ever step out of line, they can take everything away and remind us that none of it was ours to begin with. I was always afraid of that, and I ran away from it. But I don't think I want to anymore."

"You're lying. I know you haven't given up because you're not like Alex or Oscar. You're still here."

"I am a walking corpse, Via." He steps away from the railing, and only now do I see desperation under the surface like an untamed flame. "I can't go home because Dean's parents won't even look at me. Charles Brooks had to bribe them with a scholarship just to keep me around for school. You think anyone wants me there? I'm just damage control, for you."

"I'm sure that's not—"

"You think your family is any different? It's just like mine. They made a deal with the devil, but they didn't like what they got."

I search his eyes, hurt. "Let me drive you home. Or anywhere. Please."

"There's nowhere to go. I don't belong anywhere outside this balcony." He inhales the remainder of his flask. "And I don't need you coming out here to pity me."

"Don't do that," I say. "You know why I came here. Why I keep coming here."

That's when the phone in my pocket buzzes, and I pull it out to see Jimmy's name on the screen. "It must be about Elliot. I hope they left already—"

"Don't!" He grabs my arm with deadly intensity. "Don't answer it."

A chill goes down my spine.

"Listen to me," he says with piercing eyes. "By now they've probably figured out that you know everything. They'll be after you to take you back to the lab. They may even be on their way right now. Do you hear me?"

"If we get rid of the glitch, they won't have to take me." My mind reels. "We can just go to the school. That's where they moved the computer. We'll just destroy it and all the calls will stop."

"No," he straightens to his full height. He seems to have made up his mind, his jaw set in determination. "You don't have to do anything. Just stay here." And then, he pushes by me and disappears back into the cabin.

"Dean!" I race after him and follow the trail of his long coat through the log maze.

We barge back into the living room of the party, and everyone makes way for Dean as he stumbles down the stairs. Jimmy and Elliot are already gone, but Klara and Wes look at me with concerned expressions. Even they know something is off about him, more than usual. He plows through clusters of drunken bodies, and every set of eyes drink in the strange outbursts of emotion from the boy they usually pay no mind to.

I grab him by the coat and close my fingers around his collar. "Hey, look at me." I lock onto his eyes. "Nobody is going anywhere."

I see something break in his expression, something like anguish. "I'm sorry. I have to end this."

And then he charges toward the entryway, and the front door swings open behind him and lets in a wave of cold.

"Dean, what are you doing?" I sprint after him. I can hear footsteps from behind as people follow me into the night. He climbs into the nearest car, and my whole body surges with fear. The car whips out of the driveway and backs out onto the street. I'm not fast enough to stop him. I can hear Klara and Wes shout after me, but I only see Dean. *I'm not going to be the last one.* I throw myself out onto the icy road.

As I brace for the crash, my whole world illuminated by his blinding white headlights, I can't help but think: *What incredible déjà vu.*

Suddenly there's screeching tires and a bang like the crack of thunder. From the other side of the road, Elliot's car slams into the front corner of the oncoming vehicle and it lurches to the side, saving me from the impact. A million sounds of chaos break the silence of the woods, and I'm thrown to the ground away from the wreck.

A year ago, I heard those same sounds—the same crunch of metal and shattering of glass.

Almost in slow motion, Dean's body breaks through the windshield and tumbles over the hood. I watch him slam into the frozen pavement. Through the pitch black of the night, I see a glint of metal from underneath his skin. Slowly, like a drifting leaf, Dean's long coat billows in the air and alights onto the gravel in front of me.

Elliot climbs out of the other car behind Jimmy, his bandaged arm still bloody, and they're frozen in shock. From behind me, Wes's firm hands grab at my shoulders to drag me away from the damage. I break free and stumble over to Dean.

My friends watch through the dark as I kneel on the bloodstained ice, crouching over his crumpled figure. I put my hands behind his neck and lift up his head gently. He animates at my touch and with agonizing effort, pushes himself up off the ground. And that's when I notice it. It's the first time I've seen him without his long coat on, the first time my eyes have settled on his bare skin. It's a canvas of scars and burns that slash across his fair skin like wild brushstrokes. His flesh warps and twists around metal parts that fill in the gaps of his joints, his ribs, his collarbone. The metal and tissue flex and breathe, like two versions of him intertwined in a haunting dance.

Only after I've torn my gaze from his body does he draw his head up to meet my eyes.

Half of his face is torn away. Underneath the blood and strands of disheveled hair, an exposed aluminum skull stares back at me. His flesh hangs from sheer artificial bone. But those eyes, those piercing, devilish eyes are the same. He tries to look away, and I see the mechanics in every movement of his jaw and every arch of his eyebrow. I cup his scathed chin and hold it up to mine. *It doesn't change anything.* He will always be a little less flesh and a little more human than the rest of us.

A year ago it was almost exactly like this—our lives colliding on a snowy night road, a single body bleeding out on the asphalt. Dean knelt over my mangled body, a familiar stranger who held up my head amidst the falling snow. Now I'm the one who kneels over him. A year ago Alex saw Dean's face on the side of the road, a face from his past life, and it drove him into me. Years before that, Oscar saw that same familiar face outside a small cottage, and it drove him into the lake. Now, that familiar stranger is the one who drove off the deep end. The pattern keeps repeating itself like a glitch, a never-ending loop. Because life isn't a line of code, or a formula. It's irrational and infinite and circles back again, and again, so there is no start or finish.

I had been searching for something, and Dean wanted to be found. Maybe closing the loop is as simple as that.

CHAPTER 27

For the first time in months, it's warm. The trees have budding leaves now, and grass breaks through the melting layers of ice to reach up for the sun after months of frost. I can hear birds again. Snowmelt drips from the branches of the pines as thawed lakes glitter in the morning sun. The tantalizing deep green of the forest returns, and it reminds me of when I first moved to Park Falls. That feels like lifetimes ago.

I pull into the parking lot of the school and take a deep breath. I can already feel the presence of that other AI, the computer hidden just on the other side of a locked door. But even more terrifying, I can already picture the rumors—the ring of gossip around the accident at Chad's lake house two nights ago. I can already feel the stares as they pick me apart for new clues that I'm the Agent.

I slam the door shut and fix my plaid shirt in the side mirror. *Screw them. I actually look great in plaid.*

The dim morning light and scuffle of hundreds of shoes fill the hallways of Park Falls Technical High School. I forgot what it was like to be here, forgot what it was like to be around all these people. At one point I could walk through these corridors and recognize every face. I would look for a smile or wave of acknowledgment, all the while paranoid that I seemed suspicious or not quite right in their eyes. Now amidst the sea of faces, I only look for one. And I know I won't find him.

I try to go straight to my locker, but something catches my eye. I have a compulsion to stop at the side of the hallway as a current of students pushes past. The large poster on the wall stares back at me. I tilt my head. I muse at that silhouette of a nondescript person, the cheesy question mark plastered in the middle. The cartoonish letters that read "Who is the Agent?" almost elicits a laugh from me.

"I never understood the point of these things," a voice says to my right. Wes flips aside waves of blond hair and stares at the poster with me. "How are you?"

"I'm fine," I say with conviction.

"And… with Dean?" He shoves his hands in his pockets. "That may be Klara's territory, because I'm gonna be honest, our friendship never really covered boy problems. Especially ones where the guy's been kidnapped."

I know it's a joke, and he says this with sympathy, but the mention of that boy carves a deep sadness into my chest. YouTech didn't even wait until morning before they went into the hospital and took their original Agent back to the lab. The truth is, it's only been two days but his absence makes me feel like none of it even happened. Like it was just another memory I convinced myself was real or a dream that was so vivid it couldn't possibly be fiction.

"You know he did it for you. He wanted it this way," Wes reassures me.

I nod, my throat tight.

We stare up at the poster for a minute but don't say anything else. He saw the true nature of Dean on that road, same as me. It's not an image you can easily forget, and right now my mind paints it over the blank silhouette of the poster.

"I did know about you, by the way. I knew the whole time," he says quietly. Nothing surprises me anymore, but I turn to him abruptly anyway. "See, I was there at the hospital. I was by Olivia's side when they pronounced her dead. But I was also there when you woke up. I watched my best friend die and I almost followed suit because I didn't think I could handle it. The responsibility of knowing, I mean. Knowing you weren't really her."

A group of girls shove past my backpack, and I sway on my feet.

"But anyway, after I tried to die, it didn't work. I woke up in the hospital alive the next morning. God, I was mortified. I thought they had brought me back, same as you. So I spent this whole year questioning if I was really myself, and this whole year I ended up getting closer to you in the process. It was torture at first, I'll be honest. And yet, I kept coming back. Every Sunday. I kept coming back with my family to look after you and to play that game because that was kind of all we had."

I study his expression, but I don't know what to say.

"And, you know, Klara's actually not too bad." He shrugs. I raise an eyebrow at him but he just laughs. "You know what I mean. It may not be my place to share, but she also knew the whole time. And when I first found out she knew, I was really mad. She had been trying to take down the program and she was putting you in danger, so I hated her. But she didn't know she was hurting people. She was never trying to endanger Alex or you."

I think about that AI system, the one in the school right now. Something that has triggered insurmountable pain, it's so close I can practically hear it.

"That's why we started meeting up. Because after we realized we both wanted the same thing, we thought we could fix it all. We thought we could shut down the computer and you would never have to know. But her dad must've caught on, which is why it probably got moved."

"I liked the story of you guys having an affair better."

"You're the worst." He hits me, and lets out that childish giggle.

"Please, for the love of God, never make that sound in public again." Klara must've heard her name from the hall, because with a flick of her ponytail she intrudes right in between us. "What's up, guys?"

Wes makes a face at her and nods his head toward me.

"Ugh, fine." She rolls her eyes. "I've been meaning to tell you… you were right about me using my dad's obsession with his work as an excuse for being awful. To be fair, you *are* his work. So I kind of hated you for that. But I guess what I'm trying to say is…" she trails off and Wes nudges her. She sighs, "You didn't deserve it."

I raise an eyebrow at her. "Is this an apology?"

"Ew, no." She recoils. "You know I don't do those."

"So, wait, just to clarify…" I point between them. "You two aren't actually hooking up?"

"No, no way." She fiddles with her earring.

Wes turns to her. "Would you ever, you know, actually go out on a date with me? Like for real?"

"You're kidding, right?"

He sways on his feet, flustered. "Oh, come on. The whole town already thinks we're hooking up."

She faces him and crosses her arms. "Alright, let's see. I very illegally messed with thousands of dollars of my own father's equipment just because I was bored and wanted attention. Does that scream girlfriend material to you?"

"Okay, you're crazy." He shrugs. "I was convinced I was a robot for the majority of last year. Big deal."

"I'm extremely intrusive. No boundaries."

"Well, I broke into your house."

"I'm very dramatic. And I constantly do what other people do, just to fit in."

"I attempted suicide after my best friend died. I feel like that counts."

"No, that's not—" She rolls her eyes. "Seriously, you don't want to be with me. I gossip. And talk, a lot."

"So do I. Conspiracy theories are essentially gossip for geeks, so..."

A smile breaks out on her face, that kind of shy and genuine smile that I rarely see from her. "Fine. But you have to pick me up. And I get aux."

"You know, as much as I love this," I interrupt, "I can't understand why the two of you couldn't shut down the AI computer. If you tried so hard to hack it and reprogram it, why did it keep coming back?"

Wes still can't take his eyes off of Klara but shrugs. "That's the thing about technology, I guess. It just keeps going."

"I just wish we could destroy that thing. For good. I even know what room it's in right now, which is driving me crazy. But even if we wanted to, you need a key to get in. It's like the only door in this whole school that isn't electronically locked. Can you believe it?" Klara shakes her head and laughs bitterly. "If only we lived in the dark ages and one of us actually knew how to pick a lock."

A smile tugs at my lips, and Wes and I exchange glances. "Actually, about that..."

* * *

The lunch table feels fuller than it usually is, even just with Wes, Ben, and Cole. Amidst the cacophony of cafeteria sounds, Cole plays games on his phone and Ben passionately debates with Wes about joining soccer.

"Come on, I know you'd be good at it." Ben tosses a chip at Cole, who flinches. "I'm trying to get Jimmy and Elliot to play too. We'd be an incredible team!"

"First of all, Elliot and Jimmy haven't even gotten back from the hospital yet." Wes shakes his head. It makes my heart swell when I think that Jimmy stayed there just for Elliot. And Jimmy never likes to skip school.

"Dude, I'm serious. Stop it." Cole swats at Ben as he throws another chip. I laugh.

"Look, who knows what kind of secret weapon you're covering up. Max had a robotic arm this whole time and everyone just found out," Ben continues. "I mean, just look at the rumors about Dean. I heard he's not here because YouTech is replacing his whole body with metal after the crash. Did you guys see it?"

I couldn't even begin to explain what I saw, the intricacy of Dean's hybrid form. The very thought makes my heart race. Wes shrugs dismissively. "No, not really."

"Well, I hope they turn him into a superhero, like The Balancer," Cole marvels. "That would be straight out of a comic book. Lucky bastard."

"Hey, where's Klara?" Ben scratches his head. "Didn't you guys say she was going to sit with us?"

Before I can respond, I see Wes freeze and a shadow crosses his face. I turn around to see what has him so spooked, and my stomach drops. Mr. Richards hovers at the doorway of the cafeteria. Two men in sharp fitted suits flank him. His beady hawk-like eyes sweep the crowds, and I already know who he searches for.

I push my chair out with a screech, and Wes stands up to follow me. I stop him. "I got this. Don't worry." As I weave through tables of students that clatter and buzz with energy, I draw a rising tide of attention. Whispers and rumors follow me, the speculating eyes and hushed stories from kids who still play the game relentlessly.

"Olivia, I'm glad to see you're doing well." Mr. Richards crosses his arms in front of him.

"Let's talk out in the hall. I want to make this brief." I nod. I calm my palpitating heart and take a deep breath. *Are they here because they know what we're doing?* The broad-shouldered man leads me out into the empty hallway, and his two associates stand guard at the cafeteria to make sure nobody overhears.

His deep-set eyes give nothing away. I tug at my sleeves for a moment. "What's going to happen to me now?"

He drops his hooked nose. "Nothing."

"So this is just a check-in?" I scoff. "To see how I'm doing?"

I only get a nod from him. My thoughts whirl. "Okay, let's see. How am I doing?" I rub the back of my neck, where only days ago Dean had clutched me with shaking hands. "Well, over the past few days I've been realizing how much everyone around me knew, *what* they knew, and *when* they knew it. And I'm trying to figure out why they did what they did. See, some of my friends hid the truth to protect me. Some of them tried to tell me the answers or at least help me get to them myself. My parents did what any parent would do. They gave up everything to bring their daughter back. They did what they thought was best for me, and you gave them an offer nobody could refuse. Principal Conners took joy in controlling and manipulating all of us just to see what would happen. But you, you're the only one I can't place. This whole time, I was never sure."

"My priority is, and always has been, your safety."

"Do you expect me to be grateful to you?" I want to laugh. "You're protecting me because I'm your project. I'm your prized work. Isn't that why you let me find out Alex was an Agent that day in the trunk of your car? Because you could tell me enough to warn me, but only once Alex was already dead. Only after two of your Agents had died were you desperate enough to step in and 'prioritize my safety.'"

He rolls back his shoulders, and the tailored suit glints. "You remember the photo of The Balancer in my office, yes? Do you remember what it means? Sacrifices for the betterment of the world. Someone has to make them."

A tumultuous anger builds up in my throat. "Not Alex. Not Oscar. And not Dean."

His cool expression shows no signs of empathy. "All of them were already dead."

I lower my voice. "And Olivia? Was she already dead? Because just today Wes was explaining to me what happened that night. And according to him, she arrived at the hospital alive. She even made it through surgery alive. In a coma but stable. So yes, maybe she did die over the course of that week. Or maybe YouTech was in dire need of a new Agent because their other one was experiencing glitches. That would be a worthy sacrifice, to you?"

He glances around the hallway with an unsettled air. "I'm on your side. I want you to succeed. I want you to pass the test."

"And in order to do that, you have to terminate Dean."

He falls silent.

"Have you done it yet?" I fight down a feeling of disgust, wondering again how mere lines of code could ever stir up emotions of this depth. "Or do you still have him in your lab, to run a few more tests before you shut him down for good?"

"He is the source of the glitch, Via. Don't you want to live?" He raises a crooked finger. "He knew he had to die so you could go on. That's why he got in the car willingly."

In that instant, I pity him. For the first time during one of our conversations, I feel a surge of confidence. "You really don't understand the glitch. Do you?"

I finally get a rise out of him, and his face contorts into a scowl. "I've been working on this program for years. I understand more than anyone else."

A laugh bubbles up from me. "The glitch isn't some random error, and Dean isn't the one who started it. You did. You created your own downfall when you made all of the Agents from the same system." I see him straighten his tie, and just the presence of this little tick urges me on. "You tried to build off of each previous program and improve upon it. But you ended up scrambling thoughts, and memories, and code. Even then it might've still been fine. If the Agents lived separately and never came into contact with their counterparts, the shared memories might never have backfired. But instead of keeping us apart and avoiding that possibility, you decided to build a school specifically to 'contain all your variables' and brought us all together in one place."

He tries not to seem bothered, but his omnipotent disposition falters.

"That collective consciousness, though, that's just the beginning," I continue. "Then you used the very same AI system to store all your data in Charles Brooks's house. It experienced the same glitches we did, only without active functions or a physical body. But here's the thing. It only took one girl trying to get the attention of her father to turn a mere computer with a coding error into a murderous trigger. It set out to fix the glitch in the only way it knew how, which was to use its information to terminate the other Agents. So as much as you tried to update each model to withstand the glitch, it had already taken on a life of its own."

The distant symphony of buzzing conversation and clanking chairs drifts out into the hall.

"And now, hang with me, this is the best part," I say. "You've taken that exact AI system, the computer that was setting fire to your entire life's work, and you moved it right here in the middle of your simulation."

He says nothing. His stare is vacant, and he locks and interlocks his hooked fingers as if trying to put together a puzzle. That's when I hear it; soft at first and then louder, until the jarring crashes and bangs fill the school like a dissonant song. The murmurs in the cafeteria turn to excited bursts, and soon the whole student body dashes from their chairs into the hall to see what sounds like a violent robot attack.

"Don't worry. I'm sorting out your issue for you." I put on my best smile. "You can thank me later." Mr. Richards jumps at each thunderous echo, his colleagues swept up in the swarm of writhing teens.

Principal Conners storms out of the administrative office with a bulging face, red like a tomato about to explode. "What in the good name of—"

The banging stops suddenly, abruptly. A hush sweeps over the riled-up students as they clamor for a better look down the hallway at the source of the disruption. Slowly, a path cuts through the mob as everyone presses against the walls to make room. Klara saunters out from the sea of faces, baseball bat in hand.

"Did you guys hear that?" She swings the bat over her shoulder. "Must've been another power drill."

A furor erupts from the crowd as people gasp, "Klara's the Agent!" and "She's gone psycho!" and "I knew it the whole time!" She just flips them off absentmindedly.

Conners is flabbergasted. His round belly heaves in an uproar, and he can barely contain his fury. "Ms. Brooks, what on earth do you think you're doing?"

She chuckles to herself. "It's so funny. I didn't even know we had a baseball team."

"If you damaged school property, you can be charged with vandalism! I will not stand for the destruction of your peers' experiential learning environment."

"But Principal Conners, this was my final ESP project." She makes a mocking face.

"Young lady, do you hear me?" he splutters. "I can have you expelled for this!"

"Great. Feel free to take that up with my father, Charles Brooks. I'm sure you know him. After all, he's the one who funds the majority of the Agent program, along with the rest of your 'experiential learning environment.'" She picks at her long nails. "And if I were you, I wouldn't press charges. You wouldn't want the world to find out that Park Falls Technical High School and their award-winning YouTech partnership pulled the plug on a sixteen-year-old girl in a coma."

I can hardly believe the words that come out of her mouth. I should rejoice in the unraveling of Principal Conners and his incessantly joyful facade. I should revel in the way Mr. Richards sweats beneath his hawk-like prowess, the way he snaps at his associates to pull Conners into a meeting where he will have to reassess everything. But only one thought fills my head: *Dean would have loved to see this.*

Klara struts down the corridor as her dark ponytail snaps, and from across the way I see Wes's jaw dropped in awe. Cole holds his phone up as he films the entire thing. Next to him, Ben shakes his head. "I am totally writing my college essay about this."

CHAPTER 28

It's different being inside the church for once.

The unadorned building stretches above us, its tall stained-glass windows aglow in the lazy morning sun. I sit in one of the back pews with my family, and the rest of the benches are filled with people I've only seen in passing. Employees, parents, kids from a town that didn't really feel like a community until it was torn apart. Toward the front of the nave, flowers encircle a large picture of Alex. He looks younger than I ever remember him in that photo.

The service is brief but touching. Alex's father gives a eulogy, and I wonder if, like Dean's parents, this is not the first time he's had to grieve over his son's death. Or maybe he's like Jimmy's family, who was stuck in the memory of the son they used to know.

After it ends and people file out of the small local haven, I stay behind and wait for Elliot. He walks down the aisle, his long hair slicked back out of his eyes. The sight of me brings him out of his thoughts.

"You clean up nice." His features are illuminated by the soft, filtered sunlight.

I tug at the sleeves of my black dress. "So do you. I almost can't tell you have two broken hands under that suit."

"Quiet down, my coach might hear." He glances around at the empty church. "It's a small town, you know. People talk."

"Very funny," I muse. "Hey, can I ask you something?"

"Always."

"Are you still mad at me? For the way you found out about Alex?"

He runs his fingers through his gelled hair. "There's a lot I feel about Alex."

"You don't have to explain."

"No, I want to." He looks back to the sanctuary at the front of the room. "Remember that one day when we were hiking, how I said that God created humans in his image?"

"I can't recall. Did we agree God looks like Ben?"

"Right." His whole face squints as he laughs. "So all this time, I thought it was talking about what we look like. But I was wrong. I guess God's image is about our true nature."

"What does that mean?"

He shrugs at the floor, shy when asked to explain. "It means humans have the reason and the free will to be their own master."

I nod. "I like that."

"And also… it means human beings are inherently good," he says. "And I know Alex was good."

The church bell suddenly chimes, and both me and Elliot glance up at the small bell tower. I watch his eyes wander down the rafters, past the satin banners, and from each stained-glass image to the next. He takes in the entire room with a whimsical gaze.

"That's all I need to know for now. I can wait for the rest."

I smile. "Alright, well, speaking of waiting, my parents are outside. Want to walk me out? It's not necessarily a hike, but it'll have to do."

"I think I'll stay here for a minute." He turns back to the altar. "I want to pray."

"You pray?"

"No. Well, I don't know. I think I'll try."

My heart is full as I make my way out of the church. It really is divine in here. Almost makes me want to start going to services, or sit with Elliot one day and try to pray with him. I don't even know what I would say, but still, I think I would like the idea of it. It's kind of like going to an art museum and staring at a painting for a while, even if you don't get it.

I don't go to the parking lot right away.

The cemetery is especially beautiful this morning. I wander through the worn grass toward the glade, a pocket of gravestones nestled up against the quaint church. I halt at the edge of the clearing when I see Jimmy. He stands with his hands in the pockets of his suit, unmoving. His gaze is fixated on the two headstones in front of him.

I approach him leisurely to share his view. The two headstones bask in the sunlight of their resting place, both sharper around the edges than the other graves that have slowly faded. Two names stare back at us: Oscar Andrade carved into one and its new companion, Alex Brockman, on the other.

"It's nice that they did this for him," I say. "I wasn't sure if the town even cared."

He stares at Oscar's stone. "It has the wrong year."

"What?"

"I mean, technically it's the year he died. But what about all the years after? You know? Those are the ones I liked the most. The ones where I needed him." He adjusts his glasses, a mannerism I've gotten so used to. "But I have my own friends now. I don't need his anymore."

The sun warms the back of my dress. As I face Oscar's stone, memories and lingering emotions resurface to the forefront of my mind. I focus on the good ones. The ones where he's looking for Jimmy, stepping out onto the ice to save his brother because that's the only thing that matters.

As if reading my thoughts, Jimmy clears his throat. "By the way, I thought I'd give this back. I don't know if you even want it, but I have a weird feeling it belongs with you."

He pulls out Oscar's button and his brown eyes soften, noticing my hesitation. *I don't need it anymore.* But he takes my hand and drops it into my palm anyway, and I roll the familiar smooth edges back and forth between my fingers. I count the grooves. *One, two, three, four.*

"Via! Come on, honey, Beth and Lawrence are waiting for us!" my mom calls from the parking lot. I squeeze Jimmy's shoulder and notice with satisfaction that, after everything, it still makes him squirm.

I stroll over to my family's car and Josh grins mischievously. "Was that your boyfriend?"

I groan. "Don't you have your own love life to worry about?"

My mom comes up, puts her arm around me, and kisses my head. "You look beautiful in that dress." She smells of honey.

Then she leads Josh around the car to herd him in, but my dad stays behind. His stern eyebrows furrow, but it's the good kind of intensity—the one I recognize from the hospital when I woke up and saw his face leaning over me, unable to express all he felt in that moment.

"I'm sorry," I say.

He grunts, fixes his tie. "What for?"

I look back at the church, at the families gathered around their cars and paying their respects by the graveyard. "I'm sorry you didn't get one of these."

He purses his lips, nods. "We don't need one. We have you."

I exhale shakily, and before I can even find the words to say anything else, my dad points. He reaches up his arm and points over my shoulder, behind me.

I don't even have to look, and my heart lurches. A sensation builds up inside me that starts from my gut and fills my whole body. I turn slowly, and there's Dean—a lone figure on the side of the road, his piercing stare boring into me.

Before I know it, my feet move beneath me. I expect him to disappear as I get closer, but he never does. He just narrows his eyes as I approach him and watches me. I practically collide into him, and he wraps me up in his arms. It feels real. I bury my face into his stupid long coat, and his warm hands clutch the back of my neck as he holds me.

I let go and stumble back to really look at him. It's like I've manifested it from my own thoughts. Something about his face, seeing it back to normal again, makes me feel some kind of way. I've been seeing that face in my dreams, searching for him for weeks. I waited for him to walk into the room at any moment, but he never did.

"I can't believe you still have that coat."

"It's indestructible. Like me." His tongue plays on the inside of his cheek. "What, you liked what you saw underneath better?"

I can't seem to catch my breath. "But how did you… I thought you were…"

"A rather nice man by the name of Charles Brooks had me released." He scrunches his nose. "Showed up at headquarters to have a meeting with the board. He told them he no longer wanted to fund their project, something about his daughter's life being endangered by one of their Agents Sunday night… they're definitely talking about you by the way, not me. So anyway, I guess Klara has the hots for me now because she talked to him and I was one of his demands."

"Don't forget that you're the recipient of the prestigious Charles Brooks scholarship."

His mouth hangs open as he chuckles, and then he reaches for my hand. "Let's get out of here." As he does, he feels the button in my palm and swipes it away from me. He holds it up to the sun. "No way. This is my button. I've been missing it forever."

He holds it up to his long coat, and there in the middle is a gaping hole that I never noticed where a button should be. All the other buttons on his coat have smooth edges, four grooves on each of them.

"But it's Oscar's," I murmur in disbelief.

"He must've gotten it from me, the same way you got it from him." He slips the button into his pocket, and something about the whole thing seems right. *I didn't need it after all. He did.*

He takes my hand, brings it up to his mouth, and kisses it. Then he leads me down the road, but I laugh in protest. "Dean, what are you doing? My family is leaving. We're not seriously going to walk?"

"Sure, walking is nice." His eyes glint. "Want to go to that coffee shop in town? We can pretend we like coffee and sit there for an unreasonable amount of time."

"Yeah," I say and gaze down the middle lines of the winding road. "I can do that."

ACKNOWLEDGMENTS

This book started out as a personal project, my own strange way of processing and reflecting on my high school and coming-of-age experiences. I never thought that over the course of the toughest year ever (COVID, I'm talking to you), it would turn into a professionally published novel. It's mind-blowing to see what this story has morphed and developed into, all because of the tremendous support that I received this past year.

I want to firstly thank New Degree Press and Eric Koester at the Creator Institute for taking a chance on me, giving me the resources to achieve my dream. And Jordan, you know who you are, thank you. I want to also thank my marketing and revisions editor Alan Zatkow; I walked into our zoom call with a shell of a manuscript, and because of your undying encouragement and guidance I walked out with an incredible book I am so proud of. The rest of the amazing people at NDP, my editors and designers and layout team, thank you for being so patient with me. I handed you a seventy-nine-thousand-word manuscript at the very last minute, and you turned it into a masterpiece.

To my family, Dad and Mom and Grace and Leah, thanks for putting up with me. Actually, to anyone who has been forced to read my warrior cat fan fiction: look where we're at now! I'd call that improvement.

But most importantly, I want to express my deepest gratitude and appreciation to all of my wonderful Beta Readers:

Adam Work
Adele Andrews
Alex Chmar-Chmar
Alexandra Frankel
Alison Silcox
Anastasia Chunilal
Andrew Meisler
Angelina Han
Annette Meyers
Annie Kim
Anush Shah
Ashley Kim
Ashlyn Dunn
Atharva Gawde
Bapa <3
Barbara Martin
Belinda Lei
Bill Gaisford
Bolu Ojuko
Brett Neilon
Caitlyn Ark
Cally Erickson
Carbondale Middle School
Chris Kei
Chris Wendel
Christian Gagnon
Christie Jensen
Christy Falco
Corinna Czink
Courtney Waring
Dana Augustino
Darby Ferguson
Demian Detweiler
Derek Brenner
Edwin Ladd
Elisa Kodama
Emma Preger
Emme Pedinielli
Eric Koester
Esther Park

Fiona Shaw
Francesca Seeman
Gabriel Cutrone
Gabriella Sutro
Grace Ferguson
Greta Hando
Hannah Zanin
Hanni and Gavi Ress
Heather Fox
Hilary Wendel
Holly & John Martin
Holly Willson
Ingrid Lundberg
Jack & Pamela Keese
Jaime Martin Atilano
Jessie Gerdis
Jocelyn Zhu
John & Kari Hamilton
Jonathan Zybert
Jordan Fox
Josh Anderson
Josh Spicer
JP Toppino
Justin Lin
Justin Vega
Kathy Matsui
Kathy Smith Neblett
Kayla Vestergaard
Kevin Dunne
Kim Heffernan
Laurel Lamont
Laurie Cohen
Leslie Lamont
Leslie LaVey
Lexi Ferlisi
Lily Felsenthal
Liv Oksenhorn
Logan Brown
Lynda Louise
M Kay Howe
Maddy Leibinger
Mariel Gorsuch
Mary Moskowitz
Maya Krause
Maylen Hathaway
Megan Currier
Meredith Dillard
Michael Logan

Michele Gray
Molly Scharlin Ben-Hamoo
Nadine Broussard
Nakiri Gallagher-Cave
Nan Campbell
Natasha Keidl
Nile Drochak
Oz & Maralyn Howe
Phyllis Samaha
Randy Work
Reece Ettelson
Regan Tierney
Rhonda Tatham
Ricky Wojcik
Riley Engels
Rob Omer
Robin Humble
Sara Ark
Sara Collins
Sara Rees Carroll
Sarah Fick
Sarah Scharlin Ben-Hamoo
Sartaj Ahmed Habib
Simone Chmar
Sophia Wong
Stacy & Ricky Dimino
Stephanie Toppino
Susan Seltzer
Suzanne Scheer
Sydney Slossberg
Talulah Marolt
Tariku Smith (& Wellington Gang)
Tess Mahon Kuzin
Timothy Kirkwood
Ty Yocum
Vaibhav Parve

Thank you for believing in me and supporting this book. Thank you for joining me on this journey. I could not have done it without you. You have taken a girl who wrote stories about dragons and turned her into a real published author. That's pretty cool.

Simone Lamont

APPENDIX

INTRODUCTION

Hodges, Andrew. "The Turing Test, 1950." The Alan Turing Scrapbook. 1997. http://www.turing.org.uk/scrapbook/test.html.

Newman, Lex. "Descartes' Epistemology (Stanford Encyclopedia Of Philosophy)." 2019. *Plato.Stanford.Edu.* https://plato.stanford.edu/entries/descartes-epistemology/.

Turing, A. M. "Computing Machinery and Intelligence." *Mind* 59, no. 236 (1950): 433–460.

CPSIA information can be obtained
at www.ICGtesting.com
Printed in the USA
BVHW040723210621
609824BV00033B/2469/J